'I have read it at least half a dozen times and each time it seems to me as remarkable, perhaps more remarkable. I would even say it is the most brilliant piece of surrealist prose to have been written in English (if you don't count the Alice stories). It is the culmination, and justification, of the joint Mortmere fantasies so wittily described by his friend Christopher Isherwood in his autobiographical *Lions and Shadows*. One may well ask oneself what the connection is between this world and the world of Mr Upward's novels. First of all, of course, there is his marvellous use of language. As a prose stylist, in imaginative writing, only Mr Isherwood seems to me to rival him in his generation. We may never have another "Railway Accident" from Mr Upward; but the future seems full of exciting possibilities, even though of a different sort' – John Lehmann, *Sunday Telegraph*

'"The Railway Accident" could be claimed to be one of the few surrealist texts in English that is not just arch or jokey' – Robert Nye, *The Times*

'"The Railway Accident" is a private, fantastic story, in which everything is clear but nothing is intelligible; it has, as Isherwood put it, "the splendour and oddity of madness". But it has also the sharp particularity of observed reality ... an extraordinary achievement, and one regrets that there are apparently no more. "Journey to the Border" is nevertheless more fantasy than socialist realism. "Journey to the Border" is often brilliant, and most brilliant when it is most hallucinatory' – *The Times Literary Supplement*

THE RAILWAY
ACCIDENT
and
Other Stories

EDWARD UPWARD

PENGUIN BOOKS

PENGUIN BOOKS

Published by the Penguin Group
27 Wrights Lane, London w8 5TZ, England
Viking Penguin Inc., 40 West 23rd Street, New York, New York 10010, USA
Penguin Books Australia Ltd, Ringwood, Victoria, Australia
Penguin Books Canada Ltd, 2801 John Street, Markham, Ontario, Canada L3R 1B4
Penguin Books (NZ) Ltd, 182–190 Wairau Road, Auckland 10, New Zealand

Penguin Books Ltd, Registered Offices: Harmondsworth, Middlesex, England

This collection first published by William Heinemann Ltd 1969
Published in Penguin Books 1972
Reprinted 1988

Made and printed in Great Britain by
Hazell Watson & Viney Limited
Member of BPCC plc
Aylesbury Bucks
Set in Linotype Granjon

Contents

The stories collected here were written by Edward Upward between 1928 and 1942. The first of them, 'The Railway Accident', was written in 1928 and published under the pseudonym of Allen Chalmers in *New Directions in Prose and Poetry: Number Eleven* (New York, 1949). 'The Colleagues', written in 1929, and 'Sunday', written in 1931, were both published in *New Country*, ed. M. Roberts, 1933. *Journey to the Border* was published by the Hogarth Press in 1938. 'The Island' was published in *The Left Review*, I, January 1935, and 'New Order' in *Penguin New Writing*, ed. John Lehmann, No. 14, July–September 1942.

Edward Upward: An Introduction

BY W. H. SELLERS

GEORGE STONIER, writing in 1933, described the arrival of the New Countrymen on the English literary scene in these words:

> From the cactus land discovered and solely inhabited by T. S. Eliot they emerge strangely on bicycles, removing ties, waving placards, and chanting inscrutably in native argot. We catch phrases as they pass: 'Take a sporting chance'; 'It's up to you now, boys'; 'What time's the train for No-man's land?' and so on. But as our hearts rise or sink to these echoes, we notice with astonishment that the faces express something quite different: rapture, irony, surprise, rage, despair, high spirits, bad nerves – which is it? While we are wondering, the shouts die away and there is only the evidence of a thinning cloud of dust. Which, as pedestrians, we naturally resent:[1]

Less than ten years later the bicycles lay abandoned in the bushes and the band of riders had confusedly dispersed. The dust that they raised, however, has never completely settled, for the literature of the New Countrymen, because of its political nature, has provoked almost ceaseless resentment and critical controversy, the most recent incidents of which have been Julian Symons's apologetic *The Thirties* (1960) and John Mander's astringent *The Writer and Commitment* (1961).

Among the New Countrymen, Edward Upward held a place of special importance. Stephen Spender includes him in the imaginary cabinet of young university artists who were, they all felt, about to seize the centre of the English literary stage, the cabinet invented and presided over by Auden in his sunless Oxford room. Spender recalls that 'just as Auden seemed to us the highest peak within the range of our humble vision from the Oxford valleys, for Auden there was another peak, namely Isherwood, whilst for Isherwood there was a still further peak,

Chalmers [i.e. Upward]'.[2] John Lehmann remembers his awe upon first learning of Upward's existence: 'I heard with the tremor of excitement that an entomologist feels at the news of an unknown butterfly sighted in the depths of a forest, that behind Auden and Spender and Isherwood stood the even more legendary figure of ... Edward Upward.'[3] Among his New Country friends, Upward enjoyed a unique reputation as an intellectual and an artist. Auden not only alluded to him in *The Orators* but often quoted from his unpublished work in lectures.[4] Spender has stated that, as a result of conversations with Upward in Berlin, he moved closer to the recognition of the necessity of Marxism.[5] And Isherwood remarked as recently as 1961, 'He's the final judge, as far as I'm concerned, of my work; I always send everything to him.'[6] Whereas Auden excited his contemporaries by the daring diversity of his thinking and poetic practice in the early thirties, Upward sobered them by his unwaveringly rigorous criticism of both literature and life. An examination of Upward's works, therefore, should shed clearer light on some of the difficulties that not just he but, in different ways, all of the New Countrymen faced in trying to reconcile art and politics, in trying to write committed literature.

2

The Upward canon is small. Owing to what Lehmann calls 'his slow and fastidious creative methods',[7] Upward has published only five stories, two essays, and one novel. Between 1942 and 1961 he published nothing. However, the publication in 1962 of the novel *In the Thirties*, the first part of a projected trilogy, refutes the notion that Upward is artistically dead.

The earliest of Upward's extant works has only the faintest of political implications. In *Lions and Shadows* Isherwood relates how he and Upward, while still at Cambridge, invented and elaborated the mad world they called Mortmere, which in a later reminiscence Isherwood describes as 'a sort of anarchist paradise in which all accepted moral and social values were turned upside down and inside out, and every kind of extravagant behaviour was possible and usual. It was our private place of retreat from the rules and conventions of university life.'[8] Of the apparently numerous Mortmere pieces, only one has been published: Upward's 'The Railway Accident', his farewell to Mortmere, appeared pseudonymously more than twenty years after it was written.

'The Railway Accident' caricatures mental and moral disorientation before and after two apparent catastrophes. They are 'apparent' because what gives the story its bizarre quality is that, from beginning to end, the incidents that occur do so only in the deranged mind of the narrator, Hearn. From the beginning of the story Hearn's morbid tendency to detect the ominous in the obvious becomes evident; glancing about the station before his train departs, he reflects:

Other insignia of the bogus, curt and modern cathedral ceremony which in my day-dream, induced partly by the cold, I had begun to arrange were the reverberating stammer of slipping driving-wheels on suburban trains and the fussing haste of porters loading the guard's van with wooden crates. Outside the station the air would be warm and I should remember ... the voluntarily ascetic life I had often planned; there would be crocuses or vultures, it would not be the same as it was here. Immediately the train started everything would be changed (p. 36).*

Studying fixedly a nearby express, Hearn notes that its coaches seemed 'of a new triple bogie pattern crouched on concealed springs' and 'were too heavily built, almost armoured, to sustain the image'. He visualizes the coaches, 'very long, tubular, dead', speeding through the night like steel coffins. He feels as if he was plunged briefly into 'a world in which I should have felt as wholly disorientated as though, suffering from amnesia after an accident, I had found myself among hoardings bearing futurist German advertisements' (p. 39). The uneasiness lurking just behind Hearn's daydreams becomes more pronounced and terrifying when, after his own train has finally left the station and he

*Page numbers relating to Upward's stories refer to this edition.

has settled back to anticipate the pleasures of his approaching vacation at Mortmere, the inexplicable presence of Gustave Shreeve and his extraordinary and totally irrelevant introductory query 'Fond of poetry?' (p. 40) initiates a sequence of events that makes it clear that Hearn has in fact crossed into a world 'wholly disorientated', that he has indeed journeyed into the mad world of his private terrors.

From this point on the story traces the steady degeneration of Hearn's psyche to a final state of catastrophically complete horror. His tendency to see the malevolent all about him assumes increasingly gigantic proportions as the train trip continues. Shreeve, himself the personification of fear and suspicion, excites Hearn's own agitations, for Shreeve can talk only of a past train accident and of his conviction that Wherry, the Mortmere architect, caused it deliberately. Then, just as Hearn's earlier vision of futurist German hoardings foreshadowed the hallucination of Shreeve, so now Shreeve's obsession with the past accident leads to Hearn's growing realization that the accident pattern is beginning to recur. As he watches in dismay, the train plunges down an abandoned siding towards a blocked tunnel, the site of the earlier accident. Amidst squealing brakes, he and Shreeve jump. Then Hearn sees the express thundering down the same siding:

The express had taken the points. Booster-fitted, excessively rolling, the racing mogul engine rounded the curve, bounded into the rear of the carriage we had left. Coaches mounted like viciously copulating bulls, telescoped like ventilator hatches. Nostril gaps in a tunnel clogged with wreckage instantly flamed. A faint jet of blood sprayed from a vacant window. Frog-sprawling bodies fumed in blazing reeds. The architrave of the tunnel crested with daffodils fell compact as hinged scenery. Tall rag-feathered birds with corrugated red wattles limped from holes among the rocks (pp. 51–2).

In the second half of the story all mention of this catastrophe vanishes quickly, and for a time it seems that crocuses have supplanted vultures in the mind of Hearn. The main action concerns the rector Welken's absurd Treasure Hunt, in which game Hearn figures as the object of everyone's search. As in the first part of the story, however, the pattern of steadily increasing anarchy and violence repeats itself. The inverted game of hide and seek begins innocently, develops into brutality, and climaxes when the smouldering hostility between Shreeve and Wherry leads to a duel fought with pea-pistols, one of which turns out somehow to be a real pistol and permanently lames Wherry.

Both catastophes, the railway accident and the accidental laming, as well as the bizarre series of events leading up to them, illustrate an individual impotence bred of intellectual insecurity and a moral apathy to gross brutality. Hearn, under the influence of the hallucinatory Shreeve, finds himself transfixed by growing terror as the accident pattern takes shape on the train. After the collision, he dismisses it as casually as Rector Welken who, upon finding the dazed Hearn and Shreeve on the embankment, remarks heartily: 'We'll have you home in a jiffy, and then you can tell us all about it.' A similar superficial response occurs after the wounding of Wherry: 'A most amazing thing', a bystander exclaims. In Hearn's private nightmare world, the world from which he cannot escape, not only is human action illogical and violent, but human reaction lacks relevance and depth. It is, in fact, a world of total disorientation.

An abundance of fantastic incidents and details fills out this bedlam vision: the English Territorials splintering the compartment wall and then striding along the carriage roofs just before the collision, Harold Wrygrave saluting solemnly among the bushes, Wherry's Provençal hat and pirate's cape, the cruelty of Boy Radnor and the other choirboys towards the effeminately handsome Anthony Belmare, and the public measurement of Miss Belmare's forty-five-inch bust. Yet all of this fantastic subject matter Upward renders in a simple, rigorously denotative prose style that gives the story an ironically factual quality, a disturbing suggestion of reality. For instance, when Hearn discovers the treasure, an ivory paper-knife, Upward describes his impressions in this series of short, graphic sentences:

At the cool entrance brambles obstinate as wire had eaten into the doorless jambs. The beehive stood on a single-legged table spoked with warped cricket stumps. Whorled coils of black horsehair or blood sausage. It broke in my hands like cake, issuing dark treacle (p. 67).

According to Isherwood, Upward modelled this dispassionate style after that of E. M. Forster, of whom he once said: 'The whole of Forster's technique is based on the tea-table; instead of trying to screw all his scenes up to the highest possible pitch, he tones them down until they sound like mother's-meeting gossip.'[9] In Mortmere, however, the tea-table belongs to a mad hatter.

Isherwood also tells how he and Upward grew away from the cult of romantic strangeness. He observes that as a writer, however, Upward needed Mortmere and could not afford to abandon it altogether:

He was to spend the next three years in desperate and bitter struggles to relate Mortmere to the real world of the jobs and the lodging-houses; to find the formula which would transform our private fancies and amusing freaks and bogies into valid symbols of the ills of society and toils and aspirations of our daily lives. For the formula did, after all, exist ... quite clearly set down, for everybody to read, in the pages of Lenin and Marx.[10]

3

Perhaps more than any of his fictional works, the essay 'Sketch for a Marxist Interpretation of Literature'[11] has kept Upward's name alive, if only in a footnote. It expresses with emphatic clarity his complete artistic and personal commitment to Marxism.

George Steiner recently pointed out that in 1934 the Stalinists turned their official backs on Engels's belief that 'the more the opinions of the author remain hidden, the better for the work of art', and embraced as the central premise of the Marxist literary aesthetic Lenin's uncompromising demand that 'Literature must become an integral part of the organized, methodical, and unified labours of the social-democratic party.'[12] Upward's essay defends unreservedly this Party line. After positing the material basis of both life and literature, Upward asserts that 'The greatest books are those which, sensing the forces of the future beneath the surface of the past or present reality, remain true to reality for the longest periods of time' (pp. 46–7). In terms of the present, this means that 'no modern book can be true to life unless it recognizes, more or less clearly, both the decadence of present-day society and the inevitability of revolution' (p. 49). Proust, Joyce, and Lawrence, all of whom tried to tell the truth about modern life, failed because their ideas derived from a decayed social class doomed to ultimate extinction, and their failures confirm Upward's conviction that 'A writer today who wishes to produce the best work that he is capable of producing, must first of all become a socialist in his practical life, must go over the progressive side of the class conflict' (p. 52).[13]

In the course of his argument, Upward took special pains to denounce his earliest writings:

... a modern fantasy cannot tell the truth, cannot give a picture of life which will survive the test of experience; since fantasy implies in practice a retreat from the real world into the world of imagination, and though such a retreat may have been practicable and desirable in a more leisured and less profoundly disturbed age than our own it is becoming increasingly impracticable today (p. 48).

And this rejection of pure Mortmere remained in effect in 1949, at which time Isherwood revealed:

Today, Chalmers is inclined to disown Mortmere and his share in its saga – hence his wish to appear under a pseudonym. He feels that the kind of literature which makes a dilettante cult of violence, sadism, bestiality and sexual acrobatics is peculiarly offensive and subversive in an age such as ours – an age which has witnessed the practically applied bestiality of Belsen and Dachau.[14]

Despite protestations to the contrary, however, Mortmere remained an essential if subordinate part of Upward's literary style.

The three stories that Upward published between 1933 and 1935 represent attempts to solve the problem of finding a literary form appropriate to Marxist dogma. New forms were needed, for, as Upward observes later in his sketch, 'already now the old forms can no longer adequately reflect the fundamental forces of the modern world. The writer's job is to create new forms now, to arrive by hard work at the emotional truth about present-day reality' (p. 54). Each of the stories describes, with little or no plot, the intellectual awakening of an individual to the necessity of Marxism. A character, as a result of observing the decadence and deceit of the world about him, makes a political decision that promises to lead him away from an aimless passivity that foreshadows the delusory world of Hearn and towards purposeful, dynamic social action, towards orientation.

'The Colleagues'[15] portrays the psychology of two schoolmasters, Lloyd and Mitchell. In the first part of the story, the thoughts of the experienced and confident Lloyd are presented. He disapproves of much that the school stands for, particularly the educational philosophy of its headmaster Taylor:

... in Taylor's world effort and guts are vulgar; only skill is respecable. One is born either dull or bright, and nothing afterwards can change one's nature. Certainly not Taylor's own methods of dealing with the young. But if we're to get these kids anywhere we've got to cater for the average. The world's work isn't and never will be done by exceptions. As time goes on there will be less and less room for the type of person whose sole object is to evade responsibility. Whether we like it or not there are changes in the air. And the boy with guts is the one who is going to survive (pp. 73-4).

Upon seeing the new master, Mitchell, approaching him, Lloyd thinks: 'Why can't the man change into proper clothes when he's refereeing?' (p. 74). Here the point of view switches to the nervously uncertain Mitchell, whom Lloyd persuades to take on extra duties next day. In the course of the persuasion Lloyd reveals in passing that his own ideas on education, though more gutty, are no less debilitating than Taylor's. He urges Mitchell not to worry about teaching the boys: 'Charades. Games. Making up codes. Anything that will keep them amused. Provided they don't kick up a row or break the furniture' (p. 76). Though he agrees to help Lloyd out, Mitchell reviles his own weakness and conjures up absurd visions of rebellion: 'Why acquiesce for an instant? Decline utterly to be an accomplice. Queer the whole schedule. Cheap water-pistols for fussing terriers. Clear straight out of the house after lunch' (p. 77) Such romanticism collapses rapidly into impotent despair :

Nothing that happens in the school grounds has any connection with what happens in the town outside. Every day here certain ceremonies are independently performed. Latin lessons are given. Games are organized. Surplices are worn. Outmoded precautions are scrupulously taken. Nothing which a clergyman might think risky to neglect is neglected. We are the servants of the parents' most contemptible misgivings. I shall be here or in places similar to this for the rest of my life (pp. 77–8).

Then something meaningful does happen. Mitchell observes Lloyd again, this time amusing himself alone on the rugger field. But for the first time, Mitchell sees his colleagues in a startling new light: no longer is he merely the attractive personification of tradition but rather, for one brief and lucid moment, the external and material confirmation of all of Mitchell's inner doubts about the degeneracy of the educational system of which he has become a part :

He sprang, he raced towards the tennis courts. Bucking, heavily agile with jerking shoulders. Baboon or antelope. Going all out, broad-backed in a tight sweater. How terrific. How electrically vile. He plunged, he touched down, stumbling among tree roots (p. 78).

Mitchell interprets this flash of insight as the gift he needs to find the meaningfulness that his personal life has lacked :

I've had an hallucination. Probably involuntary. It's a reward. It's going to happen again. In the night. At lunch. Everywhere. An award of power. This is only the beginning. A genuinely religious delusion. I am very glad (p. 78).

'The Colleagues' lies midway between Mortmere and Marx. The Mortmere effects serve well to depict the different psychological states of Lloyd and Mitchell. But the nature of Mitchell's escape from despair lacks focus: whereas the ugly vision of

Lloyd 'stumbling among the roots' does symbolize vividly the degeneracy implicit in Lloyd's complacency. Upward's introduction of religious overtones, even though qualified by such psychological terms as 'hallucination' and 'delusion', does not point very clearly in the direction of Mitchell's earlier rebellious thoughts. Mitchell has crossed a border, has made a beginning along the road to truth, but the map that he consults remains something of a mystery.

Upward's other two stories, being considerably more tendentious, raise few problems of interpretation. 'Sunday' [16] is an interior monologue of an office worker on his way home from a walk. His political intellect has already reached a far more advanced stage than that of Mitchell; he thinks, for instance, that 'Everyone will appear quite at ease, fairly well-dressed, comfortably married, not at all furtive or sinister. Nothing will visibly suggest that they are all condemned, that what they stand for is already dead, putrescent, stinking, animated only by preying corpseworms' (p. 80). He requires no epiphany, therefore, to decide to act upon his beliefs and to join 'the small club behind the Geisha Café', the members of which 'are not content to suppress misery in their minds but are going to destroy the more obvious material causes of misery in the world' (p. 84).

Thematically, 'Sunday' is similar and obvious, more an exhortatory essay than a story. Aside from its pronounced Marxist bias, its most striking quality inheres in the speaker's penetrating eye for aspects of modern city life that suggest the bogus. He is cynically suspicious, for example, of the municipal motives lying behind the remodelling of the city park: 'I am invited, everyone is invited, we are expected to stop and look at the mandarin ducks, to use the less direct path up the side of the valley, smell the lupins, poke groundsel through the wire meshes of the aviary. Why did the council put flood-lights in the trees round the fountain and build a thatched hut for the ducks on an island?' (p. 79). Similar ominous images occur when he nears his lodgings: 'Who will be there? Only the table, the flower with protruding stamens arching from its jug like a

20

sabre-toothed tiger, the glass of custard, pleated apple-green satin behind the fretwork fleur-de-lis panel of the piano' (p. 80). Such observations, which gradually give way to more abstract patterns of thought ranging from Epictetus to Lenin, vivify this white-collar worker's contempt for the emptiness of the life he has had to lead. Marked stylistically by a shift from the first person to the second person point of view, paralleling the shift from the subjective to the objective attitude towards life, such thoughts culminate in the decision to join 'the enemies of suffering'.

'The Island' [17] resembles 'Sunday' in that it is more an exhortation than a story: dialectical argument replaces characterization and plot development. The reader enjoys a tour of the Isle of Wight, and his guide is the Marxist conscience that, presumably, lies within him. From his guide, the reader-vacationer learns that, even though he has temporarily escaped 'the bullying foreman', he has not escaped social reality even on this apparently idyllic island. Even here, where natural beauties abound and where 'No strength should be denied ... no weakness exposed or tortured' (p. 224), signs of human destructiveness and injustice protrude from beneath the island's glittering surface: the aircraft carrier anchored in the bay, the guns angled from the masked cliffside forts, and 'this woman shuffling along in dirty canvas shoes, searching among the lines of rubbish left by the tide ...' (p. 229). Such realities make bogus the gaudy amusement arcade, reveal it as a symbol of deceit and decadence: 'fraudulent as vulgar icing on a celebration cake rotten inside with maggots, sugary poison to drug you into contentment' (p. 229). Yet, while giving clear evidence of man's decay, the island also provides physical proof of his potential for progress: its rock formations illustrate his former mastery of material conditions, and its historical sites the evolution of human freedom. To realize his potential today, however, man must abandon fantasies: 'Come out of that sickly dreamland, that paradisal island of culture and everlasting joy, come and see the island as it really is ...' (p. 227). He must develop 'new eyes' so that he will not be shocked when, for instance, a group of cyclists 'wearing the badge of a worker's sports club' sing of hunger and war and revolution. He must see that the island itself confirms the burden of their songs that only through revolution will war and hunger end and will the island change from 'a ghost-place dazzling with false promise' into 'a real place, the island as it can be, a place fit for men and women, as it must be, as it will be' (p. 230).

Whereas in his earlier Mortmere story Upward used bizarre imagery and sequential illogic to create the vivid and violent world of a disturbed mind, in these three stories he relegates such effects to the minor role of imaging a pervasive cultural sickness and introduces as major emphasis the curative force of Marxism. With the exception of the indecisive 'The Colleagues', the demands of *Tendenzpoesie* seem to have forced Upward into the adoption of an exhortatory form of literature that necessitated the subordination of his most remarkable artistic talent. Like his friend Isherwood, Upward could still use the camera technique to register graphically the facts of modern life, but, because his camera carried a heavily coloured lens, Upward's photographs, though often vivid, suffer from distortion. The search for the formula that would transform 'private fancies' into 'valid symbols' may have ended, as Isherwood asserted, but Upward still needed to find the literary form that could satisfactorily accommodate both his Mortmere manner and his Marxist faith. In his novel *Journey to the Border*,[18] he tried anew to find this form, 'to arrive by hard work at the emotional truth about present-day reality'.

4

In 'Journey to the Border' Upward combines the themes and techniques of the four short stories. The novel explores the psychology of near insanity in the Mortmere manner of caricature; it introduces the inner voice of a Marxist conscience to expound the necessary political choice; and it follows a dialectical thematic pattern of initial personal dissatisfactions, a series of futile and nearly fatal attempts to escape these dissatisfactions, and a climactic recognition of the necessity of Marxism for the achievement of personal as well as social integration. By indulging in increasingly Hearn-like evasions of the glimpsed but suppressed truth of Marxism, the hero of the novel, an unnamed tutor not unlike the earlier Mitchell, travels to the borderline between sanity and insanity, at which point, no longer able to escape the inescapable, he is forced by his own desolation to hear the truth and to realize that he can find fulfilment only through identification with and participation in the workers' movement. To use the more familiar metaphors of Auden, the tutor suffers from but finally corrects 'the negative inversion' of his will, forsakes his 'coward's stance' and, by reversing himself, rebuilds his life according to 'new styles of architecture', having had if not a 'change of heart,' at least a change of head.

At the beginning of the novel the tutor has concluded that the family for whom he works, the Parkins, represents a spiritual and physical decadence that threatens to infect his own integrity. He determines, therefore, to find 'a new technique, a first step towards solving the problem of how to live in this house' (p. 86). During the remainder of this critical day, he tries to come to terms with the Parkin world, but all of his efforts prove abortive because of his failure to go beyond his own ego. Instead of fastening on to external realities, his increasingly agitated mind conjures up gross distortions of reality that reflect his own private revulsion for the world he sees about him. He sees the Parkins not as pitiful representatives of a dying culture, but as monsters crippled by disease: inwardly he mocks Mr Parkin's gimpy leg, facial twitch, conspicuous blackened tooth, red-rimmed eyes, and greasy, sallow complexion: he exults at the brief sight of the bed-ridden Mrs Parkin's fat-wristed hand; and he stares with horrified pleasure at young Donald Parkin's flabby leg and efflorescent flesh. Similarly the Parkin estate reeks of the bogus; its artificial lake, fir trees, four lawns and sprawling flowerbeds, signify to the tutor 'a faked and isolated world incompletely retrieved from the eighteenth century' (p. 86). Only after a nearly complete mental breakdown and after the Marxist truth has escaped from his unconscious does the tutor come to understand that, because of his own weakness, he has distorted the facts of life into gross melodrama:

Mr Parkin would not scream or shake his fist in the tutor's face. He was not a maniac. He was not even the unspeakable swine that the tutor had formerly supposed him to be. That supposition had been due to the tutor's cowardice, to his failure to assert himself against Mr Parkin (p. 219).

The tutor's first attempts at finding 'a new technique' consist of wilful self-delusions. Having failed to assert himself by refusing to accompany the Parkins to the races, he withdraws into the privacy of his self and tries to impose a romantic image on the world about him. But sheer will power proves inadequate, and the ugliness of life he longs to escape from remains stubbornly before him: 'he was aware of two marquees – one large and beflagged and white, the other small and dull and grey' (p. 108). He tries again, this time buttressing his private vision with an external fact. On the way to the race track Mr Parkin seemingly becomes enraged when a steam roller impedes his car, and the tutor seizes on this machine as an ally and as a source of strength in his personal battle against decadence:

Its boldness, its simplicity, its power, were what the tutor had wanted to see, had struggled to see, and now they were here before him, outside him, wholly independent of his wanting and struggling. Now he could cease to want and to struggle and the steamroller would still be there, animating him from outside with its boldness and simplicity and power. The new vision was here and it was solid and real and it could not fade (p. 112).

But the vision and the sense of power it provides do fade as soon as the steam roller drops out of sight, and the tutor remains once again locked within his frustrated self.

At the race track he passes through a series of increasingly terrifying delusions. Overwhelmed by his own inadequacy and guilt, he fabricates first the humiliating hallucination of a juggling race-track tout denouncing him in public: 'I'll tell you straight what I think of your principles. You don't believe in 'em any more than I do. You only pretend to. Because you're in a bad funk' (p. 133). Repelled by this self-truth, the tutor forces himself to join a group of bright young people whom he recognizes, but this attempt to escape soon turns into another confrontation of his own cowardice: imagining himself urging Ann MacCreath to run away with him to Reykjavik, he is appalled to hear her reject his proposal with a socialist argument in which 'he recognizes phrases which he himself had used in earlier conversations with her' (p. 139). Even in his private fantasies, he finds no escape from his conscience. From this point on, the political implications of his inner fears and failings become more marked. Unable to grasp 'the actuality before his eyes' the tutor finds himself drifting helplessly towards intellectual and political darkness. Tod Ewan's casual remarks about his bullying of Nigerian natives expand in the tutor's imagination into a Fascist harangue in which Ewan boasts of the formation of Storm Troops in England that will annihilate the socialists, 'real scum from the gutter. Most of them Jews' (p. 148). Gregory Mavors's subtle and initially tempting argument in favour of unreason — 'There is only one sin ... and that is disobedience to our desires' (p. 157) – becomes grotesque when the tutor imagines that Mavors joins the Storm Troop formation at one end of the marquee. And when the wealthy and powerful Master of Fox Hounds (the M.F.H.) enters the marquee and announces, amidst great applause, that his horse will run in the main race, the tutor's fevered mind envisions the M.F.H. launching into a violent diatribe against socialists. In the growing darkness of the marquee where he had sought refuge from his own cowardice, the tutor, sick with despair, sees finally the full horror of Fascism triumphant:

Darkness pressed in upon him once again, lifted him. Horror of the future alone supported him, kept his consciousness alive. He would be gassed, bayoneted in the groin, slowly burned, his eyeballs punctured by wire barbs. Yet it was not the thought of these physical agonies that really horrified him. He was unable to imagine them vividly enough. And such extremes of torture could not last long, could not compare in persistence with the other slower horrors which he *was* able to imagine. . . . The death of all poetry, of all love, of all happiness. Never more to be allowed to use his brain. But perhaps this stage would come first, would precede the war; perhaps it had come already. It had come, it was here, was in the marquee. They were mobilizing. Gone for ever was his hope of making friends, of establishing contact with human beings. There were no more human beings. He was isolated among brutal slaves (p. 184).

His vaguely political personal distaste for the Parkins having climaxed in this nightmarish triumph of tyrannical bestiality, the tutor stumbles from the marquee. Outside, however, he finds himself once again reduced to the 'icy vacancy' of his vulnerable self, and so, resignedly, he turns back towards the marquee 'To make a final effort to identify himself with those people. Surrender all his romantic demands, become a hopeless slave' (p. 188).

At this point the tutor's instincts revolt against his craven intellect and render him incapable of movement:

... he could not shift his left foot an inch. A glacial panic tightened round his heart. He could not do anything at all, could not even move his eyelids. He was done for, paralysed, a hopeless failure. He had become insane. Suddenly he surrendered, gave up trying to move. An infinite relief, a blissful vacancy, expanded within him. ... Now nothing existed. But out of nothing something was born. A noise, a voice. Ghostly and distinct, it came from high up among the fir trees. It spoke into his left ear (pp. 189–90).

In this state of near-suspended animation, the tutor can no longer suppress that part of his psyche that perceives reality. Earlier in the novel this alter ego had sought to break through his fears, notably in the steam roller incident, but repeatedly and deliberately the tutor had thrust it back down into his unconscious, diminished it to an occasional faint buzzing in his left ear. Now, unimpeded, it floods his consciousness and, echoing the voice heard in 'Sunday' and 'The Island', it furnishes him at last with the 'new technique' that he has so fruitlessly been seeking. Like his predecessor in 'The Colleagues', the tutor gains from his final delusion an insight into reality, but this revelation, unlike that of Mitchell, introduces no ambiguities of meaning.

The newly-released alter ego, after reviewing at considerable length the tutor's recent behaviour, concludes that he travelled to the very border of sanity because, out of cowardice, he tried, against his better nature, to substitute daydreams for realities:

... You ought to learn first of all that your problems cannot be solved in the mind alone. Nor can they be solved in the heart, in the emotions. They must be dealt with in the external world, because they have their origin in that world. You must take action — living practical action (p. 192).

And such action must be taken in the name of the workers' movement, which will demand of the tutor a complete revolution of thought and behaviour:

You will have to move out of the region of thinking and feeling altogether, to cross over the frontier into effective action. For a short time you will be in an unfamiliar country. You will have taken your so-called 'plunge in the dark'; but it will not be in the dark for very long. Out of action your thinking and feeling will be born again. A new thinking and a new feeling (p. 201).

Accepting these dicta, the tutor regains control of his senses and at once begins to see the life around him in the clear light of revealed Marxism. For the first time he sees things as they truly are: 'The huge white marquee had been a fake, but the reality upon which the fake had been based was something more than a small grey tent. It was an ordinary medium-sized refreshment tent' (p. 203). His unfamiliarity with the new perspective does, as his alter ego had warned, allow some doubts to rise in his mind, especially when he encounters a young engineer indifferent to the workers' movement and when the race track crowd exults over the victory of the M.F.H.'s horse. But such doubts disappear when the tutor sees the local curate. To the Marxist convert, the curate personifies the quintessence of the enemy, for he is the 'intransigent popularizer of a reversed, a twisted picture of the world' (p. 215). Indulging his new Marxist zeal, the tutor denounces to himself the principle of resignation:

'England need no longer be a land of poverty and of tragedy. Men had mastered nature, and the requisite conditions now existed for creating – not a heaven on earth, but a society in which every man and woman would at least have the chance to be normally happy' (p. 215). Realizing that he is once more day-dreaming rather than acting, he collapses into doubts and fears. A relapse into delusions threatens him. Then, 'While his mind fumbled, his body seemed already to have solved the difficulty' (p. 216), and guided once more by his unconscious, he moves through the crowd until he finds Mr Parkin.

'He had come back', he thinks to himself as he confronts his employer, 'to where he had started from, to the situation which had faced him in the dining-room this morning' (p. 217). Only now he sees Mr Parkin as he really is, and he knows precisely what he must do; so, with only the slightest hesitation, he announces that he will not return to the house until next day. Having asserted himself at last and finding himself not over-surprised at Parkin's sniggering acquiescence, the tutor makes his way purposely towards the neighbouring town to put himself in touch with the local workers' movement, to ally himself completely with Marxist reality.

'Journey to the Border', then, is a psychological political novel: it traces the psychological progress of a sensitive, but highly insecure young man, through a hallucinatory hell to the political 'truth' of Marxism. The tutor's grasp of reality, already shaky at the outset of the novel, loosens entirely. Among the Parkins, he is only ill at ease and disdainful; but in the marquee among the likes of Ewan, Mavors, and the M.F.H., his uneasiness grows into terror and his disdain crumbles into deep despair. For instance, upon first entering the marquee, he senses an ominous unreality: 'What luxury there was here was only an improvisation ... and he saw a frayed black overcoat hanging from a corner of one of the hampers. Or did he see it?' (p. 151). By the time the M.F.H. arrives, these details have assumed the monstrous proportions of political terrors: 'The bowls had an evil look, like objects in a devil temple. They were something more than quaint ornaments: they had a definite connection with the nasty ritual which was being performed at the other end of the marquee' (pp. 181–2). Similar disintegration occurs in all his actions as long as he refuses to accept the Marxist truth about himself and his world. When, for example, he tries to force himself, against his better nature, to act upon Mavor's philosophy of unreason by winning the love of a young woman whom he meets in the marquee, his high hopes soon fade as he finds himself being toyed with by a sexual machine, and the whole affair becomes a hideous mockery of his desperate passion when she dismisses him with the remark: 'You poor little swine' (p. 181). Only after he has explored, psychologically, attitudes ranging from pastoralism to fascism, and reached a dead end, does the tutor permit himself, of sheer necessity, to hear the truth.

Psychologically, the novel creates a vivid image of a mind almost destroying itself through a reluctance to face political truth; the tutor, out of cowardice and egotism, comes close to landing permanently in Hearn's mad Mortmere. And politically, at least from the point of view of Marxism, the novel meets the requirement so often, according to Upward's 'Sketch', unmet by modern novels: 'it recognizes, more or less, both the decadence of present-day society and the inevitability of revolution'. Aesthetically, however, the novel founders before the end: after depicting brilliantly a mind journeying towards madness, it suffers from a jolting and bathetic descent from subtle fiction into *Tendenzpoesie*. The alter ego's lengthy Marxist discourse resembles too much an extended footnote that Upward affixed to his obliquely political psychological novel to make absolutely sure that the reader did not miss the point. Similarly, the facts that the tutor hears first a buzzing, then the voice of his Marxist alter ego only in his *left* ear and that it is his *left* foot that he cannot move towards the marquee seem at best crudely symbolic in contrast to the subtlety Upward employs elsewhere in the novel. Such blatancy both insults the reader's intelligence and wounds his aesthetic sense. Being a completely committed Marxist, however, Upward had to tell what he considered to be the whole truth about the dominant forces at work in the modern world, and this required a climactic recognition by his hero not only of the necessary choice of Marxism but of the full implications of that choice. Political necessity, therefore, drove Upward into blatancy and prevented him from finding the new literary form that would permit a truly satisfactory union of his Mortmere gift and his Marxist faith.

Unlike his more famous contemporaries and friends, Auden, Spender, and Day Lewis, all of whom either began as or soon became at best reluctant fellow travellers in the New Country, Upward dedicated himself wholly to Marxism. As late as the early 1940s, in the essay 'The Falling Tower' [19] and in the short exhortation 'New Order' [20], he did not swerve from the path he had chosen. And, as a result, he paid the high price of maiming his artistic gift on the monolithic demands of his political faith. As Lehmann wrote regretfully in his autobiography, Upward gave 'evidence of an imaginative gift ... the fate of which one will never cease to mourn, slowly killed in the Iron Maiden of Marxist dogma'.[21] The recently published novel, however, provides new hope that Upward may yet find the artistic wholeness he sought unsuccessfully in that decade of political delusions, the decade of the thirties.

Notes

1. *Gog and Magog*, London, [1933], p. 171.
2. *World within World*, London, 1951, p. 102.
3. *The Whispering Gallery*, New York, 1954; London, 1955, p. 195.
4. ibid., p. 244.
5. Spender, p. 133.
6. 'A Conversation on Tape', *The London Magazine*, New Series, I, June, 1961, pp. 45–6.
7. *New Writing In England*, Critics Group Pamphlets No. 12, New York, 1939, p. 43.
8. Foreword to 'The Railway Accident', *New Directions in Prose and Poetry: Number Eleven*, New York, 1949, pp. 84–116; this volume p. 33.

9. *Lions and Shadows*, London, 1938; Norfolk, Conn., 1947, pp. 173–4.

10. ibid., p. 274.

11. *The Mind in Chains: Socialism and the Cultural Revolution*, ed. C. Day Lewis, London, 1937, pp. 41–55.

12. 'Marxism and the Literary Critic', *Encounter*, XI, November, 1958, pp. 33–4.

13. Stanley Hyman, in *The Armed Vision*, New York, 1948, p. 193, disinters Upward's essay and derides it as 'probably the most stupid single piece of Marxist criticism ever written, an argument that the way to become a good writer is to become a good Marxist ...' Conveniently and unjustly, Hyman ignores Upward's qualification that 'Having become a socialist, however, he will not necessarily become a good writer. The quality of his writing will depend on his individual talent, his ability to observe the complex detail of the real world, p. 52.

14. Foreword to 'The Railway Accident', this volume, p. 34.

15. *New Country*, ed. M. Roberts, London, 1933, pp. 174–82; this volume pp. 71–8.

16. ibid., pp. 183–9; this volume pp. 79–84.

17. *The Left Review*, I, January, 1935, pp. 104–10; this volume pp. 221–30.

18. *Journey to the Border*, London, 1938; this volume pp. 85–220.

19. *Folios of New Writing*, ed. John Lehmann, Spring, 1941, pp. 24–9.

20. Penguin New Writing, ed. John Lehmann, No. 14, July–September, [1942], pp. 9–11; this volume pp. 231–3.

21. *The Whispering Gallery*, p. 244.

Reprinted from *The Dalhousie Review*, Volume 43, No. 2, by kind permission of the *Review* and with grateful thanks to the author.

Mortmere & Environs

S E W N

THE ATLANTIC (?)

FURZE ETC

BELSTREET DOWN

SUMMER COLONY

MARSHES

AMHERST RAILWAY & LIGHTS

MUD FLATS

RIVER STOOL

MUD FLATS

RICHMOND COLLEGE FOR BOYS

HAINWORT WOODS

TOREMERE

Skull and Trumpet

SITE FOR PARISH HALL

miss Belmaris cottage

BLAKE

BELMARE HALL

THE BELMARE ESTATE

WORMWALD (?) HILLS

GIRLS SCHOOL

HAINWORT FIELDS

The Amherst Railway

The Railway Accident

Foreword by Christopher Isherwood from *New Directions in Prose and Poetry: Number Eleven*, in which Edward Upward's 'The Railway Accident' was published under the pseudonym of Allen Chalmers.

Anyone who happens to be familiar with my autobiographical book, Lions and Shadows, *need not bother to read what I am going to write here. For* Lions and Shadows *is, among other things, a detailed introduction to* The Railway Accident *and to 'Allen Chalmers', its author. Chalmers – as I shall call him from now on, omitting the quotation-marks – is known by his real name as a distinguished British prose-writer, not yet as widely popular as his admirers could wish, but profoundly and subtly influential. His pseudonym is attached to this story at his own request, for reasons which I shall mention in a moment.*

When Chalmers and I were undergraduates together at Cambridge, in the mid nineteen-twenties, we invented a fantastic village which we called Mortmere. Mortmere was a sort of anarchist paradise in which all accepted moral and social values were turned upside down and inside out, and every kind of extravagant behaviour was possible and usual. It was our private place of retreat from the rules and conventions of university life.

We wrote many stories about Mortmere – entirely for our own amusement – and created a lot of Mortmere characters, nearly all of whom appear in The Railway Accident, *often quite casually referred to, like old friends. This is no place to describe their various peculiarities and adventures; they are all set forth in* Lions and Shadows. *And* The Railway Accident *doesn't need such annotation. It can stand alone, as a complete, self-explanatory work of art.*

Written in 1928, it is the last and longest of the Mortmere stories – a farewell to Mortmere, which left Chalmers free to

33

develop his extraordinary technique in other, more fruitful directions. Nevertheless, Mortmere was the mad nursery in which Chalmers grew up as a writer, and no future evaluation of his work will be able to ignore it.

Perhaps The Railway Accident can best be described as a dream, or a nightmare, about the English; Gunball, Welken and Shreeve are all dream-distortions of classic English types. At moments, they seem nearly normal, nearly convincing; and they appear to be taking each other quite seriously. But this is only a part of their basic social pretence. Life in Mortmere is like a poker-game between telepathists, in which everybody is bluffing and nobody is fooled. We too, in the everyday world, have our social pretences. For us, too, there are fantastic realities which we conspire to ignore. The Railway Accident may, therefore, be regarded as a satire. But it is something more than that; it has an extra-dimension. It is, so to speak, a satire on satire, a parody of parody. Satire requires a norm, a sane observer, a standard of contrast. Where can we find one here? Hearn, the 'I' of the narrative, is just as crazy as the people he describes. Indeed, he may be crazier – for we begin to suspect that this entire journey and its sequel may be taking place only in his own imagination. Even his style of narration has the splendour and oddity of madness. The purple passages are just a little too purple, the seemingly-reasonable dialogues often run abruptly into a blank non sequitur. And there are strange sly echoes of Proust, Joyce and Henry James which suggest an anarchic mockery of all literary values whatsoever.

Today, Chalmers is inclined to disown Mortmere and his share in its saga – hence his wish to appear under a pseudonym. He feels that the kind of literature which makes a dilettante cult of violence, sadism, bestiality and sexual acrobatics is peculiarly offensive and subversive in an age such as ours – an age which has witnessed the practically applied bestiality of Belsen and Dachau. I respect this scruple, and I agree with it on general principles. But I do not agree that it covers the case of The Railway Accident. Indeed, The Railway Accident seems to me to be fundamentally anti-sadistic, anti-pornographic. Its

ludicrous exaggerations, its antiseptic spirit of parody, its inno-
cent extravagance produce an atmosphere in which the real
sadist suffocates for lack of hatred and the real pornographer is
revealed as a dreary little bore. And so we must admit a para-
dox: this insane story is, after all, a touchstone of sanity. It will be
best understood and appreciated by those who, like its author,
are most immune from the infectious evils of our neurotic epoch.

*

'ONE more.'

'Thanks no, really.'

But Gunball had already signalled with a slow regardless movement of his forefinger to the girl wheeling a dumb-waiter on rubber tyres quietly through the tin wailing of milk-cans and the drawl of trolleys. I leant on the wood of the lowered carriage window, observing with the sharpened pleasure of an antici-pated farewell the metropolitan morning striking down through risen straw specks, dust of horse dung, beneath the glass arch of the Terminus roof. A horse-drawn mail-van flickered red at the interstices of the platform barrier, there was frost in the air and I had, not intellectually but sensationally, a conviction of warmth which remembrance of the falsely tender coaching litho-graphs in Gunball's sitting-room would not have destroyed, since they would have been irrelevant to what seemed an im-pression quite unassociated with the past. Beyond the barrier a soldier in khaki carrying full marching kit was watching one of the horses. Another soldier had passed the ticket collector and had begun to walk up the platform. More were coming.

'What's the idea, I wonder?'

'Idea or no, the whole pack of them are getting on your train,' said Gunball. He carried two cups of coffee. I took both while he fetched out a flask from one of his angler's pockets.

'You'll need it. There's a nip in the air this morning. Spring-cleaning the gravestones. Well, I wish I were you. Give them all my love and tell them how sorry I am to miss the Treasure Hunt. My word, you'd not know we were in sight of the first of May.'

Nevertheless he wore no overcoat, seemed warm, and I recognized in his remark that advertisement, blatant or discreet, of the power of the weather which is necessary to most sportsmen who have left the country even for a few hours. Through the roof panes the sun froze whey-white on steam columns from the waiting engines. Other insignia of the bogus, curt and modern cathedral ceremony which in my daydream, induced partly by the cold, I had begun to arrange were the reverberating stammer of slipping driving-wheels on suburban trains and the fussing haste of porters loading the guard's van with wooden crates. Outside the station the air would be warm and I should remember clock-golf in the rectory garden, or there would be heavy snow recalling the voluntarily ascetic life I had often planned: there would be crocuses or vultures, it would not be the same as it was here. Immediately the train started everything would be changed.

'Just like the rector to have forgotten where he'd hidden the thing.'

'And then to have lost the plans.'

'Isn't it?' He guffawed, without spite. 'All the same, beggared if I'd travel up there myself on a day like this *solely* in order to remind him. Besides, we could have done that by wire.' He smiled, ostentatiously shrewd. 'Who's the skirt?'

'Oh, the barmaid's Angora rabbit. Well, I'll remember to give him that message in your words.'

'Which?'

'"Try squinting under the damp beehive in the summerhouse."'

'All right: but don't harp on it for too long or he'll get fussed with the idea that one of the competitors might overhear you.'

'Anyway, what exactly is the treasure this year?'

'An ivory papercutter. Given by Henry Belmare. Good thing you took a first-class ticket. By the time they've loaded on the China Expeditionary Force, or whoever they are, there won't be room for a dry hug in the whole train.'

'I suppose Anthony Belmare's term won't have begun yet.'

'Probably not. That's another reason why I'm not over keen to be at the Hunt. The boy's all right, of course. It's the effect he seems to have on the others that I don't fancy. Shreeve and Wherry prancing about and imagining they're school kids again. Ten to one someone'll get a cricket stump pushed through his eyeball. Of course, I'm exaggerating but that's the kind of thing. You've got the carriage to yourself. You'll find chocolates in that newspaper and here's my reserve flask. Think that's gunpowder they're shoving into the van? There'll be meringues for tea if I know the rector's baker. My, I've a good mind to chuck up this shooting in the Black Forest and take a snooze on those cushions. Heads or tails, heads – tails, as it happens. Well, perhaps after all if it had been heads and I'd bought a ticket, something else would have gone against me; Griever might have got hydrophobia. Porter!'

'Yes, sir.'

'Just take a look in at this window for a moment. No, not over there; it's this corner, I mean. Anything attract your attention?'

'I don't think so, sir.'

'You couldn't suggest a certain rearrangement?'

'Well, sir, there's those golf clubs on the edge of the rack.'

'Oh, those are safe enough. Mr Hearn's not off on a sea voyage. But you might have noticed that the heating pipes are under the right-hand seat and that a suitcase placed against them is sure to protrude a few more inches than it would from under the seat on the left-hand side. You don't expect Mr Hearn to rub his ankles against that during the whole journey. Well, make a note of it. Myself, I've always found it a good plan before breakfast every morning to rehearse in my mind what I intend to do during the day; it lessens the chance of small oversights. Ah, one thing more: if you could procure an extra rug from somewhere I'll see you get a couple of pints for lunch. It's none too warm this morning by God.'

'What with the heater on and three rugs I shan't feel it much unless I pop off to sleep after ten miles.' I again glanced past him to watch a long corridor train with restaurant and sleeping cars which had drawn up on the opposite side of the platform. I should have taken a no more detailed mental photograph of it than most poets do of elaborate architecture if I had not been able to give it a place immediately in one of those non-technical elastic classifications, which alone satisfied my intelligence, of objects describable only by their effects on persons. My first thought was of a day spent in a racing motor-boat on a very calm sea. But the coaches, which seemed of a new triple bogie pattern crouched on concealed springs, were too heavily built, almost armoured, to sustain the image, and I remembered the picture in an illustrated journal of a man-carrying rocket designed by some scientific advertiser to be fired towards the moon from a gun. My instantaneous caricature of my own impression spoilt my chances of discovering what it really was; but there could be no doubt of the interest displayed by a middle-aged man wearing a plaid overcoat in the couplings and buffers between two of the coaches most nearly opposite my window. He was testing them with the end of a walking-stick. He turned, rapped heavily with his boot against the incurve of the coachwork, which I then knew to be what I had not supposed from distant inspection, cast steel. I remembered the face of George Wherry, architect to the Mortmere Rural Council, but was not sure that I had identified him.

'All those rats,' Gunball said, not explaining that he meant the soldiers, small cockneys with bow legs and peg teeth who now occupied the platform in groups from end to end of the train.

Wherry had finished his examination and had entered one of the restaurant cars. His face barely above the level of the lowest part of the embrasure peered from an oblong window. Like an electrically moved cardboard football in a sports outfitter's window it shifted almost surprisingly without revolving, devoid as cardboard of animation, towards the left-hand or rear-most corner of the window, then passed out of sight. The cast steel coachwork was painted grey, studded at intervals with visible rivet heads such as one sees on girder bridges or in the saloons of smaller paddle-steamers. Less space than I thought usual had been allowed for the windows. The panes, which seemed dark, were on the streamline principle, distinctly curved inwards towards a roof surmounted by scarcely projecting cone ventilators. However, I hardly supposed that the coaches were lit by gas and I wondered why ventilation could not have been obtained, as it usually is, through superimposed movable hatches above the windows. My impression of most details in the design of this train was that they were unnecessary or, if necessary, belonging to a world in which I should have felt as wholly disorientated as though, suffering from amnesia after an accident, I had found myself among hoardings bearing futurist German advertisements. I pictured myself leaning over a level crossing gate watching trains; I could not see this train pass until I altered the scene to weak moonlight with ravines and a sharp curve in the line allowing me to include all the coaches in a single and close view. Very long, tubular, dead, they turned with mournful speed at the bend, did not sway, plunged into the red earth and tree-roots of a landslip, emerged with the ease of a saw. Chambers of oblivion in which not one of the passengers returned to consciousness until a porter opening the carriage door shouted that the train had reached its destination.

'So I suppose this one will go there too,' I heard Gunball say.

'Where? Which one?'

'The train you're leaning out of at the moment. To Mortmere. But I was just saying I'd noticed that the other one certainly does. Look at that end coach; you don't see many of those on the main lines.'

It would have been too late to change. An eddy of hustling soldiers clashing water-bottles, trenching-tools, ration-tins, flooded between myself and Gunball who, like a bather surprised in the middle of a facetious gesture by a heavy wave, was scarcely able to shout: 'Anyway, yours will arrive somewhere.' A whistle blew with vicious sharpness, the train had started, the guard had rerolled his flag and vaulted on to the running-board of the luggage van. Then only, glancing through shifting gaps in the thinned but still racing groups of soldiers who had not yet been able to mount the train, was I convinced that the carriage which Gunball had designated was certainly of the out-of-date refitted type usually employed on the Mortmere slip-line. The narrow high body-design, compared with that of the preceding corridor coaches, had the topheaviness and antique lines of an extended sedan chair, but it suggested also that this carriage could have negotiated very deep cuttings where the brambles had been neglected for years by the rural officials and where, as I indolently began to imagine, the signalman's eye must not be distracted by the vivid colours of fresh paint moving among the trees. If my train did not go to Mortmere I could get another the next day, or Welken might guess what had happened and send his car. The first gasometers, restful, solemn like stumps of semi-amputated breasts, curved past the window in frost-bright air. Wireless poles and drying pants in soot-black gardens with mustard and cress sprouting from window boxes would soon follow. Now for many months of complete summer I should idle in gardens warm with croquet and the tinkling of spoons, shadowed by yews. Naked bathing would be usual and the rector would fish for pike off log-rafts. Only the King may shoot swans. Do you eat mango salad, Mr Hearn? Yes, oh yes, certainly yes, though I have not ever, I now will.

'Fond of poetry?'

'I say, I'm frightfully sorry, I mean I'd no idea there was anyone else in the carriage.'

'Hadn't you, ah ha. Well, I'll admit I slipped in rather on the quiet. Part of my trade you know. Otherwise you could never be sure what they weren't doing in the dormitories.'

By chance I recognized him as Gustave Shreeve, but I knew that he did not know me and that it was only his exceptional self-conceit which made him forget that he wore no visible decoration to show that he was head-master of Frisbald College. His large ears protruded almost at right angles to his temples — always a sign, to my mind, of an assertive, fussy temperament. He brought down a small suit-case from the rack, searched with vicious haste in the pockets of his country overcoat, mustard-brown and reminiscent of frosty afternoons on the touchline, for a pencil. He drew a fairly straight line freehand on a writing pad which he had produced from the case, stopped, glanced up to speak.

'Are you for Mortmere?'

'Yes.'

'Ah so am I.'

'Good, then I'm right after all.'

'Well, I see we've managed to secure a carriage in the safest part of the train.' I supposed he meant the rear. He laughed like a clergyman who has made a joke about a subject in which secretly he is seriously interested; then as if regretting his perhaps after all risky levity he added didactically : 'The safest part of any *long-distance* train.'

'You're not a keen railway traveller, perhaps?' I asked with deference.

'Very keen indeed. Of course I was joking just now. I'd as soon take my luck in the cab of the engine. Set me down anywhere on the track between here and Mortmere and I guarantee I'll tell you to within a sixteenth of a mile where I am. And not many regular travellers could do that. You know, speaking quite seriously, I believe there is nothing in this world of ours which if regarded from the right angle will not seem vitally interesting.'

'Yes, that's what I've always felt.'

'Yet you yourself,' he went on with approval, 'must already have knocked up against persons who can find nothing more intelligent to do during long railway journeys than sleep or read a novel.'

'I know.'

'Or play some footling card game on a mackintosh.'

'Not much chance of those chaps next door doing that.'

'Ah, why's that?'

'Well, look what a crowd of them there was at the station.'

'That's so,' he agreed with noticeable eagerness. 'Wonder who they are. Market gardeners, perhaps.'

'No, it's the troops I was thinking of.'

'What do you mean, troops?'

'You know, all that gang on the platform.'

'Ah, but they didn't get on to this train,' he informed me. 'In fact, I should hardly expect to find troops travelling at all today, but if they did you can be pretty sure they would go by the other one, which is considerably the faster.'

'Then I'm afraid things have changed since you last came this way. Look at that door.' I pointed to the varnished partition separating the third from the first class section of the corridor. 'Well, I'll wager my return fare that that bulge in the upper panel isn't caused by the damp. Besides you must have seen them boarding the train when it started. The only thing I can't understand is why they're all keeping so quiet.'

'Probably you were misled, quite naturally, by seeing a few regulars giving their friends in this train, civilians of course, a good old military send-off.'

'Surely you can't have helped noticing at least one of them getting into the carriage next door to this — or next door to wherever you were when we left the station? It isn't as though their boots were soled with velvet.'

'Oh, I arrived pretty late, a last moment dash in fact, too late to have noticed my own daughter if she'd been there. But the fundamental point is this: You'll always find that troops, if they are present in any number, travel by express.'

'Well, if you arrived late I can't help feeling that that's just the time when you'd have had a very good chance of seeing them with your own eyes.'

'Excuse me, but this isn't the fast train.'

A terse crash of glass from the hidden corridor proved me right. Organized deafening laughter announced the success of some well-prepared booby-trap. At last they had begun. Hobnails rasped against varnish, rifles fell, a choir using toilet paper and combs played the first bars of the Forfarshire Stallion. The communication cord suddenly sagged, hung in a slackening useless loop.

'Lord. Well that's judgement with costs all right. So I suppose this must be the fast train after all.'

'Fast be damned,' he said with excessive vehemence. 'I'm

sorry, but if you took the interest in railways that I happen to do you wouldn't make a statement like that quite so casually. I can tell you that alterations in the scheduled times aren't made over the breakfast table. If they are, well, God help us.'

'I know. Ten minutes late for an appointment and you lose a rattling good post in the colonies which would have made you for life.'

'GUARD.'

'Good God, what's happened?'

'GUARD.'

'Well, sir, I can't stand much nearer.'

'Of course this isn't the fast train, eh?'

'No sir, you're right.'

'There you are.' Shreeve turned to me, less with triumph than with an absurd relief.

'Well, it seems the subject of our discussion has undergone an important alteration. The only statement of yours which I disputed was that there were no troops on this train.'

'Ah, I can see you are in the legal profession. It's a clever point. But I'm afraid the judge in this case is too old to lose sight of the issue. By the way, Guard, how is it that these soldiers have been planted on us at the last moment?'

'Change in the orders I suppose, sir.'

'But doesn't the Company raise any objections to this kind of thing?' I pointed towards the dangling communication cord.

'They get reparations, sir. Of course, we've come to expect trouble from these Territorials by now. The worst lot in the country. Colonel Moxon's English Rifles: though I believe Major Wherry has the command this Summer as they say the C.O. has gone abroad.'

'I saw Wherry in the other train,' I said absently.

The Guard's information exhumed no memories in Shreeve's mind. He seemed pleased, had an idea. The lax introverted smile of a nervous fisherman suddenly successful after hours of tension in a trippers' pierhead competition. He brought out an enamelled pencil sharpener barnacled with small wads of blotting paper, hair balls, husks of chicken food, from a waistcoat

43

pocket, and used it rapidly on the pencil with which he had already made marks across his note pad.

'That sounds as though they're getting up a tug of war in the corridor,' I said. 'I wonder how much more the door will stand.'

'I don't know what it'll stand,' said Shreeve, 'but I know what I won't, and that's all this damned row they're making. Like a pack of girls.' He stood up.

'You'll only irritate them if you do anything,' I said. 'We don't want them all in here fooling about with bayonets.'

'Irritate them?' He was half-humorously amazed. 'Well that's one way of looking at sound discipline. Do you think the Colonel keeps a record of their individual fads and consults it every time he gives an order to form fours?'

'That's rather different.'

'It's a difference which made a tenth of the map red.'

The Guard had stepped out of the compartment and begun to retire towards his van. Anyway, that ought to show that the partition door is already locked, I thought. I turned to Shreeve: 'But seriously I think it would be better not to call attention to ourselves just now.'

'Well, if you'd rather not,' he said tolerantly, 'but I think it's a bad principle. Not because I'm a rabid spit-and-polish man. Only because I foresee that if we don't warn them of our presence now we shall certainly have to later on in the journey. I'm not going to suffer for any volunteer officer's incompetence.'

He replaced the sharpener in his pocket, began to draw carefully, his rigid knees resisting the jolts of the now racing train. I thought out what I should do when the English Rifles burst the partition door. Here's the man who thumped on the panel. Here; I've been cursed with him and his insults against the Army for over an hour. If as long. Probably longer, since we were passing the aerodrome and Camber Woods already. It wouldn't matter how ignominious: Shreeve would never be there to tell them. An airman in furs swung the propeller of a small monoplane. Someone was killing a rabbit with wire in the spinney. Seagulls on arable land far from the sea estuary circled for worms. A dung heap smoked in the damascene steel air.

Woods passed like frozen paper. Further on, the girders of a bridge receded obliquely, very close to the window; the train's clatter changed to a lulling profounder rhythm.

'I suppose you've been wondering all this time what I'm up to.'

'I have, yes.'

'I'm making a rough map of our route, the various land-marks, you know, bridges, signal cabins, the main branch lines, etcetera. Any objects which can fairly be said to have a connec-tion with the railway. It's a small thing I always like to do dur-ing a journey. If you were to ask why, I'm not sure whether I should be able to tell you concisely in a few words. I suppose it's because I've always felt impelled to take an interest in whatever happened to be going on round about me at a given moment. And, do you know, the man whom, as I realize more and more every year, I have truly to thank for that little habit is my old headmaster?' His wholehearted smile left no doubt that that gracious portrait had in a very few seconds been discarded in the portfolio for another more striking.

'I wish I had the knowledge to do something of that kind.'

'But it's not knowledge you need,' he urged keenly. 'Anyone could do it. Just take a look at this. Here's our main line — pretty roughly drawn, of course, but that's from memory — here's the central signal cabin at Belstreet Junction, here's where they control the points leading to the new slipline. Damn.'

The tug of war had probably gone to the team nearest to the partition door. A sharp crack from thin wood interrupted Shreeve's voice and I saw that the upper panel had split down the middle. It still screened from us the adjacent section of the corridor. I waited for laughter but heard only the exaggerated cheers of the winning team. Probably none of them had noticed.

'That's as much as I intend to stand.'

'Well I don't know. After all, they haven't been kicking up quite so much noise until now. I expect they'll get bored. They'll settle down on their own accord before we've done another few miles.'

'All right, here's an agreement we can come to between our-selves,' he said definitely. 'If there's any further trouble I go and tell them exactly what I think. That settled?'

'And ask them whether they're really there,' I evaded.

'Ah, now you're chaffing.'

'Well you'll admit that at first you didn't altogether believe me.'

'Yes, I admit. But then, not seeing them myself, and arriving as early as I did. . . .'

'Early?'

A slip of the tongue. He flushed. 'I told you I was late, I know. I'm afraid that was a bit of a fib. But when I've ex-plained the circumstances I think you'll understand why.'

'Of course.'

'The truth is I was in the W.C. at the end of the corridor.'

'Ah.'

'Not actually using it, of course. Not while the train was standing in the station. There's nothing I detest more than that kind of failure to consider the comfort of others.'

'Yes.'

'You're wondering what I was in there for at all, no doubt. Well, it's not a long story, but it's one which I don't care to re-peat often. It might give the impression, quite unjustifiably as it happens, that I was patting my own back.'

'I see.'

'Well, some years ago I was taking a stroll one half-holiday . . . it was in June I think, as the river had sunk quite three or four feet below its normal level on the banks . . . near Gatley Weirs just outside Mortmere. All of a sudden I head a splash. A large salmon leaping, I thought. Actually it was a man who had slipped off the foot-bridge and couldn't swim a stroke. I didn't see him till he had passed me by about ten yards. It was going to be a race; the question was, should I overtake him be-fore he reached the weir? I hadn't time to take off anything more than my mackintosh. Well, I got there, just on the edge. It had been devilish hard going, I can tell you, with that icy cur-rent against me all the way. I brought him round with artificial

46

respiration. Both of us had our clothes frozen almost stiff on our bodies. I got a passing farmer to loan me his trap and we drove to the nearest cottage. I thought this chap would never stop thanking me for having saved his life. Well, about a year later I met him again. He was still harping on his debt of gratitude, as he called it. I told him I had only done what any man in my place would have been bound to do. We met several times after that, and every time it was the same story; I had saved his life. What could I say? And when he started going over the whole thing in detail in front of my friends I at last felt I couldn't bear it any longer. Now the point I've been coming to is this: I saw him today at the booking office, fortunately he didn't see me, and I heard him ask for a ticket to Mortmere. Wouldn't you, if you'd been in my place, have made yourself pretty scarce?'

'I suppose I should. All the same I can quite see that he's got every justification for being very grateful.'

'Ah, rubbish,' said Shreeve, pleased. 'Anything to escape a scene on the platform.'

'So you don't think there's any chance of running up against him in the train?'

'Oh, he's sure to have gone by the other.'

'Now there's a point which has been puzzling me. The other does go to Mortmere?'

'Of course. It's the better train of the two, in fact. Starts twenty minutes later and arrives a quarter of an hour earlier.'

'I wish I'd known that before. It would have given me time to get a decent breakfast.'

'Well, perhaps you won't regret it.'

'Why's that?'

'Those new coaches they've been putting on lately are a bit stuffy.'

'That's what was my impression. Not from a close inspection, of course, and I really know nothing about the technical side of the thing.'

His smiling attention had wandered back to the map. He added a few lines, a semi-circle, began shading, did not look up to see whether I was watching. Another train going in the opposite direction to ours passed with a single sound. Watchers on a rapidly curving platform stared like dummies, were swept away by the burnt side of a steep cutting. Massed telegraph wires rose evenly and were flung downwards again at the pole. The river reappeared, passed slowly. The workman driving a tractor could never get on to this train. Nor could any of the married women or chauffeurs living in any of those houses. Metaphysically we were as remote as Saturn or the Plough. Our times differed. Between the dipping of the iron ladle and spilling of the tar on a road dotted with navvies, Shreeve had drawn a line more than a hundred yards long, though it looked only three inches on the paper. Another hour. Cucumber sandwiches. Afterwards the bed among birded wall-paper, feeling very full, sure of dreams. And in the morning at twelve I should go to the Skull and Trumpet for news and a game of darts.

'Yes, perhaps it's as well we're on this train,' Shreeve again smiled. 'I suppose you wouldn't remember the account in the newspapers some years ago of an accident which took place in Hainwort tunnel?'

'I don't think so.'

'Well, the train that was buried was the Mortmere express. And it started at the very same time as the one you regretted you'd missed will have started today.'

'Really. And what do you infer from that?'

'Nothing exactly.' He grinned with a mystifier's conscious relish. 'But I know that if you'd been travelling then and had gone by the slower train you'd have been saved.'

'There are two ifs to that proposition,' I readily argued.

'I don't see it.'

'All logical assumptions are quibbles.'

'Anyway in real life it was the faster train which went wrong. And one of the few survivors, a great friend of mine, gave me a peculiarly interesting account of something he'd noticed about twenty minutes before the disaster.'

'Did he?'

'Yes. It was like this. The train was passing certain grounds belonging to the Belmare estate (remind me to point them out to

48

you) and there, not more than twelve yards back from the river, he plainly saw a fisherman dressed in green standing among the rhododendrons and winding his reel. Nothing queer about that. But when he looked again he saw only a horned sheep and two swans.'

'Pretty nasty.'

'It was, wasn't it? He looked again ... his attention had been distracted for less than a second, perhaps by some slight movement in the carriage ... and all he saw was a horned sheep and two swans.'

'So what did he do?'

'I never asked.'

'Now frankly, did you believe him?'

'I did. And I think you would have done if he'd told you the story himself. It was not the words that convinced me, they might have appeared in any book or play, but his face. That's a thing that never lies.'

'If it had convinced me I should not have cared to travel by this line again.'

'You would if you'd thought the position out. You see, the warning only applied to the faster train.'

'Then it'll be a sinister lookout for your admirer if we spot anything in the shrubs.'

He had a brief suspicion: 'For whom? Ah, you mean the cove who thought I saved his life. I wonder if he saw me.'

'Why?' I frankly asked.

'Because, well, if you'd care to know ...' His voice stopped, far ahead of his fumbling experimenting thought. 'Because if we were to notice anything in the rhododendrons and the chap you mentioned happened to be one of the survivors, well, I know he's superstitious. ... I mean he might even attribute his escape merely to having seen me on the platform.'

'And follow you about Mortmere telling everyone what a hero you were.'

'Ah.'

The interesting, superficially obscure explanation he had given me seemed to linger unpleasantly in his mind. A weasel looking out of a stone dyke, scared by footsteps. By bootsteps idly drumming on the sweaty tobacco-streaked floor. By Jewsharps and thudded tins. No, again he had not heard. Or perhaps he had, and what he'd said before was all bluff. Leaves were falling outside, from the woods. There were no woods and it was March. Of course, they were birds. Cigar-shaped like brown seagulls. Without wings. One of them struck the pane, softly, flattened out into a brown uneven paste. Ruffled cones of soiled toilet paper blew past. Shreeve was marking a corner of his map very heavily with the pencil. And of all those boys who through the changing years would constantly look up to him, not one dreamed that in the privacy of his room their headmaster was, profoundly and irretrievably, a coward. Ploughed fields were succeeded by grass, a lake, a private golf course. Gentleman's country. Here Disraeli wrote his novels. Breakfast is served from the sideboard. Turf mounds rotted in the damp shadow of the cypress avenue. The head gardener had invented but could not afford to advertise a herbal balm for eczema. It had cured the master and several of his friends. There were iron railings round the trees.

'We're not far from the place now,' Shreeve said.

'And is this part of the estate?'

'It is. Though we've some way to go yet before we reach the river. What's that?'

'Only those Territorials.' My tone excused him from remembering.

'You know what we agreed.'

'Yes, I do,' I risked.

'You'd think it wise to warn them now?'

'Probably.' I became confident.

'I mean you don't feel they might calm down on their own accord after a time?'

'Not now,' I definitely cornered him.

'Very well.'

I was quite wrong; he had hesitated merely out of consideration for my own opinion. Christ. I had sprung on to the seat, fumbled for the handle of a golf club, futilely released it.

Shreeve was at the partition door, his hands curved to a megaphone. He shouted in padre's affected slang: 'Here, cheese that row you fellows.'

'Bligging spak a flunka blicking spug!' A few laughed. The lower panel split noisily. 'All together, ram the fliggering backer to bitching hell.' But already some other interest deflected them. 'Chuck over and hand back me Tin Lizzy. Look at this you gowks, Sandy's gone and cut his bum. That's his own funeral for shoving it through a closed window. Bleeding like a pig, is he? Here, take my neb-wipe.' Slowly they subsided, their voices merging in the clatter of the train. Probably we were safe.

'That's settled 'em.'

'Jolly fine the way you did it.'

'Oh, well, not really. I'm pretty used to having to deal with all kinds of ragging. Boys and soldiers, they're really just one big family. Of course I don't often address my boys in that particular tone.' He smiled finely. 'It was a bit of a joke. Anyway, how can it matter so long as they don't see me?'

It was true that they seemed to have quietened down. Too much so, I thought. But perhaps Shreeve was partly right about their being like boys. During the journey they might go through at least five successive crazes. They wouldn't persist in any of them for long. Perhaps they had now returned to the boobytrap. Well, at best all they could do would be to squirt urine at us through the crack in the panel. But then I could move my seat to the other side.

'Hi.'

'What is it?'

'Look.'

'A river. Ah, you mean we're somewhere near?'

'We are. It's just beyond that first clump of pines. Ever seen a lawn kept quite like that? Think of the generations of gardeners who must have been born and died before they made it what it is now. Be ready to look along my arm when I point. A panther might come out of those trees in the height of the afternoon and you wouldn't hear even so slight a sound as an ant might make on lichen. Till it had sprung at your deck-chair. If ever in any age men have seen ghosts, I do earnestly believe that it is here, in gardens such as this, frosty, at full noon, that they have seen them. Not in the moonlit chancel or the abandoned graveyard.'

'Got the salts ready?' I partly sneered.

'Mind you,' he seriously, theatrically commented, 'I'm not guaranteeing you'll see anything. And if by any wild chance you do, it will be something so indefinable that afterwards you won't be sure that you haven't imagined it. The ghoul on the corkscrew stairs and the corpse in the frozen reservoir don't cut much ice in these critical days. No, it would be very different from that. Something, a stiff hedge or perhaps a tree which some fancy-gardener has been busy on, would deceive the eye. Or let's say that some pattern in the landscape would strike a sympathetic chord in your brain. You know how in large cathedrals sometimes a certain note from the organ has sympathetically affected the roof, and suddenly a chandelier weighing many tons has plunged into the crowded nave. Perhaps it would be like that. A certain vibration of light. Do you notice anything to the right of those bushes?'

'No.'

'Very well. What's *that*?'

'I don't see.'

'Quick man, THERE.'

'Where? Mind out, you'll drop your handkerchief.'

'Oh, to hell with that.'

Straining from the opened window he violently, erratically pointed, his stiff arm shaken in the racing outer air, his fingers clutching a mere corner of what seemed less like a silk handkerchief than a small green flag.

'Didn't you see anything?' he absently hoped.

'No. Not where you were pointing.'

'What's up?' He suspected suddenly, with a forced explosive laugh: 'You're looking as pale as a horse. You didn't think I was serious, did you?'

'I really couldn't say.'

'Catch a glimpse of the fisher, eh?'

'I'm afraid not. But I saw someone I happened to recognize.'

'Well, considering the pace we were going I should think you were quite probably mistaken.'

'Why?' I flashed. 'Do you know who it was?'

'Of course not. I mean, how can I guess when I don't even know who you *thought* it was?'

'Harold Wrygrave. I saw him in a car. Standing up.'

'You're wrong,' he said with noticeable readiness, 'Wrygrave always takes the Upper Fourth in French at this hour on Wednesdays.'

'Well, he must have mislaid his timetable this morning. I know I'm right because I distinctly noticed that he'd recognized you as we passed. And I rather fancy that he was standing at the salute.'

'I'm afraid it would take more than that to convince me,' Shreeve said with faint irritation. 'Of course, if you're really quite *sure* that you recognized him, well, it is just possible. He's rather a harebrained sort of cove. And there's just the chance that knowing I'm temporarily out of the way he might have risked taking a short holiday. Even the salute which you say you noticed mightn't have been altogether imaginary. You know the truth is, unaccountable though it may seem, that that fellow thinks absolutely no end of me.'

'Does he?'

'Yes. Mind you, I don't want to boast. It isn't because of any striking virtue he may have detected in me. If anything it's what might almost have been called a weakness on my part that he admires. On a certain occasion. I wonder if you can guess what I mean?'

'I believe I do. There were rumours at the time, you know.'

'Ah, then I shan't feel I'm giving the fellow away. What happened was that I surprised him in the act. I·suppose he thought that no one would visit the dormitories during the afternoon. Perhaps I ought to have brought the matter into the courts. But then, though I'd be the very first to condemn that particular offence, when I considered that it would be generally known that one of my own masters ... well, I think any man in my shoes would have hesitated.'

'Certainly.' I wondered what far more interesting subliminal train of thought had allowed him to expose so mechanically to me an incident which officially he would have been the first to deny.

'I look at it like this. Either you take action publicly and ruin the fellow for life, or else you deal with him on the spot in your own way, and instead of making a dangerous enemy you'll have a, if one can use that word, friend who'd do anything in the world ...' He broke off with sudden, almost fanatical inspiration: 'Perhaps you *imagined* you'd seen him.'

'I thought I'd told you pretty clearly that I was certain of it.'

'Ah, you don't understand. I mean perhaps what you saw was not Wrygrave at all but a shape, a simulacrum with his form and features.'

'A different kind of fisher in green,' I supposed.

'Yes. Yes. That's it. An omen, a warning in the quiet of the day, a visible prefiguration it may be of death as we comfortably roll through the frozen countryside.'

'Well, it's true I thought he looked ill.'

'Pale, was he?' Shreeve subtly foreknew the symptoms: 'Looked as though he'd had a shock? As though he'd seen an apparition himself? I quite understand. That's my friend's impression all over again. But let me tell you this; both that shock and that pallor were not his but yours, transferred from you to him, to it, to the *thing* which some premonition in your brain had conjured among the rhododendrons.'

'Conjured, ah ha.'

'Well, if you think I'm yarning there's nothing more to be said. For the present. Perhaps you're right, perhaps I am. Let's hope I'm wrong. But we shall know quite soon I think, as unless I've totally misread the timetables for the last six years the other train should overtake us in a very few minutes, and then it'll have less than twenty miles to go before it arrives in the vicinity of Hainwort tunnel.'

'Why "in the vicinity"?'

'You don't suppose it's actually going into the tunnel do you?'

'I'm sure I've no idea.'

'Haven't you? Well, that's the richest I've heard for many years. No idea whether it's going into Hainwort tunnel. Lord, man, if it went into that not only would it never come out but every passenger on board would be killed as surely as though the train had fallen five thousand feet into a ravine. Every man. Not one would escape. Not a single one. You see, it was the extraordinary collapse of that tunnel, on the first day of its use, which caused the original disaster. It has never been repaired. In fact, the slipline leading to it has only once been used.'

'Well I hope it won't be used today,' I sneered.

'Ah, God forbid. Let us try to believe that Wrygrave himself may really have played the truant this morning after all. It's best not even to imagine the horrible death which for the second time in the history of that train hundreds of persons would suffer owing to the incompetent engineering, or as some are inclined to think, the criminal guilt of one man.'

'But how can you assume, even supposing there's the least detail of truth in your so-called omen, that it will be that train and no other which will crash?'

He ignored my irritation: 'Oh, *we're* safe enough, if that's what you mean. And I think if you look at my map for a moment you'll see why.' He offered me the pad, adding: 'No one to interrupt our meditations this time.'

'Yes, it's extraordinary how quiet they've been since you warned them.'

'Oh, they know well enough whether you mean business or not. Now, where was I? Belstreet Junction? Follow my finger along this line. There it is. What I want you particularly to notice is that before we reach the Junction and for some three miles after we have left it the track consists of four parallel sets of rails. You may not know why that is. I'll tell you. These two lower lines, an up line and a down, are used exclusively for express traffic, but the other two, the ones nearest the top of the page, are for goods trains and slower passenger traffic only.

Now, we are at present travelling along one of the slow lines. And the reason why we are doing this is that in a very few minutes we are going to be overtaken by the Mortmere express, the train to which my friend's delusion, if you like to put it that way, referred. Look along the page a little farther to the right. What do you notice now? *That the four parallel sets of rails have become two.* You can understand that it would be impossible for any train to overtake another here. Therefore by the time we have reached the points uniting the slow with the fast line the other train will have had to pass us already. Follow my finger. Now we have reached the spot where the disused slipline branches off the main track. I want you to tell me: Which train do you think will arrive here first?'

'The other, I suppose.'

'Quite right. The other. And, God permitting, it will be the first to draw up in Hainwort Halt, the first to deliver its passengers to the care of the Mortmere busman. How simple, how ordinary that sounds as I say it. And yet this slipline, so easily rubbed out on paper, might be the indirect cause of death to all those people.'

'Why should it?'

'There you are,' he shrugged, 'why? Why did the tunnel collapse in two places almost simultaneously ten years ago? A minute error in trigonometry. Some urchin comes during the lunch hour and fools about with the surveyor's instruments, and afterwards nobody notices that one arm of the theodolite is bent a mere division of a centimetre out of the straight. You could pretend to accept that explanation, like the coroner. But if you'd stood as I have done for many hours among those terrible ruins it might have occurred to you to wonder whether after all it was an accident, an error, that the distance between the two collapsed sections of the tunnel almost exactly corresponded to the average length of an express train.' His spittle inspissated to a jellied cord clung between his softly gabbling lips, his hot face neared me, absurdly, disproportionately excited: 'No, my friend, there is only one explanation which will fit that fact. Deliberate foul-play.'

56

'And I suppose you've got a pretty close idea who did it.'

I had gone too far. For a moment his voice was suspicious: 'No, I can't say I have, myself.'

'Of course not. How absurd of me. As though anyone could possibly know; when even the coroner had to accept the other explanation.'

'Well, as a matter of fact there is someone who does know. Or says he does. A great friend of mind, the same chap, as it happens, who saw the fisher and was one of the very few survivors. I'll give you his words: "As surely as Wrygrave's vice is branded on his face, that maniacal crime is stamped on the face of the fiend who did it." He declined to say anything further at the time, but from various hints he had let drop I got the impression, perhaps wrongly, that he was referring to the designer of the tunnel, the man who is at present architect to the Mortmere Rural Council.'

'Wherry?'

'You know him, do you?'

'Quite well.'

'Oh, I can guess what you think.' Shreeve was on his feet and had begun to pace the compartment: 'That he's one of the most amiable and casual of men, the last fellow in the world to have carefully planned out even a comparatively innocent practical joke. I thought so too. But when my friend, though it's true he had not actually mentioned Wherry by name, began to tell me a few things about the man's record, how at school he had been known as a liar and a cheat and in later life had even been implicated in a scandal connected with the cricket-club funds, I almost wondered whether perhaps I hadn't been mistaken, whether after all this same man mightn't have had some presentiment of the Hainwort disaster.' It was plain from Shreeve's sweating face and the vicious jerking of his clenched hands that whatever crime of Wherry's he had in mind it was not one which had been committed some ten years before. He seemed to suspect my thought, for he soon added:

'The points leading to the disused slipline are hidden from the view of the nearest signalman by a bend in the mainline cutting. A child could tamper with them. Now suppose that the man who was at least partly responsible for the first accident is still living today and that his name might be Wherry. Suppose that there are several persons on the other train who are travelling to Mortmere in order to take part in a certain Treasure Hunt and that the treasure is known to be of considerable value. Mightn't he think it expedient to delay them?'

'It would be rather short-sighted considering he'd be on the doomed train himself.'

Shreeve was perceptibly checked: 'Yes, that's true.' He frowned, withdrew into his fanatic's incomprehensible daydream, suddenly resumed: 'That's true. You saw him, I know. But what if by some amazing coincidence something did happen to that train while he was on it. Nothing serious, of course. Just something that would make him believe for an instant that at last he had been called upon to give account for the part he may have played in the wrecking of that very same train, ten years ago. I am not a vindictive man, I shouldn't like to hear that he had lain for hours slowly bleeding to death in the suffocating darkness of the tunnel which he himself had designed. But somehow if he were to receive a severe shock or even to break an ankle I couldn't sincerely feel that the retribution had altogether been unjust.'

He mused, shaking with restraint, semiconsciously fumbled for his watch, regarded its face for some seconds evidently without reading the time. I noticed that we were passing through a large station.

'That train's overdue by two minutes,' he at last said, sharply.

A faint shattering of glass surprised us. The electric-light bulb above our heads had burst and fallen into the bowl-shaped glass shade which subtended it. A slurred thud sounded from the next compartment.

'Sympathetic vibration. Perhaps they're tossing one of their comrades in a blanket and he's hit the ceiling.'

'Well, I've had enough of it,' Shreeve said.

'But that's the first sound we've heard from them for over half an hour.'

58

'It's the last we'll hear for the rest of the journey.'

I had followed him into the corridor, ready to move towards the guard's van. He rapped briskly on the upper panel of the partition.

'Unless I have complete silence for the next twenty minutes the whole lot of you will spend the week-end in the guardroom.'

There was no response. From a more distant section of the train the thudding sounded again. Like careful heavy footsteps. Shreeve was peering through a crack in the panel.

'There's no one there. They must all have gone up to the front part of the train.'

'I don't see how they could. It would be far too crowded already.'

'All right, then they've all fallen through the windows if you like. It wouldn't be so very surprising; considering the lacka-daisical bolshevik they've got for one of their officers.'

The problem did not occupy him for long. Outside three sets of rails raced backwards along the cindered surface of a high but gradually descending embankment. He tapped the glass of his watch, frowned. We had returned to the compartment.

'I shall positively have to get this old turnip of mine over-hauled.'

'Really?'

'It's gained quite five minutes since I put it right by the station clock.'

'Awful curse when the things begin to go wrong. Once a watchmender gets his fingers into them they're done for, in my opinion.'

'Ten minutes, more like. You see, we've got some way to go yet before we reach Belstreet Junction.'

'I thought we'd passed it already.'

'Did you?'

'Well, we've just passed through some large station.'

'You're quite wrong. Because if we had the express would have overtaken us by now.'

'Anyway you know the line better than I do. Look out of the window and judge for yourself.'

'Of course, I can quite understand what gave you the impression,' he maintained. 'We were passing through a wood. I noticed myself that the carriage had become darker for a moment.'

'I daresay. All the same I saw the platform with my own eyes.'

'Damned rubbish,' he almost shouted. His direct obstinate regard unapparently focused some object moving outside the window, became suddenly attentive: 'Good God.'

'Well, am I right?'

He was stiff with nervous terror: 'Good God. We're done for.'

'What on earth do you mean?'

'He may have time to pull up yet. A quarter of a mile. Listen. The brakes. Thank Christ. Don't you think you can hear them?'

'I think that if you indulge in much more of this bloody nonsense you'll make yourself mentally ill.'

'Oh my God, too late.'

'What for?'

'Christ forgive me.'

A self-balancing toy bird. He rocked woodenly, lightly on the seat. I turned to my window, less with ostentatious disgust than with irritation that his nervousness had genuinely infected me. Through the interior shadow of a passing signal cabin I thought I'd imagined I'd seen a man swinging an unlit danger lamp. The fields rose slowly to the level of the embankment. Cows moved against a large rock, across grass lozenged with flat stones. A cutting interposed, shallow-sided, deepening, slagged with frosted pebbles. The train suddenly swerved. We must have branched off from the main line. What an idiot, I almost thought we had. But of course it must have been some sideline that branched off from us. I did not look at Shreeve, unwilling to let him know how much I had been scared. In these parts they allowed weeds to grow between the sleepers. Reeds. They flickered against the pane. Oh my God. Where are we? Try not to be quite such a fool. You see, rector, I really couldn't for the moment remember that I'd ever heard that there were mountains. I can tell you I almost swore I'd attend Matins for six years. What makes the rocks look so white? Struth I'm sweating. Yes, and of course those blackbirds are really condors. How extraordinarily white. Rock above rock. When you get out of this you'll wonder how on earth you ever let that bloody imbecile half-convince you that something might happen. All the same, looking at it quite disinterestedly, you'll admit that the height of this cutting must be a record. For anywhere in Europe.

'This was my work. In a moment of jealousy temptation overcame me. Now I must pay the price.' Withdrawn into a trance of fear he had begun mechanically to confess. His pudding cloth face wilted. A pool of urine increased round his feet.

He would not see me at the window. I had rammed down the sash, leant out. Like a canyon the cutting deepened among organ-pipe rocks towards the still distant mouth of a tunnel. The English Rifles were walking on the carriage roofs. Some had already reached the engine. Exceeding sixty miles an hour it visibly left the rails, jogging the foremost coaches through spraying wood from ploughed sleepers, mowing the reeds. A blinding jolt had us into the inverted rack, dazzled with glass showering like luminous fish, ricocheting between punching upholstery. Jump. The brakes savaged the wheels. Calvary. Mater. The roses. Vesperal. Burial at sea. Slowing down. Shreeve stood at the uncertain door. He jumped like a rat. Had jumped, falling softly, not stunned, not even bleeding, my spine uninjured, my eyes safe. Buried in reeds.

Shreeve called, close by. On my knees I peered, saw the train entering the tunnel. Slowly. It had almost pulled up.

'Quick. Out of this.'

An iron echo approached us. Clambering the lower rocks I turned. The express had taken the points. Booster-fitted, excessively rolling, the racing Mogul engine rounded the curve, bounded into the rear of the carriage we had left. Coaches mounted like viciously copulating bulls, telescoped like ventilator hatches. Nostril gaps in a tunnel clogged with wreckage instantly flamed. A faint jet of blood sprayed from a vacant window. Frog-sprawling bodies fumed in blazing reeds. The architrave of the tunnel crested with daffodils fell compact as hinged scenery. Tall rag-feathered birds with corrugated red wattles limped from holes among the rocks.

'Another thirty seconds in that carriage and we should have been . . . well. It makes you think. And I'm afraid poor Wherry will never see Mortmere again.' Shreeve gravely turned, designated the externally undamaged cast-steel coaches of the other train. Now hedged by flames. I noticed that the out-of-date sedan carriage which in the station I had seen at the rear of the train was no longer there.

'I am truly sorry,' Shreeve added. 'He was one of the best-hearted fellows I have known. You mustn't take too seriously the things I may have said under the stress of excitement before the accident. He was a white man all through. And there's another thing I believe I said which might have misled you. Didn't I at one time make some remark rather to the effect, "This is all my own doing"?'

'You did.'

'Well, I can explain to you *now* what I meant. The fact is you must have been right after all in supposing you saw Wrygrave in a car. At first I was rather inclined to fancy you had been pulling the long bow. But from the moment when the train took the points the whole truth flashed on me. This was his revenge. He had waited to make sure that I was on the train, then raced us to the slipline. Because two years before I had justly thrashed him after making my discovery in the dormitories. That's what I meant when I said it was my doing. If I had neglected my duty this awful disaster would not have occurred.'

'Wrygrave's no more capable of a calculated revenge than a hen. It's malicious bunk. Though I admit I couldn't answer for what he might do under the influence of blackmail. You suggest that he bore you a grudge for thrashing him; but how could he foresee that contrary to all timetables the slower train would reach the points before the other did today? No,' I emotionally accused, 'if he intended to wreck any train at all it was not ours he had in mind.'

Shreeve made no defence. Above us a voice suddenly shouted: 'Here they are.'

'Lord, forgive me.'

'SHREEVE. HEARN.'

'You fool, it's Welken.'

'God. That you, Rector?'

'Yours ever. Either of you hurt? Eh? Well, take it easy, old boy. No hurry. Got the car here waiting for you. We'll have you home in a jiffy, and then you can tell us all about it.'

The arum colocasia, lupines, lentils, the pomegranate, syca-more, date palms, yew, beech and privet, fenugreek, the meloukhia, the Acacia Farnesiana, carob tree, mimosa habbas, lemon verbena, nasturtium, rose and lily. Snakes hung from the elm branches; pigeons rose from black curtains of leaves, startled by the engine of the car. The river coiled through the woods, avoiding boles of pine and willow. Across the waters of the sun-white marshes alligator fishermen punted their raft. The sea-man's monument on Belstreet Down like the gnomon of a sun-dial cast its shadow over the roofs of the village. A quarter to five. Blue-tiled houses which had grown like bushes out of the ground.

'Well?'

'"Try squinting under the damp beehive in the summer-house."'

'Hoch, of course! Can't think how I forgot.'

Welken had manoeuvred Shreeve into a seat beside the chauf-feur and was sitting with me in the rear. Descending rooks perched on the lowered hood. At the horse-trough outside the Skull and Trumpet, Alison Kemp balancing yoked milk pails returned the rector's amiable wave. Ducks slept on the toad-green water of the pond. Nothing has been moved. A fringe of chopped straw moustached the louvre slits in the church tower. Sergeant Claptree wore a joiner's green baize apron, was re-tenoning the struts of his hen-house. Facetiously he sprayed the chauffeur with disinfectant from a brass syringe. Ernie Travers opened the rectory gates.

'Are they waiting for me, my lad?'

'Yes, sir. Oh thank you, sir.'

Up the bleached gravel drive, oppressed by ink-dark trees. Lilac bifurcated past the windscreen in perfumes of wan blue gauze. Odours of chimes of croquet hoops, tango of views of choirboys through the rustling privet. A lawn-mower wove its rainbow fountain among imagined rock and fern. Shreeve had fainted. The front door was held open by the brass head of a fox. Summer mildly billowed into a hall shadowy as a cave where Welken's geographical globes faded beneath clusters of hats. A rubber ball struck one of the windows.

'So Wherry's safe after all,' I said.

Shreeve's drugged face was instantly alert. Round the screen of privet Tod Erswell and Boy Radnor swerved, Wherry overtaking them.

'Sloshed you both by inches. Now let's see if you can *run*.'

'Hullo, George.'

'Gustave by God.' But he easily deflected whatever amazement he may have felt into: 'Hullo Hearn. No idea we'd have the pleasure of seeing you after all these years.'

'The two rivals,' Welken shrewdly winked. 'Who's it to be this year? Gustave looks the more determined, but George managed to arrive earlier and I'll bet you he's been out with his footrule surveying the ground.'

'Pardon me. Just a moment.' Shreeve turned and hurried from us towards the garden.

'Watch him, George, ha ha. Stealing a march, eh? But perhaps you've got the Treasure in your pocket already, have you, George?'

'Didn't I see you on the fast train today?'

'Daresay you did. That's the one I came by. Slipped a coach at Belstreet Junction. It's far quicker than going on to Hainwort Halt.'

'Quicker than you may have thought. There was an accident.'

'Whew. Anyone injured?'

'Come on boys. Time we started the Hunt. I'm off.'

'Ta-ta rector. We'll be with you in two shakes. How many?'

'All your Territorials.'

'Poor beggars. They were looking forward to the holiday camp in Hainwort marshes.'

'Lucky you'd decided not to travel with them.' I couldn't repress a certain admiration in my tone.

'You're right. A word in your ear: I had a premonition.'

'I'll wager you did.'

The trellised verandah supports. The lemon verbena like a tropic creeper. Wherry's Provençal hat and pirate's sash. How quiet and how hot the air is. You might drop a bomb into the sea and it would leave a more permanent sign than the shouts and chatter of the crowd on the lawn will leave. Welken mounted a wicker armchair:

'Before we begin I have a most interesting announcement to make. News has lately reached me of an engagement between Miss Belmare and Mr Reynard Moxon. They are to be married in July.'

Bellowing cheers. Centripetal faces turned. Miss Belmare with Dr Mears following curtly pushed her way to the front. He brought a tape-measure out of his waistcoat-pocket; ceremonially encircled her bust.

'Forty-five inches.'

'Hooray.'

Among the crowd Shreeve noticeably showed another immediate interest. In profile his chattering face aided by descriptive arm-gestures futilely strained to intercept Anthony Belmare's view of the ceremony. An interpreter. Grudging the boy's independent impression he was evidently explaining the scene. Anthony absently responded. An absorbed reader evading a wasp.

'Our only regret is that Mr Moxon has been unexpectedly detained at Karlsbad by the customs officials.'

Bombs of laughter.

'Otherwise I think you'll all concede there would have been

little doubt, to use a pet expression of my old Dean's at St Salvador's, as to who would have been the successful *agonist* in today's contest.'

Serious cheers.

'I will now make the customary résumé of the rules. Ladies, gentlemen and boys, one of your number has been preinformed of the whereabouts of the Treasure. When or if unobserved he will seek, unearth and clandestinely pocket it. (No, Sir Napier, "Unearth" is not an accidental hint.) The rest of you will have exactly half an hour in which to spot the concealer. The spotter wins the Treasure. If there is no spotter the concealer has it for keeps. I declare the prime of the hunt. You are advised to draw the kitchen garden.'

Wrecking shouts. They faded into the trees. The crowd separated into groups, solos. Miss Frorster in hygienic sandals and a hand-woven skirt. Sir Napier Bevan blue-lipped in the heat, gaitered and spurred, with checked breeches. Caesar Wrygrave sweating under the eyes, oyster-faced, deliberately observant. The boys from Frisbald College. Charles Wrythe. Andy and Mundy Shanks with a privately-made chart of the grounds. Gaspard Farfox with a terrier. The girls from Miss Frorster's Modern Academy. Mr Hards, scales of graveyard mud on his corduroy knees. Hynd and Starn, wearing faded college rugger caps. Wherry last but two, seriously conversing with the three choirboys. Ernie Travers, Boy Radnor, Tod Erswell in knickers. All descended the steps through the yew tunnel into the hedged kitchen garden. Only Anthony Belmare, still followed by Shreeve, remained on the lawn. Curtained by verbena on the shadowy verandah Welken said:

'I believe that boy's spotted you. But he can't get at you without being seen by Shreeve.'

'What,' I mused.

'Great Scott, I believe I forgot to tell you. You're the concealer. Hope you won't mind.'

'No. What do I do?'

'Simple as winking. Just walk into the summerhouse round

the corner when no one's looking and lift the beehive. Pocket the treasure. Then mix with the crowd. There are no bees, I may say.'

'But someone is looking.'

'Never mind. The boy won't do anything while Shreeve is with him. Really it's hardly fair. I know what, I'll go and have a talk with Shreeve and give Anthony a chance to get away. Then if you're quick you can slip into the summerhouse without being noticed.'

'All right.'

Carefully parting the hanging verbena, Welken stepped out on to the lawn, approached Shreeve:

'Well, Gustave, got any ideas?'

'No.'

'I should try the kitchen garden. That's where the rest of them have gone. The concealer will probably be there.'

'Will he?'

'Ah, that's asking.'

Welken laid an emphatic forefinger on the lapel of Shreeve's coat. Anthony had already left them, begun to descend the steps through the yew tunnel. Shreeve's back was towards the verandah. The cowl on the blue cone-roof of the summerhouse veered as the damper air from the interior rose towards the sun. At the cool entrance brambles obstinate as wire had eaten into the doorless jambs. The beehive stood on a single-legged table spoked with warped cricket stumps. Whorled coils of black horsehair or blood sausage. It broke in my hands like cake, issuing dark treacle. Fortunately there were mulberry leaves. I cleaned the ivory paper-cutter, concealed it in my shirt.

'Here he comes, boys.' Wherry's voice. At the back. A square in the trellis window was unblocked by leaves. Wherry with the three choirboys waiting in a clearing among the laurels. Bushes arranged like pincers having their axis at the summerhouse and a narrow gap between the far ends where Anthony Belmare carefully appeared.

Unnoticed, Wherry quickly hid.

'Challenge,' Ernie Travers shouted.

'Sucks, you're wrong,' Anthony said. 'Same to you.'

'Are we?' Boy Radnor ignored the returned challenge with a seriously spiteful sneer. 'How do we know you aren't lying?'

'How do I know you aren't?'

'Never said anything. What's more we've had enough of your cheek.'

'At him, dogs.'

'Go and eat worms.' Anthony briefly put out his tongue, began to run.

Ernie Travers smartly tripped him at the gap, had him by the ankle. Tod Erswell took the other leg. Boy Radnor's warted hands clipped beneath his armpits violently raised him. Anthony struggled with mock anger, the sleeves of his blazer slipping to his elbows, the thin watch-strap breaking on his wrist.

'You'll find some string in my pocket,' he offered.

'Pooh. We could fix you up with cotton.'

'You're going to be jolly well searched.'

Boy Radnor wrenched open Anthony's blazer, fumbled for the buttons of his silk tennis shirt.

'I don't know what you think you're doing.'

'Stop his gab, Ernie. The sash will do.'

'Dashed clever, aren't you. Three to one ... You beastly rotters.'

Lost in pleasure, Wherry had frankly come out from the bushes.

'Look out, there's someone running.'

Wherry had no time to disappear. Branches snapped from the bushes at the gap, Shreeve plunged in like an escaped pony. Already before he had rounded the corner his arm had been raised to point; now it fixed on Wherry: 'You bestial fiend. I'll make you pay for it.'

'Buzz off.'

'They shall know about this.'

'Admit you've been properly fooled.'

'Rector. Here.'

A party of treasure-hunters whom Shreeve had easily outraced had now arrived at the gap. Charles Wrythe led them, sweating in drab herring-bone reach-me-downs, all out for the treasure, limping in tough boots through the hot grass. Miss Belmare followed, strong-buttocked, planting her heelless shoes heavily. Welken with a preconceived explanation of the scene scarcely observed it, was twisted with laughter :

'Blowed if they haven't almost torn the clothes off the boy's back. And the scream of it all is that you're both quite wrong.'

'The man who designed Hainwort tunnel ...' Shreeve sinisterly began.

'Whooha ha ha whoohaha ha.'

'Wouldn't go far out of his way for a treasure you could put in your pocket.'

'Whooha ha. Now Gustave, don't take it to heart. You're both in the same boat. And you've a clear twenty minutes to make it right or, whoohaha, wrong if we look at it from George's point of view. Try again.'

'Not until I've made an important statement.'

'If it comes to statements,' Wherry said, 'I believe I could make one about the headmaster of Frisbald College which would put daylight through several none too recent events.'

'What about a duel?' A voice asked.

'Whoo ha. Come now, shake hands like the pals we all know you really are. On with the Hunt. Time's precious.'

'What about it?' Miss Belmare persisted. 'With pea pistols. Reynard gave me a couple when we were engaged; he used to use them when he was a boy.'

Miss Frorster faintly sobbed.

'By great luck I have them with me,' Miss Belmare surprisingly drew two small revolvers from the V slit in her blouse, handed one to Shreeve.

'Gentleman to see you, sir.' Whinny Saunders the rectory maid standing at the gap addressed Welken.

'Tell him I ... Who is it?'

'Sergeant Ganghorn, sir. Motored up from the police station.'

'Very well. Awfully sorry, you people. Shan't be long.'

'May the worse man lose.'

He had gone. Miss Belmare handed Wherry the other revolver. Above the bushes I thought I saw the roof of a black motor van. Drawn up under the elms, on the drive.

'Is that a pea-shooter?' Charles Wrythe seriously asked.

Miss Belmare scoffed: 'It's a sweat syringe.'

'More like a six-shooter.' Sir Napier Bevan had come critically forward. 'If you value the judgement of an old sportsman you'll both put them away where they came from.'

Miss Belmare blushed.

Wherry: 'By God, I believe you're right. WAIT.'

SPAK. Shreeve had opportunely fired. Dropped the revolver with theatrical horror. Started forward. Mumbled: 'Awful mistake.' Dr Mears intercepted him:

'My job this time.'

Wherry writhed sneering like a rat on the ground with a bullet through his groin. Far off, from the sea, a first phrase of thunder warned. The crowd stood posed in self-conscious inactivity, aware of the tableau they formed. The laurels signalled in a faint damp breeze. Bees whirred. Beyond Belstreet Down the marine sky glittering like tin seemed the cymbals on which the vibrating note of a steamer's siren had been sharply struck. Dr Mears prised open a nickel instrument case. Everyone was chatting. At the gap, Welken had excitedly reappeared.

His face changed with difficulty: 'What's the verdict Doctor?'

'Not fatal I think, unless gangrene supervenes. Though I fear he will be permanently lamed.'

'That's a pity.'

'I can't imagine how Reynard made the mistake,' Miss Belmare said.

'A most amazing thing.'

Taut with news Welken finally released: 'Then what do you say to this: Harold Wrygrave has been arrested on a charge of train wrecking.'

The Colleagues

Now the sergeant's contrived to get laid out I shall have to re-arrange the scouting for tomorrow. But with all due fellow-feeling I'm not over-regretful that I shall have a pretext for in-ducing Mitchell to take a more responsible interest in the doings. I fancy offering him an emphatically free hand might meet the case. Suggest nothing, but ask if he'd mind amusing a combina-tion of my lot and the babes from two-thirty to four. The sig-nallers I'll manage. The usual with variations: something involving recognition. Fix one of those wooden grid mats across a bath in the upper tubroom and stand young Gilchrist on it against the window. The rest of the section I'd have in the ash yard, with pencils. Afterwards, unless there's frost, we might give the new tracking irons a trial. Parade at two-fifteen. An inspection by patrol leaders of badges and neckerchiefs. No, it's important at least in this way – that unless the scouting and everything else the kids do here is to be quite indistinguishable from an unorganized nursery game, some sort of antidote to the exemplary vagueness of their headmaster is urgently neces-sary. 'Well, Mrs Taylor and I rather *thought*, with all these coughs and colds hanging over us just now, that if the actual parades could be managed temporarily inside the hut –' Today after lunch I could have kicked Taylor extremely hard on the bottom, but the feeling has worn off. There are other things to do.

'Kingsley! Come here a moment.' Lloyd propped his bicycle against the wired library window, hooked a rugger ball from beneath the pedals. I must remember to say something before prayers about putting the yard balls back into the drying-room. 'What were you shouting just now?'

'Sir, I wanted to ask if I can fetch a book from the dormitories after I've changed.' The boy, wearing football clothes beneath an unbuttoned overcoat, stood almost at military attention. A slow water-drizzle echoed minutely in the adjacent lavatories.

'If you *can*? Well, I hope so. We don't want to have to hire a bath chair for you just yet. Presumably you can still use your arms and legs now and again, if not your brains.'

'May I then, sir?'

'May you what?'

'May I get my book, sir?'

Lloyd whispered: 'A word in your ear, King. When we want to ask a question in civilized society we usually try to do so as quietly as possible. We don't stand at the door of the house and shout across the ash yard.'

'No, sir.'

'Well, think of that next time. All right – get out of my sight.'

Boys returning across the yard to the house after football side-glanced at Kingsley. Lloyd called:

'There will be no tubs this afternoon. See that you're all changed and downstairs in ten minutes.'

Kingsley waited. 'May I fetch my book, sir?'

'Yes, yes. Hurry up and change. Oh – Kingsley – who's pill fag for this week, do you know?'

'I'm not sure, sir. I think Moffat is, sir.'

'Quite probably. You might find out, will you? And send the little brat along to my study as soon as he's changed. You needn't tell him what I want him for, though.'

'Right, sir.'

Master Moffat badly needs waking up, but I can hardly smack him for leaving a yard ball lying about after lunch. Taylor, of course, if by any startling chance he'd happened to notice, would have done nothing at all. No, I'm wrong, he would have passed some remark to let them understand that he didn't mind in the least. Remember when I told him that I'd caught Williams pinching biscuits in his study: 'Did he really? Ha, ha, ha. Cheeky little blighter.' It's such rotten luck on the kids themselves; or it would be if Taylor had the least influence with them. Imagine how young Kingsley might have turned out. At first I was inclined to agree with what Pa Kingsley frankly said about him. Now he's probably one of the best types of boy we've got here. A thoroughly reliable customer, and he's really beginning to pull his weight in the house. As a matter of fact we think a good deal more of him here than they do at home.

A final couple of boys, comparing mock ballet gestures, shuffled brick dust with studded boots, approached slowly. Lloyd pointed: 'You. Get a move on. Run.'

We note the intense anxiety caused at headquarters by impending coughs and colds when they don't happen to hang over my scouting arrangements. I'm afraid one doesn't need peculiarly good eyesight to be able to see right through comrade Taylor. Not that one objects much to his spending the whole afternoon reading the *Church Times* in the drawing-room when theoretically he's on duty. But he might have taken the trouble to tell either Mitchell or myself what he intended to do, and have asked one of us to keep an eye on the kids while they were changing. However, that would have meant pushing extra work on to us, and for some reason he dislikes doing this. The extraordinary thing is that his attitude doesn't seem to be entirely due to a consciousness of glass houses or even to grudging us our influence with the kids; there's a definite motive of benevolence behind it all. Work is so frightfully unpleasant. One does it and one is paid for it, but one avoids discussing it more than is necessary. To talk shop in the presence of a man who is new to the place would be a kind of inhospitality. If Mitchell's the right sort he'll get into the swing of things by pure instinct. If he isn't he won't, and no amount of prompting will have the least effect. It would be ungentlemanly even to suggest that he might make himself useful. Because in Taylor's world effort and guts are vulgar; only skill is respectable. One is born either dull or bright, and nothing afterwards can change one's nature. Certainly not Taylor's own methods of dealing with the young. But if we're to get these kids anywhere we've got to cater for the average. The world's work isn't and never will be done by exceptions. As time goes on there will be less and less room for the type of person whose sole object is to evade responsibility. Whether we like it or not there are changes in the air. And the boy with guts is the one who is going to survive.

Watching the upper tubroom windows Lloyd lifted the ball slightly with the toe of his boot, jerked it upwards, but did not attempt to catch it. *I shall take a look round later; they're fairly quiet.* He gathered the ball. *I've had quite a full day today.* He grasped the ball firmly, swung it swiftly from his right to his left hip. *Locker lists revised. Twice telephoned during lunch. Run before breakfast. I ought to be feeling tired.* He braced himself, sidestepped, prepared to sprint, became aware that Mitchell was approaching him from the far end of the ash yard. He nodded, dropped the ball to his feet, glanced again towards the tubroom windows. *Why can't the man change into proper clothes when he's refereeing?* Mitchell hesitated, about to come towards him, grinned experimentally. *A rather sordid mistake. No response.* Mitchell quickly fixed the grin on to the gardener, who was standing at the door of the greenhouse fifty yards away. *How really loathsome. As though I imagined that the least gesture made by anyone else must necessarily be addressed to me. Well, and suppose you do, great Christ. You won't be killed. The truth is I'm developing into a curate.* Lloyd kicked the ball against the wall. Without looking away from the windows he said:

'Game go off all right?'

'Yes, quite well.'

'Good.'

'I borrowed your whistle.' Mitchell handed it to him. 'I hope you didn't want it.'

'Not at all. I've got another as a matter of fact.'

'My penny one isn't much use. It sounds as though it had come out of a cracker.'

'What about getting a scout whistle?'

'I know. I've thought of that. But none of the ordinary shops seem to stock them.'

'I can send up for one for you if you like.' Lloyd became off-hand: 'Not that it matters really, but if you're going to do a fair amount of refereeing I think it might be worth while.

There's no harm in being rather fussy over the minor details when one's dealing with lower game. As a matter of fact the kids here respond particularly well to that kind of thing.'

'Yes.'

A boy, already changed, strolled across the yard towards the lavatories. Lloyd threw the whistle to him. 'Put that back into my study, Simmy.' He returned to Mitchell : 'Excuse me.'

'I was wondering whether it would be worth while my changing into football clothes,' Mitchell said. 'I don't get much running to do.'

'Well, I generally change myself. I think it's a good thing on the whole.'

'I shall have to overhaul my sports outfit. I rather suspect that I've left my shorts at home.'

'It's a pity you don't play fives.'

'Yes. Did you get a game this afternoon?'

'I meant to. But I haven't had time.' Lloyd mused, brightened. 'By the way, you've heard all about the accident?'

'No. Who?'

'What, hasn't Taylor told you how he leapt from the window to render first aid?'

'I haven't seen him since breakfast.'

'Oh, that accounts for it. I can tell you there's a treat in store for you. A good half-hour's worth, not counting the repeats. But as far as I can see all that actually happened was that the sergeant tripped over his bicycle when he was wheeling it away after taking drill.'

'Wasn't he damaged at all then?'

'Well, he didn't have Taylor out of the window absolutely for nothing, you know. He must have been shaken up a bit.'

'Extraordinary thing to happen.'

'He was lying down when I went round to look at him after lunch. He'll probably be taking things easy for the next day or two.'

'Oh !'

'The scouting will have to be rearranged, by the way. I wonder if you'd mind lending a hand tomorrow afternoon? I should

75

be very glad if you would. There won't be much to do. I can manage the signallers.'

'I wish I could. But I really know almost nothing about scouting. I've never done any before.'

'You could keep a few of the kids occupied for half an hour or so.'

'I'd like to, but I really don't feel I'd be much use. I shouldn't have the least idea what sort of line to take.'

'Any line you like. Charades. Games. Making up codes. Anything that will keep them amused. Provided they don't kick up a row or break the furniture.'

'I suppose I could think of something. But I don't see myself giving them straight talks about the Empire or the dangers of secret smoking.'

'Well, I'm not very keen on that sort of thing myself.'

'No, I know. I didn't mean that.'

'It's all right in its way, but I'm not sure that it's altogether suited to the class of boy we get here.'

'It's the one thing I do rather jib at.'

'I generally get over it myself by leaving it in the hands of the patrol leaders. They're quite good on the whole. If you like I can send young Kingsley along to you tomorrow. He could take over the babes for a time.'

'Oh, thanks very much. I shall be pretty hopeless, I'm afraid.'

'I don't think you will. I can lend you the book of words. It won't take you more than a few minutes to read up about knots or the flag. Or you could give them a spot of first aid if you feel that way.'

'Well, I'll make an attempt.'

'Right. Good.'

'I suppose I'd better be getting along to tea.'

'Half past two tomorrow then?'

'Right.'

This evening I take prayers.

'Cheer-oh.'

My God, I am a swine. Why couldn't I have trumped up some definite engagement? Why acquiesce for an instant? Decline utterly to be an accomplice. Queer the whole schedule. Cheap water-pistols for fussing terriers. Quite frankly repudiate the obligation. Clear straight out of the house after lunch. Perfectly unassertively and not very far. Not farther than the post office. Not at all. Realize that every word of this is going to happen over and over again. Each time I shall commit myself and have the same daydream plans for evasion. I shall take prayers, I shall go to camp. I shall probably talk to them about the dead on Armistice Day. And all this will really be due to a footling design on my part. I see now. It's deliberate. I want to involve myself. Resistance would be romantic. Any attempt to do what I like would smell of desertion from real reality. Vulgarly duped by mushroom psychology advertisers. Tracts written by self-confident quacks. Don't stand on the defensive against Life; step out and greet it in the open. Bathe boldly in the arduous modern *continuum*. Accept everything. Have no opinions. Don't be naïve. Never risk being thought to imagine yourself Shelley. Be passive. Be active. Be nothing. Be a schoolmaster.

At the greenhouse Mitchell stopped to avoid the gardener. I know nothing about the Test Match. Yes, but he'd like telling you. Quick, look at something. The bell of the chapel, stuck on the downswing, jutted from its concrete shelter. No, he's going away. In the tool-shed well-oiled sacking covered the motor-mower. Bast hung from a nail on the open door. There was a smell of grass seed or weed-killer. Oblongs of sacking protected the lavatory windows from frost. Weeds had been raked from the edges of a path. Felt strips held the branches of a pear tree nailed against a wall. The roof of the chapel was thatched. The wire fence of the tennis courts rose beyond elm trees. From the house an imbecile clock face stared. Nothing that happens in the school grounds has any connection with what happens in the town outside. Every day here certain ceremonies are independently performed. Latin lessons are given. Games are organized. Surplices are worn. Outmoded precautions are scrupulously taken. Nothing which a clergyman might think risky to neglect is neglected. We are the servants of the parents' most contemptible misgivings. I shall be here or in places similar to this for the rest of my life.

I shall be here. Grinning at breakfast, amiable at lunch and supper, always agreeing. Imagining myself a spy of manners. Wholly scientific. Stopping without disgust to watch Lloyd punt a ball across the yard. Telling him I like cricket. Seriously discussing the sermon. I shall become less and less convinced that I dislike anything. I acknowledge his prestige. The enormous inescapable weight and dullness of his impersonal backing. The sanction of thousands of the dead. It would be futile to resent. No, I want to applaud. Lloyd had regathered the ball. He's perfectly aware that I'm watching. Receiving a long pass and holding it neatly he began to run. He swerved, sold the dummy, fended off a tackle, punted well over the head of the fullback. Knee up, rigid, a clean full punch with the instep. He sprang, he raced towards the tennis courts. Bucking, heavily agile with jerking shoulders. Baboon or antelope. Going all out, broadbacked in a tight sweater. How terrific. How electrically vile. He plunged, he touched down, stumbling among tree roots. It's a vision. I am palpably standing here. There are no other witnesses. If there were they would have nothing to report except that a young preparatory schoolmaster has kicked a football. I have seen a horror which no one else here would have been privileged to see. For an instant I must have been authentically insane. Bunyan saw mountains shining above the houses. I've had an hallucination. Probably voluntary. It's a reward. It's going to happen again. In the night. At lunch. Everywhere. An award of power. This is only the beginning. A genuinely religious delusion. I am very glad.

Sunday

I AM going back to lunch. There is no ambush, no one will ask me to show an entrance ticket, I have not tampered with the motor-mower, no butcher-boy has chalked my name on the basin of the fountain. This is a public path, no discrimination is made against persons not moving on a definite errand, against women without tennis shoes, men who aren't easily called Freddy by their colleagues. I have as much right to walk here as anyone. I am invited, everyone is invited, we are expected to stop and look at the mandarin ducks, to use the less direct path up the side of the valley, smell the lupins, poke groundsel through the wire meshes of the aviary. Why did the council put flood-lights in the trees round the fountain and build a thatched hut for the ducks on an island? Not merely in order to give the contract to their friends or because it's the fashion, but also because they want the town to have a good name with visitors. That's what civic consciousness really means, and it's a perfectly sound business proposition I suppose. They are really gratified that people come here, we are doing them a service, all kinds of people, dwarfs with diseases, young men with temporary jobs in the town, airmen and sailors, old women and public schoolboys returning from church, girls. There will be no inquisition at the park gates, no one is curious about your face, it is quite unnecessary to cross the grass in order to avoid seeming to follow the women who happen to be walking in front of you. Probably no one here knows anyone else. And suppose someone who did know you came up to you and suddenly asked what you were doing, you could say quite naturally 'I am going for a walk' or 'I am looking at the ducks'. You wouldn't have to pretend that you were exercising a terrier or going to buy a Sunday newspaper. That's the advantage of a place like this in a large town. There's no need to suspect that people are watching you from behind window curtains and wondering what you are doing. If anyone looks at you, you can see that he is looking at you, and you know he thinks you are merely walking through the park. And suppose everyone here were actually staring at me, suppose I were dancing or wearing sensible clothes, I should probably feel rather exhilarated. But as it happens I shall not be accused of anything, there is no kind of danger, not the least need to want to escape like a cat under the laurel bushes. I can't even flatter myself that I'm ill.

I am going back to my lodgings for lunch. Who will be there? Only the table, the flower with protruding stamens arching from its jug like a sabre-toothed tiger, the glass of custard, pleated apple-green satin behind the fretwork fleur-de-lis panel of the piano. The whole afternoon and evening will be free. Realize that, realize what I could do. All the possibilities of thinking and feeling, exploration and explanation and vision, walking in history as among iron and alabaster and domes, focusing the unity of the superseded with the superseding, recognizing the future, vindicating the poets, retiring between pillars as Socrates, desperate as Spartacus, emerging with Lenin, foreseeing the greatest of all eras. But unless I am very careful I shall sit on the sofa trying to decide not to go on reading the paper. I shall look out of the window. People will pass carrying neatly rolled umbrellas and after tea bells will toll. Everyone will appear quite at ease, fairly well-dressed, comfortably married, not at all furtive or sinister. Nothing will visibly suggest that they are all condemned, that what they stand for is already dead, putrescent, stinking, animated only by preying corpse-worms. I shall begin to doubt whether they are dead, whether it's not merely my own inefficiency which vomits when I hear them hint: 'In this funny old world of ours one must be a realist.' Hypocrisies which during the week seemed irrelevant abstractions will palpably promenade, bow, exchange smiles. I shall suspect that my work has been a drug, that all the week I have evaded this reality, that in future my leisure – the gaps between drug-takings – will become more and more impossible to bear. And the drug itself will never be anticipated with pleasure, it will always be feared. Perhaps that's why I've got nervous diarrhoea now. I feel as though I were in a waiting-room. Tomorrow I have to use a rotary duplicator for the first time.

Ah-ha, we are getting nearer to it now, we are becoming quite daring. The modest little secret has popped out at last. Now we are in our birthday suit. Oh, look, mother, there are spots all over his back. So that's why he was explaining that sunbathing permanently injures the brain cells. Is it credible? Yes, I am vulgarly anxious about my work. All other explanations are mainly decorative, shamming a greater horror, demon masks to divert attention. I am afraid that I shall not be able to understand the mechanism of the duplicator, that I shall not know how to fit the stencil on to the roller, I shall not get through what I have to do in time, shall perhaps damage the machine, be warned that my work must improve. Unless I am very careful I shall spend the whole of this afternoon uselessly trying to elaborate my fear into something monumental and flattering, and in the end quite frankly thinking of tomorrow.

Epictetus advised contempt for all things not dependent on choice. What's the worst thing, excluding murder and arson, in which I might be implicated tomorrow? I might be sacked without a testimonial. Epictetus would tell me that this is something outside my control, that I ought to be ready to accept it without complaint if it comes, that I should set my heart only on things which no external accident can endanger. He forestalled the 'His will is our peace' idea in less mystical language. Of course the idea is useless now, worse than useless, dangerous, sinister. Whether I am sacked or not depends at least partly on whether I make up my mind to understand the mechanism of the duplicator. I can't just forbid myself to be seriously interested in the success or failure of the copies, and then, if they fail, highmindedly submit to a thrashing. No one would attempt to thrash or torture me, I should simply be asked to find another job. And if I found one the same process would begin over again, till in the end I should have no job at all. Things may have been different under the feudal barons. Then you were someone's serf and you might be thrashed but you wouldn't be abandoned. That's what gave colour to the God the Father theory. But today real passivity is only possible to the leisured. Nevertheless there are thousands of people even now with jobs in this town who are made miserable by the idea that they ought to be at peace with their own souls. Though it's true they may not formulate it to themselves quite in that way – they may feel remorse for hating their wives, or they may wear an enamelled badge with the inscription 'Prepare to meet thy God', or they may make useless resolves to do their work at the office cheerfully. And what happens if they succeed in doing their work cheerfully? Suppose I became cheerful, suppose I refused to be alarmed by the duplicator. Then very soon I should be put on to something more difficult. And suppose even then I didn't revolt – I should soon be put on to something more difficult still. And in the end I shouldn't be a subordinate at all. I should have become one of those responsible liars and twisters who make a profit out of believing that drudgery and servility ought to be accepted cheerfully. But I am not likely to reach that position. I am much nearer to those other blunderers who, cynically regarding as a dishonour and horror the work they have to do every day, try to preserve the old integrity intact within the blind enclosure of their minds. That is the maddest mistake of all.

It is mad to be content to hate every external danger, to be an ostrich, to accept any explanation which minimizes the importance of material gains or losses, to fail to try to find a real solution. It's no use pretending you are splendidly or redeemingly or even interestingly doomed. If you are doomed at all, and it is still possible for you not to be one of those who are doomed, you are doomed like a factory which excludes the latest machinery or like a migratory bird which fails to migrate. Don't flatter yourself that history will die or hibernate with you; history will be as vigorous as ever but it will have gone to live elsewhere. No, you are not a martyr, you are not a conqueror, you recognize that, you are aware that only history which is already living elsewhere can make martyrs and afterwards conquerors. Then where is it living, how can you get to it? Can it have disguised itself as a rotary duplicator, as traffic fussing in a smelly street, as electricity, as lying advertisements, as dingy and crowded tenements, as factory hooters, as any or all of those things which are so uneasily reflected on the surface of the old passivity? Stop just a moment. Aren't we becoming a little extravagant, almost metaphysical? Don't you think so? Because it's well known that comfortably-paid university experts have warned us again and again against mistaking abstract generalizations for concrete things. Don't you suspect that after all they may have been right, that history is nothing more than a convenient figment, an abstraction, and that only concrete things like motor coaches and duplicators and ultimately electrons – which though not perceptible to the senses would be if they could – are real? And why not go one step farther, why not say that electrons and duplicators and motor-coaches are nothing more than abstractions? Isn't that what you have been trying to convince yourself of all along? Day after day you have walked to work in the morning, trying not to feel sick, trying not to be degraded by petty fears, despising the genuine Jesus-gang who at least believed that evil was real, trying to dismiss the office buildings as an inconvenient dream, as a boring abstraction, as something neither pleasant nor unpleasant, without colour or shape or substance, finally as nothing at all – and every day you have failed completely. You have been jarred and stung beneath your pretences by the very reality which your pretences were designed to disguise. You have failed to deny history, as you always must fail until you are mad or dead.

History is here in the park, in the town. It is in the offices, the duplicators, the traffic, the nursemaids wheeling prams, the airmen, the aviary, the new viaduct over the valley. It was once in the castle on the cliff, in the sooty churches, in your mind; but it is abandoning them, leaving with them only the failing energy of desperation, going to live elsewhere. It is already living elsewhere. It is living in the oppression and hustle of your work, in the sordid isolation of your lodgings, in the vulgarity and shallowness of the town's attempts at art and entertainment, in the apprehensive dreariness of your Sunday leisure.

83

History is living here, and you aren't able to die yet and you can't go mad.

But history will not always be living here. It will not always wear these sordid and trashy clothes. History abandoned the brutal fatherliness of the castle and it will abandon Sunday and the oppression of the office too. It will go to live elsewhere. It is going already to live with the enemies of suffering, of suffering beside which yours shows like silly hysteria, with people who are not content to suppress misery in their minds but are going to destroy the more obvious material causes of misery in the world. And the man who doesn't prefer suicide or madness to fighting – and how could anyone who has been at all near to suicide or madness prefer them? – will join with those people. He will look for history not in a Sunday afternoon's reading at his lodgings, not even in reading Lenin, nor in any of the excitements of thinking and feeling, but in the places where those people are. He will go back to his lodgings for lunch. He will read the newspaper, but not for more than a quarter of an hour. He will look out of the window and see the black hats and rolled umbrellas, but he will no longer be paralysed by disgust or apprehension. He will go out into the street and walk down to the harbour. He will go to the small club behind the Geisha Café. He will ask whether there is a meeting tonight. At first he may be regarded with suspicion, even taken for a police spy. And quite naturally. He will have to prove himself, to prove that he isn't a mere neurotic, an untrustworthy freak. It will take time. But it is the only hope. He will at least have made a start.

Journey to the Border

'We shall not perish, because we are not afraid to
speak of our weaknesses, and we shall learn how
to overcome our weaknesses.'

I

EVER since breakfast the tutor had been preparing to tell Mr
Parkin that he would rather not accompany him and the boy to
the races. 'Why should I?' he thought. 'I may have been forced
to sell myself as a purveyor of the kind of trash that's required
for a public-school Common Entrance examination, but that
doesn't mean I'm going to act as footman as well.' He was
standing at the window of the dining-room, waiting for Mr
Parkin to come downstairs. The pure-bred terrier puppy lay
weakly outside in the sun, muzzle on paws, watching the chaf-
finches pick up bits of monkey-nut from the gravel drive. The
boy had got tired of experimentally dropping very thin shavings
of nut into the tadpole jar on the window-sill, and had probably gone off to the garage to fool round and irritate the chauf-
feur. Soon his father would become anxious and start shouting
for him from upstairs.

'Presumably after three months of this I've a right to a few
hours' leisure,' the tutor thought with fury. He quickly checked
the feeling. The important thing was to remember what he had
discovered at breakfast. Going from the table to the sideboard
in order to avoid implicating himself in the advice which Mr
Parkin had been giving the boy against over-excitement at the
races, he had felt for the first time since his arrival that he
wanted to spend a day at this house. On previous mornings the
gilt and white dining-room with its window view of an artificial

85

lake, fir trees, lawns, huge flowerbeds, had suggested nothing to him except that he was wasting his life in a faked and isolated world incompletely retrieved from the eighteenth century, but today the unpleasant prospect of standing about for hours in a field and of meeting the cheerful MacCreath girls or Humphrey Silcox the ship-owner's son had inversely reflected a fictitious value over everything unconnected with the races. The lake, the four lawns all at different levels, the blue stable clock, pigeons, the whitish-green sword-like leaves of the irises, even the scalloped ivory knob of the silver-plated chafing-dish on the sideboard, had seemed to offer possibilities of enjoyment which at all costs he must not fail to follow up.

What he would do here if he managed to escape the races had been and still was uncertain, but it would be something important and at the same time deliberately queer, some act which would violently break the continuity of his life as a hired tutor. It might be a bogus ceremony of purification, performed in the kitchen or in the stable loft or under the dining-room table or on the croquet lawn. He would symbolically wash off all the dismal servilities of the past three months. He might even climb a fir tree, or go for a forty-mile bicycle ride, or drop one of the boy's exercise books into the lake, or simply peer in through the broken pane of the outhouse where the electricity was made. And the interesting point, as he now began to realize, was that whatever form the act might eventually take it wouldn't be altogether a farce. It would be something more than a frantic and temporary reaction against three months of self-effacement. Yes, it would be the beginning of a new technique, a first step towards solving the problem of how to live in this house.

Standing at the dining-room window he became aware that his valuation of the Parkins had hitherto been quite inadequate: he had disliked them because he had wrongly taken them, not for freaks belonging to the same order of reality as the characters in a Grimm's fairy story or a cinema film, but for ordinary living people. Instead of recognizing their queerness, and of using it as a pretext for being equally queer himself, he had inexcusably stood on his dignity, suspected petty insults, tried to think of stinging retorts. But in future he would be quite different. From this morning on he would be as fantastic, as expansively imaginative, as he liked. He would do just what he liked. More than that, he would do it in such a way that no one would realize he was doing it: they would merely think that he was at last settling down to country life. He saw it clearly now – he would pretend to be one of them. He would wear a check cap, borrow the boy's fishing-rod, examine rabbit-holes, shoot at bats from his bedroom window with an air pistol. He would be the maddest, the strangest of them all – with the advantage that whereas for them their behaviour came naturally, for him it would have all the attractions of a voluntary, a limitless extravagance. He would be invulnerable. Never again would he have to be on the defensive. He would see the house in a new light, would want to live here, would even choose to live here rather than elsewhere. It would have become the sole place, perhaps in the world, where he could get just this kind of pleasure.

There was one imminent danger, however. He might be tricked into a sordid quarrel with Mr Parkin about the races. He mightn't find it easy to put the new technique into operation straight away. In fact it was precisely this uncertainty which made it all the more essential for him to have the day free for thinking out the technique in detail. That was why he couldn't submit to going to the races. But an emotional scene with Mr Parkin might poison the whole morning. Not only that – it might disenchant the tutor with the new technique altogether. 'No,' he decided, 'I've got to begin to learn to control myself. Hysteria, however impressive, merely puts me at the mercy of these people.'

If Mr Parkin, who was now coming down the stairs after leaving his wife's bedroom, had been aware of what the tutor had just decided he would have been doubly surprised. He not only had no suspicion that the tutor wasn't perfectly contented in his house, but he had always regarded him as a rather frigid little man. Rather too unresponsive to be an entirely suitable companion for the boy. It wasn't that the Agency had recommended a tutor who hadn't the manners of a gentleman – and after all there was a very real risk of that happening nowadays – but Mr Parkin would have preferred, or imagined he would have preferred, someone more sympathetic and at the same time capable of exercising a stricter discipline. Actually, though he didn't realize it, no sort of tutor would have satisfied him. Fussing about the boy had been, along with midday drinking at a small hotel in the company of well-to-do local farmers, his chief interest since he had given up playing at farming ten years before. Even this morning, in spite of counter-excitement at the prospect of the races, he had chosen to open a nagging discussion with his wife about making the boy wear two scarves in the car – a detail on which they were really agreed from the start.

'Above all, no fireworks,' the tutor warned himself. Mr Parkin had stopped for a moment outside the dining-room door. He shouted up to his wife: 'I'll tell Stokes to bring the plaid rug.' She screamed an unintelligible answer. He peered round the door.

'You here?'

The corner of his mouth gave a suspicious twitch, exposing a blackened premolar tooth. He came into the room.

'Where's the boy?'

'I think he went to the garage.'

'I don't want him playing about with that motor-mower.'

Surprisingly Mr Parkin made no further comment. Wincing a little, he limped over to the window, supporting himself on the way by sliding a clenched hand along the edge of the table. His swollen knee was evidently painful this morning – as it perversely always was now whenever there seemed a chance of his getting a day's sport of any kind. But no doubt he was able to compensate himself with the theory that the swelling was hereditary. He had often proudly told the boy that he, too, when the time came, would develop the same trouble as his father and grandfather before him. The tutor had wondered whether the trouble might simply have been due, in both cases, to gonorrhoea.

'That's a nasty dirty messy thing to do,' Mr Parkin suddenly said.

'What?'

'Look at it.'

He pointed to the tadpole jar on the window-sill. The tutor noticed that the boy had dropped into it not only thin shavings of nuts, but also bits of shell.

'I didn't know he'd done that. I'm sorry.'

'It's mucky.' But Mr Parkin felt, in view of the tutor's apology, that he was going too far. He became affectedly thoughtful: 'I can't help thinking that some change has come over Donald lately. He always used to be such a neat-minded boy.'

'Perhaps it's due to his illness.'

'No, I don't feel it's that. Naturally, that makes him a bit feckless at times, poor chap. But he's become so untidy during these last few months. His mother and I can't account for it at all.'

'It certainly is rather extraordinary.'

Half smiling, half doubtful whether his remarks had gone home, Mr Parkin nodded. An involuntary nervous tremor gave a mock obsequiousness to the downward movement of his head. His red-rimmed, slightly bloodshot eyes fixed the tutor for a moment, then glanced out of the window. He abruptly, almost violently, asked:

'Hasn't Stokes come round to fetch the hamper yet?'

'I don't think so.'

'I wonder what the devil's happened now. It's going to be bad enough not having the Daimler today. It's a confounded nuisance he didn't discover there was something wrong with it yesterday evening. I'd be glad to know how he imagines he's going to get four of us into the Austin. We'll have our legs knocked to pieces with that damned hamper on top of us. I suppose he's forgotten all about that.'

Mr Parkin's irritation, which he would never have indulged if he'd been speaking to Stokes in person, seemed to be directed chiefly against the tutor.

'If Mrs Parkin is going with you perhaps it would be more

comfortable for her if I didn't come in the car,' the tutor said. 'I could ask Donald to lend me his bicycle.'

'Mrs Parkin isn't going with us.'

'But I thought you said there would be four in the car.'

'Quite right. I did. And with Stokes there'll be five.'

Mr Parkin smilingly declined to offer any explanation.

The tutor was confused, remarked insincerely :

'I hope Mrs Parkin is better this morning.'

'Well, I can't say she is. She's about the same.'

'I'm sorry.'

'Of course, as you know, it's only what's to be expected at her time of life. All women have to go through it when they reach a certain age. Just like horses. You know what I mean.'

'I see.'

'That's all it is. It's only what's to be expected.'

Watching the tutor's face, Mr Parkin added :

'Naturally, she doesn't want to go with the whole crowd of us in the small car just at present.'

'No, I suppose not,' the tutor said. 'As a matter of fact I was thinking that if someone else were going in the car instead of Mrs Parkin, then, perhaps, all the same, it might be more convenient if I didn't come with you.'

'I don't advise you to try to get to the races on a bicycle. You'd find yourself in for a longer ride than you think.'

'But, surely, if the car will be uncomfortable for you –'

'Pah, I was almost ashamed to invite MacCreath to come with us when he rang up this morning. But what else could I do? His wife's going to the dentist and she wants the Bentley and those daughters of his have had the cheek to drive off for the day in the two-seater – with friends from London,' Mr Parkin sneered. 'Caw – a couple of them were over here in the garden last year. They couldn't bear seeing anyone picking up worms, they said. The stuck-up effeminate young puppies. I could have slashed them across the faces with a whip.'

The tutor, conscious that Mr Parkin's anger was not altogether retrospective, said casually :

'If Mr MacCreath's coming I might as well stay here and leave room for him in the car.'

Mr Parkin stared at him with excessive surprise.

'Why, of course not. That won't be necessary at all.'

'But I'd really prefer spending the day here.'

'Absurd. How do you suppose you'd get anything to eat?'

'I can get it at a pub. I was thinking of going for a walk.'

'There's no need to do that. Everything's arranged for you to come with us.'

Mr Parkin's voice was insultingly soothing, almost sing-song. The tutor flushed, was on the point of retorting that he wasn't in the least interested in the races. But he remembered that he must be very careful. The new technique. He mustn't be tricked into making a naïve declaration of independence. That would be fatal. He mustn't feel angry. And almost immediately Mr Parkin added:

'Mind you, I don't want to hinder you in any way if you'd prefer going for a walk. But it seems rather unreasonable to choose the one day when you've a chance to go to the races.' Mr Parkin smiled slightly. 'Surely any other day would do just as well. Why not tomorrow? As soon as Donald has gone off to church. I'm only too glad that you *want* to get out into the country for a bit.'

The tutor stared coldly out of the window.

'That's to say' – Mr Parkin was suggestive – 'unless you've got definite plans for meeting someone today.'

The tutor wavered.

'No,' he admitted. 'I haven't.'

He felt at once that he had made a mistake. Mr Parkin was contemptuously triumphant:

'Well, then, you don't want to miss the races, do you?'

The tutor didn't answer. He wondered whether he ought to have lied about meeting someone. Perhaps he ought to have suggested that he was going whoring. Any lie would have served, the more startling the better. He must never forget that he was dealing with a moneyed imbecile. Nothing could be more degrading than to tell Mr Parkin the truth. But after all the tutor had not told him the truth. He had not made a mistake. He had been right to give the impression that he had surrendered. Because he would take good care to contradict the impression at the last moment. He would be frankly irresponsible. He would run away, go to bed, hide in the kitchen garden, jump out of the car, vanish, escape anyhow. Perhaps it might have been better still if he had consented outright to going to the races. That would have been even more in keeping with the new technique. Up to the very last minute he would have pretended to be delighted by Mr Parkin's generosity in offering him a seat in the car. He would have chatted enthusiastically about the races. He would have got all the facts about the horses out of the newspapers, would have appeared to be an expert, would have known far more about the races than anyone else in the house. Then, just as Mr Parkin and the boy were stepping into the car, he would unaccountably have walked off into the kitchen garden. Would he? Would he do it now? And even if he did, even if these proposed antics weren't just desperate fantasies, even if he lay flat on the drive and refused to be moved, did he want to behave like this? Was it good, did he prefer these contortions, the elfish independence of an ill-treated child, to the ordinary satisfaction of everyday wishes, did he choose the equilibrium of madness, would he rather tell lies, was it even necessary?

Mr Parkin stood grinning, gratified by the tutor's awkwardness. He grinned like a panting collie-dog. His head nodded jerkily, his mouth hung open, his tongue quivered. A look of spiteful cunning crossed his face. There were small pockmarks in the shaven flesh round the corners of his mouth beneath the points of his moustache. The conversation with the tutor had stimulated him, toned up his nerves.

It was not necessary. The tutor was not destitute, not driven to trickery by poverty, Mr Parkin held no whip, was not a feudal serf-owner or a public-school prefect, could not punish or coerce him. His three months' surrender to Mr Parkin had been due to nothing but cowardice. Why hadn't he at the start insisted that he should have at least one hour every day off duty, away from the boy? Mere weakness: and soon he had begun to justify his weakness by pretending that servility was inevitable, a necessary condition of modern life, that it would have been the same or worse anywhere else, that he would be petty or romantic if he attempted to gain any concessions from Mr Parkin. The new technique was simply the latest phase of this pretence, the most frantic cowardice of all. It was a day-dream victory. He had surrendered to Mr Parkin. To an ignorant snob who couldn't spell properly, who regarded himself as an old English squire, who held theories about women and about servants which would have seemed out of date even to the editor of a stunt newspaper.

Mr Parkin had suddenly noticed something on the sideboard. His grin changed to an absurd pout of fury. He fumbled in one of the pockets of his waistcoat, brought out a small key. He limped over to the sideboard. The tantalus had been left unlocked. Eyeing the levels of whisky and brandy in the cut-glass decanters he ostentatiously locked it. He looked briefly at the tutor and saw that he was smiling. He hesitated, lost control, spoke:

'Some drunken devil has been stealing the brandy again.'

His face relaxed instantly, became placid. It was greasy and sallow as though he had been rubbing olive oil into it. He bent down, brought out another key, opened the sideboard wine cupboard. The tutor watched him with hatred. 'This well-fed swine,' he thought. A swine, a swine who had never doubted his power to impose his trivial swinish standards on everyone in the house. And who had had no reason to doubt it. Who poisoned the whole district. Who succeeded in making the farm labourers play up to his conception of them as simple rustic toadies. Who bribed the cobbler and the grocer with whisky to come and consult him about their family troubles. Who despised the village schoolmaster as an upstart earning far too large a salary. Whose power extended even beyond the district, touched London, could buy up an expensively educated young man at any time to dance attendance on his boy. But the tutor had been something more than a mere obedient attendant, a mere passive jumping dummy. It was no good day-dreaming that he had been persecuted by an ineluctable Power. If he had been compelled with whips, dragged into the workroom every morning and made to teach Latin and Scripture at the point of a rook rifle, kicked into church every Sunday, forcibly hustled into a dinner jacket by the butler or the contemptuous Scottish chambermaid every evening – then he might have been able to forgive himself. But the truth was that long before any pressure had been brought to bear on him he had deliberately chosen to be a lackey, had been active, not passive, had almost fallen over himself in his shy hurry to comply with what he had assumed the Parkins wanted. No one had told him to teach Latin and Scripture or to wear a dinner jacket or to take the boy to church. He had done these things because he had guessed that Mr Parkin thought they were good for the boy – and consequently Mr Parkin had felt quite safe in boasting that he himself regarded Latin as a waste of time and religion as worse than useless to people who could go straight without it. The tutor had consented to traffic in hypocrisies which even Mr Parkin was glad not to have to dirty his hands with. He had catered for the meanest uncertainties of a reactionary snob. He had been useful to Mr Parkin rather as a police spy is to a bishop, relieved him of a doubtful job, and now Mr Parkin was able to adopt the pretence of not being in the least responsible for the sort of education the boy was getting and to give the boy the impression that it was a sham imposed upon both of them by a shabby genteel scholastic hack.

Watching Mr Parkin lift out and examine bottles from the wine cupboard, the tutor for a moment suspected himself of exaggerating. How could a person of intelligence take anything that happened in this household seriously? Instantly the tutor repudiated the question, condemned it as a relic of his worst cowardice. His contemptible pose of detachment, trying to see himself as a sinister observer, as someone perfectly disguised as a hired tutor but really far far different, altogether inscrutable. Viler still, his attempt to pretend that the Parkins were not quite living people, were modern goblins, unbelievable freaks to be amusingly described in amazing letters to his friends. And he had imagined that these childish deceits preserved his independence, his integrity. As though his nature would have received some subtle everlasting stain if he had once admitted to himself that he was a tutor in an ordinary country house. The horror of being subdued to what he worked in, like the dyer's hand. But it was just his hand, his body, his real life, his leisure, which he had allowed to be subdued. While his nature, the soul for which he had been so meanly alarmed, had performed its invisible fairy-story acrobatics, he had smiled daily at table, agreed with everything the Parkins had said, drunk their beer and obeyed their orders, given up his whole time to the boy. Any effort to assert himself in practice he would have considered degrading, petty, a danger to his soul. But he had failed even to save his soul. Its wilful fairy stories were no more than twisted images of his real predicament. He had failed, prostituted himself in every way. He had wasted in trivialities and dishonesties his one and only life, his life which might have been so full of, bright with, ardent for – what? Oh, wonders: love and knowledge and creation, history, science, poetry, interesting daily work, revolutionary politics, discipline, self-sacrifice, holidays, joy. He had voluntarily thrown all those away.

For the sake of snugness, for beer at lunch and dinner, for early morning tea and a bright bedroom with a view of rooks' nests among the tree-tops, for the sake of preserving a small private room in his mind to which he could always retire and in which he could pose as an intellectual experimenter, for the hope of holding a job which was after all less strenuous and less likely to encroach on his imaginary leisure than most other jobs. He had preserved nothing. He had become a mule, a eunuch, quite sexless, too listless even to kick. But there was going to be a change. Suddenly. A flash, a concentration of revulsion, an insurrection of the nerves, a Leviathan of fury turning over in the black ocean of apathy. He would tell Mr Parkin what he thought about country life and racing. Now. Instantly.

A large saloon car, grinding the gravel, spitting small stones from beneath its semi-balloon tyres, passed by the window and drew up outside the front door.

Mr Parkin shut the door of the wine cupboard and stood up. He smiled with pleasure.

'That's MacCreath,' he said.

Now. Quick.

But MacCreath was quicker than the tutor. The rooks, scattering from the trees at the sound of the car, were quicker. The boy, racing across to the lawn from the garage, treading down the crocuses between the trees, shouting 'Uncle Hamish', waving a fishing-rod, was quicker. To defy Mr Parkin now would be merely theatrical. The tutor's resolution had become a dream from which he had been jerked awake by the ordinary noises of the daytime. Defiance would be as ridiculous as rushing down to breakfast in pyjamas and shouting 'Shut the greenhouse door against the tarantula', or 'What have you done with my dancing-girl?' And already MacCreath was standing in the room, saying with smoothest cordiality:

'Good morning, Jim. Looks as though we're going to have a beautiful day for it this time.'

'Yes, it looks like it,' Mr Parkin said cautiously, controlling his excitement.

MacCreath directed a very amiable nod of greeting towards the tutor. The boy lunged into the room, followed by the frisking terrier puppy.

'Steady, steady,' Mr Parkin snarled. 'Do you want to smash up the whole house?'

'I haven't smashed anything,' the boy said pertly.

Mr Parkin exploded: 'If you're going to fool about and get over-excited you're not coming with us to the races. We don't want you laid up for months in the house with a strained heart.'

The boy, though he didn't believe that his father would stop him going to the races, was temporarily cowed by the words.

MacCreath changed the subject: 'Well, how are the lessons going, Donald?'

'Oh, all right.'

Outside, MacCreath's chauffeur had turned the car and was repassing the window. Mr Parkin looked at his watch.

'I can't think what's making Stokes so late. I shall have to ring him up.'

He went out into the hall.

No one would compel the tutor to get into the car. Even now he needn't go to the races. He had only to stand still at the window of the dining-room and watch the others get into the car. Or suppose they spoke to him and asked why he wasn't coming. He needn't answer. Then probably they would ring up a doctor. But why shouldn't he tell them frankly that he intended to stay here? Why hadn't he told them? Because of Mac-Creath. Because it would have been impolite to have made a scene in front of MacCreath. Because MacCreath was a gentle-man. Because he was smooth-spoken and had a sportsman's open-air complexion and was wearing an unassertive tweed overcoat and a milky-tea-coloured shirt and collar. But that was just why the tutor ought to speak out, ought to slash out, to rip to shreds this Philistine's cocksure affability.

In reality MacCreath was not cocksure. He was quite aware of the tutor's hostility. And he partly understood it. He wanted to say something which would show that he wasn't as unintelli-gent as Mr Parkin, that in spite of being a friend of Mr Parkin's he regarded him as a bit of a joke. But the tutor was inaccessible, frigidly avoided his glances. MacCreath spoke to the boy instead:

'I shouldn't put your face too close to the dog's if I were you.'

'Why? Ronald's quite clean. Aren't you, Ronald? Eh, boy? Haven't you a nice clean wet kisser?'

'Well, I shouldn't do it. You never know what germs a dog mayn't pick up.' MacCreath added a generalization in the friendly hope of drawing some remark from the tutor: 'It's a queer thing that the better bred a dog is the more he'll poke his nose into any filth he comes across.'

'Yes,' the tutor said mechanically.

MacCreath wasn't offended. He appeared not to have ex-pected any further comment. His attention tactfully strayed to the door. Mr Parkin could he heard telephoning: 'and bring the plaid rug.' MacCreath smiled. He seemed to appeal, to be on the point of asking serio-comically : "Did you ever hear anything like it?' But his gentlemanly clothes, his insinuating good humour, the soft confident aggression of his voice whenever he spoke, contradicted this impression. And actually he asked :

'Are you going to the dance at the town hall this evening?'

'I don't know.'

'My little girls would be very glad to see you there.'

The tutor was surprised. He had imagined that people like MacCreath would want to guard their daughters against young men without money. But MacCreath was almost apologizing for bringing his daughters to the tutor's notice. Was this humility simply a trick, a super-politeness designed to be so overwhelming in its condescension that the tutor would automatically give up all thoughts of going to the dance?

'It ought to be quite a good show,' MacCreath said. 'No evening dress, of course.'

'I don't know whether I shall be able to get away.'

'I hope you will.'

Again the suggestion of diffidence. As though MacCreath doubted whether the tutor would want to go to a dance at which no one wore evening dress.

'By the way, do you play bridge?' MacCreath asked.

'No.'

The tutor was quite startled at the effect of his abruptness. For the first time MacCreath looked hurt. His smile weakened to a meek weariness, his forehead wrinkled helplessly. He seemed to have lost all his confidence, to be incapable even of resentment. A suspicion occurred to the tutor : perhaps MacCreath wasn't really at all sure of himself, wasn't sure that he could pass as a gentleman. Perhaps he hadn't been to a public school, had sold newspapers on the streets of Glasgow, owed his present position solely to his wife's money. Perhaps his good humour, his tolerance, his popularity at the golf club, with the local farmers, with servants, with the Parkins, were due not to any sense of power but to the sense of a weakness in his social armour. Worse, perhaps he regarded the tutor as a gentleman, even admired him, was trying to adapt himself to him.

On the floor the boy was playing with the puppy. One of his stockings had slipped down to his ankle, exposing a flabby white leg.

'We're brothers, we are. Yes, Ronald, yes. Come on, say yes. You're human, aren't you? What's my name?' The puppy yapped. 'My name's Donald. Quite right. Well done. Now don't forget it. Ronald, Donald. We're brothers, we are.'

On the shiny flesh of the boy's calf, bulging from pressure against the carpet, the tutor noticed a soft brown mole. He had an impulse to kick the leg. If MacCreath hadn't been there he would probably have said something spiteful to the boy about the puppy. And MacCreath, almost as though he had been aware of the tutor's childish irritation, seemed to recover, to regain confidence. He asked the boy teasingly:

'You don't really believe he can understand what you're saying, do you?'

'Of course he can. Dogs are human beings.'

'That's not saying much for human beings.'

The boy looked puzzled. MacCreath couldn't forbear trying to catch the tutor's eye. Soon he would speak to him again, make another advance. Not assertively or revengefully, not humbly or forgivingly, but comfortably and with good humour. His blue-grey eyes, shallow and shiny as though they had been painted on bits of talc, would fix the tutor's with a temperate semi-blind stare. He would accept the tutor. Just as, after the initial shock, he would possibly have accepted a theft or a sexual indiscretion if one had been committed in his presence. Just as he accepted the boasters and drunks at the golf club or the respectable farmers and the village postman at the pub. His weakness was that he could never in any circumstances feel sufficiently secure to be able to reject the actual. His strength was that he felt comfortable enough to be able to eject a cloud-screen of tolerant kindliness against anything angular or rebellious. That accounted for his popularity. He would always decline to take sides. He would not be in favour of a surgical operation. But suppose the operation really wasn't necessary, suppose after all the abscess was nothing more than a pustule. What if the tutor, not MacCreath, was contemptibly in the wrong? Wasn't it possible that the tutor had become a social hypochondriac, that his isolation in this house had made him over-introspective, psychologic, almost unbalanced, ridiculously ready to see the habits of the Parkins and their friends and servants as all-important horrors? Was anything that happened in this house worth going to extremes about?

No one sane could regard Mr Parkin as a dangerous power. He was a weakness – freakishly sprouting in the accidental manure of his inherited money. He was childish, quite as excited as his son about the races. Perhaps more excited. He came in from the hall carrying an aluminium shooting-stick, his nostrils twitching, his eyes wide open. He seemed on the point of making a tremendous statement.

'Stokes will be round in a couple of minutes,' he said. 'Then the music begins in earnest.'

At once he started laughing. MacCreath joined him. They were trying to control themselves and failing wildly. They were like young girls with a daring secret. What was it all about? Probably a horse they had backed – or they might for some reason be laughing at the tutor. He didn't know and hadn't the energy to think it out.

MacCreath was the first to recover. He said gravely:

'It's a shame Monica can't come. It would do her good.'

'Well, it might, but I think she's wise not to take any risks.'

Mr Parkin was probably going on to explain once again that it was just like horses, but the boy interrupted him with a dutiful whine:

'I'm so sorry for poor Mummy.'

And why dutiful? There was no reason for thinking the boy wasn't sincere. In fact, the hypocrisy and the whine were simply another hypochondriacal delusion of the tutor's. He must be slightly unwell. This house must have tainted his nerves, made him narrow, venomous, dehumanized him. MacCreath's attitude towards the Parkins wasn't morbid, though it might be complacent. Mr Parkin might be a fool but he wasn't the medieval devil that the tutor had imagined. The boy was an ordinary boy, rather spoiled by his mother. The races would be boring, but they wouldn't be the end of the world.

Already the car could be heard coming up the drive. What would the tutor gain by bursting out into diseased heroics? The races wouldn't be altogether loathsome. That idea had been a delusion due to his tainted nerves. Nothing that happened while he was with the Parkins could be in the least frightful or important. Therefore he must kill the nerves, put an end to feeling. He must mechanically follow Mr Parkin and MacCreath out of the room and into the hall.

He was already following them. Mr Parkin, limping, recklessly digging his shooting-stick into the carpet, paused a moment, asked MacCreath whether he would like a drink. MacCreath said that his doctor had ordered him on to the watercart. Mr Parkin was amazed. The tutor stared glassily into the hall. Someone had fetched his overcoat for him and put it over the back of an antique chair. He picked it up. His nerves were dead. He was as nerveless as the sandwiches in the hamper which the butler was carrying through the hall to the front door. He had killed feeling, because feeling had been diseased. He felt nothing except a slight flatulence. The hall was only a hall, not a lethal chamber. The two copper warming-pans, the oak barometer, the brass-handled drawers of the huge tallboy, the grandfather clock with moon and stars across its face, the oil painting of bottle-green waves towering against an ochre lighthouse, the brilliantly white circular skylight above the stairs — were not in any way ominous or detestable. They were what they were, and all feelings about them were only feelings. But from now on there would be no more feelings.

He followed Mr Parkin and MacCreath and the boy out of the front door. There was a prolonged far-away ringing in his left ear. The butler was lifting the hamper into the car. Mrs Parkin, clutching a quilt to the bosom of her nightdress, leant out over her window-box of daffodils, smiling. Stokes, uniformed, gaitered and gauntleted, looked discreetly sardonic. Holding open the back door of the car he detained Mr Parkin for a moment after MacCreath and the boy had stepped inside.

'About that horse, sir.'

'Fritillary?'

'Yes, sir.' Stokes was impressive: 'He may not run today, sir.' Mr Parkin, one foot on the running-board, writhed as though he had been struck lightly across the calves with a cane.

'Why?'

'I've had information, sir.'

Stokes prepared to shut the door. Mr Parkin wanted to resist, but his legs appeared to disobey him. He got into the car. He had the stunned air of a savage who has been told that an enemy has stolen one of his toe-nail parings. But he couldn't bear to let Stokes go without saying something more to him, however irrelevant. Just as the door was closing he said:

'You'll remember to come round again this evening with the emulsion?'

'Of course, sir.'

'I think my knee is a little worse this morning.'

'I'm sorry to hear that, sir.'

Stokes shut the door. Getting into the driving seat he side-glanced knowingly at the tutor. The tutor sat down beside him. Mrs Parkin waved a fat-wristed hand from the bedroom window above the box of daffodils. The car turned and made up the drive towards the gates. Stokes sat rigid as an idol at the steering-wheel. Outside the gates he changed gear with the minimum of movement, his hand stealthy on the gear lever, his foot on the clutch pedal hinging gently from the ankle. At a sharp bend in the road a wall of dark fir-trees made a temporary mirror of the wind-screen, showed him pug-nosed, hemisphere-eyed, faintly grinning with mumbo-jumbo insolence. He *was* an idol. The Parkins depended on him, thought him infallible. He was their doctor, their adviser. He had invented an emulsion and a car polish, and Mr Parkin believed that he could have been a rich man if he'd wanted to. Above all Mr Parkin was impressed by his memory: when he went shopping he never forgot any of the orders which Mrs Parkin had given him, and he never had to write them down. Mr Parkin once, after sneering at education, said of him to the tutor: 'Stokes never had any education, not more than two years at the outside – and look at him now; he could wipe the floor with both of us.' Stokes was the real ruler of this household, the tutor thought. A kind of lay Rasputin, without, so far as the tutor knew, Rasputin's expensive vices.

What trash. Theorizing again. As the car, riding between beech hedges across the huge landscape, wove its sheltered equable hum, so the brain wove its neat private opinions and theories in an immense unconsidered wilderness. The ringing in the tutor's left ear grew louder. Any opinion, any theory, was as good or as bad as another. Think of Mr Parkin as a devil or a devil-worshipper or a hero – it didn't matter. Thinking was only an exercise, a weaving of decorations. You looked through the wind-screen and saw something and thought 'beech hedges', and imagined they were brown, but you might as well think 'parrots', and imagine they were black. You looked and saw the miles of country and a river and you thought 'the North of England', but you might as well think 'Switzerland'. Hence the futility of all travel. Why go to Switzerland and say 'mountains' when you can just as easily say 'mountains' here and now? Why go anywhere, why *be* anywhere? You look through the wind-screen now and you think – 'There is a river, there are corrugated iron roofs of farm buildings, there farther off is a mining town, there very far off a harbour, here the road reaches the top of a hill' – but all these names are only mental decorations foisted by you and other 'thinkers' upon a non-human world which, but for your interference, would have had no names. Can this hill think or feel or speak, can it say 'I am Belstreet Hill,' can it even say 'I am *something*'? It cannot even say that. It has nothing to do with names or with thinking or feeling. It is not ugly, it is not beautiful, does not owe its shape to volcanic eruption or to erosion by wind, water or ice, has no shape, has no colour, knows nothing of science or aesthetics. Describe it, give it whatever qualities you like, but don't pretend that the description and the qualities have anything to do with the real hill. Don't even pretend that what you see with your eyes has anything to do with the real hill. Because eyesight no less than description is merely human. The hill cannot see. The real hill is something about which you cannot know anything at all.

And in fact this was how the whole landscape began to appear to the tutor – as something dead and boring, not worth thinking about or looking at. Stokes, driving downhill, did not allow the car to increase its pace. He rarely drove at more than thirty-five miles per hour, perhaps in mock deference to Mr Parkin's dignity. Farmhouses, barns, brick-kilns, a pond, a heron, crows, gulls, plough furrows, earthworms, dogs, a woman in an apron. Did it matter which you called which? All names were interchangeable. Any description, any explanation, was as futile as another. Think of all the moods, attitudes, opinions, theories, which the tutor had got through in a single morning. Which had been right? None. There was no such thing as being right. There were only mental and emotional exercises, some of them prettier than others, and at present they all seemed equally spiritless and flatulent. What was Mac-Creath talking about at the back of the car?

'They say that the depredations always occur after cubbing.'

His tone was ponderous, careful, as though he were afraid of exciting Mr Parkin by some accidental reference to the races. Mr Parkin said:

'When I lived in Ireland the farmers boycotted foxhunting, and after a couple of years they were down on their knees to us, down on their knees. They put crow's feet in the hedges – you know what – boards with nails sticking out of them. Caw – no use. They were down on their knees to us.'

That was what MacCreath and Mr Parkin seemed to be saying. Seemed. But were they really saying that? Hearing, no less than seeing, was only an exercise, a decoration. The tutor might just as well have heard them saying:

'There's going to be trouble at the races this afternoon.'

'Lucky I brought my six-shooter.'

Perhaps that's what he did hear them saying. It wasn't important. Hearing was something which happened inside your head, not outside it. All sounds were interchangeable and any one sound was as good or as bad as another. Take your choice, invent whatever sounds you like. Don't say — 'the breath force, rising through the glottis, strikes the vocal chords and makes them vibrate'. That is only an explanation, a theory; it tells you nothing about the real human voice. You would have to *be* a human voice before you could know what a human voice really was. And this is everlastingly impossible. The real human voice is unknowable: it belongs to the same unknowable world as beech hedges, farms, crows, hills. The unknowable blurred world slips past the windows of the car. It is eternally heartless, mindless, dead. It is dead even though it moves.

How much better to the eternally dead. Not to think or feel that you are sitting in this car, going to the races. To be dead like this car itself, even though it moves. To be dead like Donald's flesh and bones, even though they grow. To be dead like your own unknowable flesh and bones. The tutor must kill thinking and he must really kill feeling, which still lingered on in spite of his first attempt to kill it. Because if he killed thinking and feeling he would automatically destroy the world of his serfdom, the only knowable world, which after all was nothing more than an evil decoration created by thinking and feeling. He believed that he was beginning to succeed. He sat slack as an old sawdust-filled doll beside the rigid idol Stokes. Or didn't he believe he was succeeding? Was it just another pretence, a faintly interesting affectation of madness? But even if it was an affectation, that very affectation was a sign that he had become mentally queer. Yes, he was beginning to succeed. First the blurred landscape went grey, then it stopped moving, then it went white. Voices at the back of the car became thinner and thinner. Feeling persisted for a time, but at last Stokes dwindled from beside him, slowly, as though he had been withdrawn by the hand of a thoughtful chess-player. Feeling shrank inwards from the extremities of the tutor's body, left his hands and arms nerveless, his eyes unseeing, his ears deaf. Thinking moved outwards. Thinking moved in widening circles, getting slower and slower, vaguer and vaguer, like the movement in a cup of tea which has been stirred with a spoon. The violent vortex became smooth, the outer circles moved more and more sleepily.

But, for all that, thinking was not dead, would not die. It was shamming dead. And feeling would not die either. Thinking and feeling had disguised themselves, taken on a new form. Far in the core of his consciousness the tutor was aware of them still. He was aware of a burning area of misery somewhere in the centre of his body. The burning became more and more intolerable. He wanted to be sick, to collapse, to be dead. But it was no use wishing to be dead: he could never become dead by mere wishing. Thinking and feeling would go on happening. Better they should happen as before than as they were happening now in their new form. If they didn't stop soon he must burst or go mad. This was what going mad was like: it didn't kill thinking and feeling, it made them far, far worse than ever. He must get back to where he was before this started. He must get back. Make an effort, however difficult. Try to see something, hear something, move an arm and touch something. Try. Try.

It was startlingly easy. His elbow touched Stokes. He was sitting beside Stokes in the car. The narrow road came towards the wind-screen, bringing a copse and a signpost. A night-dress on a washing line, seen through trees. Voices came from the back of the car as before. MacCreath was talking about fishing.

'A clean-run fish with sea-lice under its gills.'

The tutor had recovered, become normal again. Thinking and feeling had come back as before. After all, the abnormality had probably been a fake, a deliberate experiment. He had tried to kill thinking and feeling and he had found that it was impossible. He had found also that it was dangerous. Experiment or no experiment, for a moment he had been dangerously near to insanity. He wasn't quite normal even now. The ringing in his ear still went on.

But what a relief to be able to see and hear again. The change made him almost happy. He realized that it was possible for him to be happy. He had taken no fatal step, there were no insuperable obstacles. He realized that for the last three months he had not tried to be happy, had preferred to be miserable. Day after day of cloudy, flatulent misery. Thinking and feeling had been poisoned and had in turn poisoned sight and touch and hearing. Thinking and feeling had poisoned the whole world. And thinking and feeling could not be killed. But couldn't they be changed, couldn't they be healed, drained of their poison? If they could then the whole world would be changed. Because the whole world was a world created by human thinking and feeling and seeing and touching and hearing. Whatever was outside that world didn't count, was dead, couldn't even be called 'something'. He believed it would be possible to make that happy change. He even knew now how he would begin to do it. He would begin again on the lines of the new technique. But the new technique had not gone far enough, had been a wretched half-measure, almost worse than no measure at all. The new technique would perhaps have half-changed thinking and feeling, but it would not have changed seeing or touching or hearing. It would not have changed the appearance or the manners of Mr Parkin, it would not have changed the shape of the house or enlarged the tutor's bedroom or shortened his hours of work. It would have accepted these so-called conditions and would merely have altered the tutor's attitude towards them, made him pretend to enjoy them. But the change that the tutor was going to bring about now would be immeasurably more far-reaching. He would change his so-called surroundings, he would not only think and feel different-ly, he would see and touch and hear differently, as he wanted to, happily. Was that fantastic? He could only know after he had tried it. Better try it at once. Make a bold attempt, look at something, listen to something, see and hear what you really want to. Try. Try.

It was almost a success, seemed at first altogether a success. The landscape, seen through the windows of the car, had lengthened and broadened, become a tremendous panorama. It was like an infra-red photograph. The tutor had the impression that he could see at least fifty miles. And not only had details at a great distance become extraordinarily clear but colours also had become far more vivid. Emerald green and earth-red and ink-black and sea-blue. White insulators on telegraph poles and new copper wires gleamed along the coast road. Behind the town rose a wooden brewery tower and farther off up the coast double-wheeled pithead gear. A moving coal-conveyor crawled with rattling buckets to the top of a power station. A small lighthouse stood at the end of one of the stone arms of the harbour. Motor-coaches advanced along the coast road, leaving the town. A crowd of walkers extending over the whole visible length of the road, here scattered and there concentrated in groups, moved in the same direction. At the top of a wooded slope, not very distant now, the grandstand of the racecourse was visible. Far out from the coast a motor-driven fishing-boat showed ink-black on the mounting dead-blue sea. In the foreground a small ivy-grown church stood isolated among variously coloured rectilinear fields. The sky was quite cloudless. The racecourse at the top of the wooded slope appeared to be on a kind of tableland. The tutor noticed, to the right of the grandstand, a large marquee. Its sloping canvas roof was very white. Flags were flying from the roof. The lower part of the marquee, which did not receive the full light of the sun, was grey rather than white. But the roof itself was not so dazzling as the tutor had at first supposed. It seemed to grow dimmer as he looked at it. The sun remained as brilliant as before. The shape of the marquee was changing, was becoming less distinct against the sky. Finally, he was aware of two marquees – one large and beflagged and white, the other small and dull and grey. And the large, the original marquee, seemed to be imposed on the small one, like a superimposed photograph. But the large one grew fainter, became a mere bit of whited gauze, hardly visible.

The same process was going on elsewhere. Everywhere the tutor's original vision was fading and another vision, less generous, less detailed, was becoming more and more clearly defined beneath the filmy covering of the original one. The long crowd of walkers dwindled to a few isolated groups, the town seemed much smaller, he could only see two motor-coaches, the lighthouse turned out to be pure gauze, without anything behind it. Nevertheless, the gauze remained gauze, did not altogether vanish.

Much the same thing happened to the tutor's experiment with hearing. He wanted to hear differently, and at first he was startled by his success. Every word of the conversation at the back of the car became as distinctly audible as though Mr Parkin and MacCreath had been alternately whispering into his ear. And not only the vocal pitch but also the subject-matter of their talk was new. They were openly discussing the races.

'It wouldn't surprise me if the M.F.H. withdrew Fritillary and Willie Winkle as well,' Mr Parkin said.

'Why on earth –' MacCreath was astonished, then he laughed. 'You don't believe these tragic stories of ruin he's been telling about himself for the last ten days, do you?'

'There must be something in them.'

'Pure grouch and nothing else. He enjoys it. Ever since he came into his father's estate and paid half a million death duty ten years ago. First he was going to give up fox-hunting. Of course, he did nothing of the sort. Then he couldn't afford motoring. So he bought a new Rolls. Then came the miners' strike, and he was going to be forced to sell his estate and close down his stables and take a small flat in London –'

'It would have served them right if he had,' Mr Parkin interrupted hotly. 'It would have served them right if he'd closed down his estate and his mines and his stables and cleared out of the country altogether. That might have taught them something. All these damned spongers. That would have put them in their place. They think they're too good for the Prince of Wales, let alone the Master of Foxhounds. What's more they get away with it. And the idiots in Parliament wonder why the country is going to ruin.'

'We're a long way from ruin yet,' MacCreath said mildly. 'As a matter of fact, the M.F.H. has been doing very well lately. All his talk about giving up racing is just one of his lighter amusements. And even if he weren't doing well he wouldn't be so foolish as to cut off his nose to spite his face.'

That was the conversation which the tutor heard at first. But as he listened it grew fainter and fainter, became a mere ghost-gauze of sound. And beneath the ghost-gauze another conversation, briefer and more indifferent, grew louder and louder. It was about fishing and fox-hunting:

'... Greenwell's Glory, March Brown, a red-tipped spider.'

'They say that a fox will never kill in his own locality.'

'Ever seen a weasel after a rabbit? No matter how many of them cross in front of him that's *his* rabbit. Stops and squeals. Always caught in the end. It's a cruel sport, ha, ha.'

This second conversation – like the second, more meagre landscape – showed that the tutor had not yet conquered his old habits of perceiving. He was still seeing and hearing the same sort of things as before. He must conquer the old habits. He knew now that it was possible to conquer them. After all he had been remarkably successful already – he had seen a new landscape and heard new voices. But he had lacked faith. At the back of his mind he had been unable to believe that the new perception was anything more than a fake. Well, suppose it was a fake – wasn't the old perception just as much a fake, a foisting of human consciousness on to a non-human world? What he had to do was to substitute one fake, the more vital, the happier one, for the other, the habitual one. But could this be done by an act of the will, by mere wishing?

He certainly wished hard enough. He looked again through the car window at the marquee on the tree-surrounded table-land. The gauze outline was still there. It was like a white reflection on the glass of the window, very faint. It was much nearer to him than the other, the grey and smaller marquee. But, as he looked, the larger marquee moved farther away from him, keeping the same size though now seeming outside the glass of the window. It was about half-way between the car and the top of the wooded slope. It was moving, approaching the smaller marquee. And as it moved it grew more distinct, more solid. And at the same time the smaller marquee began to fade. Yes, the smaller marquee was fading, but the tutor could not make it disappear. Behind the brilliance and the flags of the white marquee it showed small and grey, like a dingy tent seen through a luminous transparent screen. And the tutor was aware that he must not for an instant relax his effort to suppress this small grey remnant. If he did the new vision would fade to a bit of gauze. He must go on wishing the old vision away. But for how long would he be able to go on wishing? He would get tired in the end. Wishing was not enough. There would have to be some change greater than any change that could be brought about by the conscious will. The new vision would have to be independent of his will, would have to be there whether he wished the old vision away or not, would have to be there even if he changed his mind and wished the old vision back. How could that happen, how could the new vision become independent? Could it happen now, at once?

The table-land and the marquee were suddenly removed from his view altogether. The car was descending into a narrow V-shaped valley. Across the valley the road rose in a wide curve along the right-hand side of the buttress-like wooded slope. Steeply rising trees blotted out the table-land and the marquee. The car approached a bridge at the bottom of the valley. A stream slid over flat rocks. At the end of the bridge the beech hedges on either side of the road were taller than any the car had yet passed. A signpost board was just visible above the hedge on the left-hand side of the road. The tutor regarded it simply as a decoration, and he got a shock when he saw a steam-roller coming out from the concealed side road. But Stokes, who had no visions, had already slowed down. He changed gear, preparing to drive on again. He drove on, passing the steam-roller.

The tutor had time to look carefully at the steam-roller. He looked carefully because it reminded him of something. After his shock he saw it at first as something dangerous, but he soon realized that it was not a danger – it was a power. It was simple and bold and powerful, crested in front with a rampant brass unicorn, thumping with its pistons like a thumping heart. The echoing of its roller over the stones was like the hollow sound of skates on ice. It was bold with the gala boldness of engines stared at by children from a nursery window – big traction engines dragging gipsy caravans to a fair, engines with wire guards over their funnels and with funnels protruding through their long decorated roofs, engines with their long roofs supported by gilded pillars and with dynamos in front of their boilers for making lights on roundabouts in the evening. It was bold with a reminiscent boldness. It was bold with the naïve boldness of a child who sticks out his stomach and makes piston movements with his arms in imitation of a big locomotive. It was bold, too, with a maturer efficient boldness, with the boldness of its tall austere-looking driver. It was simple with a generous mechanical simplicity, with the simplicity of its whirling governor and of its ponderous flywheel, of its burnished steering-wheel, and of the wheel at the back for lowering and raising its steel road-breaking teeth. It was powerful with the chuffing indifferent power of a train carrying away a boy to a school which he hates and fears but which he knows nothing can save him from. It was powerful with the gay sun-glittering power of a motor-coach in which a middle-class young man sets out for an unfrequented part of the country where he thinks he is going to live the just life, like Socrates. It was powerful with a steaming sighing power, a power not of despair but of compassion and understanding, as though someone were saying gently to the tutor: 'Remember your past. Look how you have betrayed yourself, wasted yourself, you poor blunderer. How you have brought disaster upon yourself, trying to go your own way. But from now on you will go my way, will be iron, be new.' It was powerful, more powerful, far, far more powerful with the power of a great mountain which no apathy, no forgetfulness, no wishing can ever destroy. It was the victory of the new vision. Its boldness, its simplicity, its power, were what the tutor had wanted to see, had struggled to see, and now they were here before him, outside him, wholly independent of his wanting and struggling. Now he could cease to want and to struggle and the steam-roller would still be there, animating him from outside with its boldness and simplicity and power. The new vision was here and it was solid and real and it could not fade. It was here, it was everywhere. He hardly needed to look elsewhere to prove its ubiquity. He was certain of it. His eyes were full of tears. He had triumphed.

He looked up and saw, only just rising above the trees, the sloping roof of the white marquee. Yes, it was there, real, not gauze. The car was ascending the long curved road up the side of the wooded slope. The steam-roller was already some way behind, at the bottom of the hill. The car was going more slowly. Not only because of the steepness of the hill, but also because of the people who had begun to cross the road. They were evidently taking a short cut to the racecourse. They clambered up the slope to reach the road, crossed the road, slowly climbed the final slope among trees to reach the table-land. Some were shouting, some were chewing stalks of grass, some were smoking, one carried a rucksack, one wore a dirty white sweater and canvas shoes, one a neat blue serge suit, one had the face of a hero, one had a watch-chain hanging from the lapel of his sports coat, one was exuberant, one carried on his shoulder a child waving a cheap Union Jack, one had a flattened syphilitic nose, one played a mouth-organ, one was strikingly good-looking, one had a camera, two were arm in arm, three were playing catch with a rubber ball, all were on the move. They were crossing the road at intervals along a stretch of about a hundred yards. It was like a migration or the storming of a fort. And even when the car had got past this cross-current of walkers, Stokes was unable to drive any faster. The obstruction now was a motor-coach, the last of three that could be seen ascending the road ahead. There was a gilt inscription across its bulging rear-side – *Sunrise Coaches*. Its passengers, who were mostly women, were sitting bolt upright and singing. One of them suddenly turned round and leant over the folded hood at the back. She looked at the car attentively, then waved to Stokes with mock coquetry. She quickly turned round again, bursting out into a strong, rather hostile laugh. The coach was very gay. People were holding up sticks with brightly coloured pieces of material, flapping like flags, tied on to them. The tutor noticed that the pieces of material were really various kinds of underclothing –

drawers, brassières, garters, even corsets. No one in the car except the tutor seemed to be at all amused. Stokes was gloomy, the boy leaned over the tutor's shoulder and stared, and Mr Parkin and MacCreath were talking in very serious tones.

'I didn't like it,' Mr Parkin said.

'Well, whether it was deliberate or not he hasn't done any damage to the car.'

'I didn't like it at all. I'll ask Stokes what he thinks. Stokes! I say, Stokes, what the devil was the driver of that steam-roller up to?'

'Imagined he was at the races, perhaps, sir.'

'There you are,' Mr Parkin said to MacCreath. 'He was driving all out round the corner, and he deliberately tried to cut across in front of us. No doubt he'd have liked to send us into the ditch. I've a good mind to inform the police as soon as we arrive at the racecourse.'

'That would make us rather ridiculous,' MacCreath laughed.

'Not ridiculous in the least. Did you notice the fellow's face? Looked as though nothing would have pleased him better than to smash into us. The insolent mucky rat. And he'd have done it, too, if Stokes hadn't slowed down.'

'We can hardly give him in charge for having an unpleasant face.'

'Sneering like a rat looking out of a garbage bin,' Mr Parkin went on pigheadedly. 'Envy and spite are what's at the back of it. The same as with that mob crossing the road just now. Not one of them showed the least sign of making way for us. If I'd been Stokes I'd have been tempted to run the lot of them down. What the devil are they all doing away from their work in the middle of the morning, anyhow?'

'It's almost one o'clock,' MacCreath said. 'And personally I must say I'm glad to see so many of them up here at the races. Much healthier for them than getting into mischief in the town.'

'Tcha, it makes me sick. All these rats. Nothing's good enough for them nowadays. Muck, that's what they are.'

Mr Parkin's voice stumbled into silence, finding no adequate words. He was less angry, the tutor thought, than alarmed. The rounded world of his self-importance, more fantastic than any caricature could make it, yet substantial and unique within the bounds of his own household, had collided unpleasantly with a larger world outside. The tutor had found an ally. Mr Parkin was no longer formidable, could even be excused. His frank venom was far less offensive than MacCreath's smug reasonableness.

The car, moving slowly behind the motor-coaches, had almost reached the top of the wooded slope. The white marquee was still there, rising more fully above the trees.

2

The white marquee was here. The car followed the motor-coaches and several other cars into the parking enclosure. A section of the racecourse intervened between the tutor and the marquee. Hundreds of yards of wooden railing, bookmakers' blackboards and giant striped umbrellas, caravans, feet and faces perpetually shifting, gipsies, race-card vendors, miners and office workers, women in hiking shorts and women in expensive toilettes, middle-class young men in tweeds and sleek rentiers in grey top hats, crowds interpenetrating crowds. Single and tall the marquee was here. It was here and it was white and triangular flags flew from its roof and there was nothing visionary about it. It might still seem to have a certain transparency, but that was due to a natural cause – the warm glow of sunlight on an interior canvas wall visible through the turned-back flaps of the entrance. It might seem to have porthole-shaped dormer windows, but that effect was accounted for by the ventilator flaps on its sloping canvas roof. It might look like an airship: that was because of its rounded ends, its whiteness and its lightness. It might remind the tutor of an aviary: that was explained by the birds flying round it and by the resemblance to thin wires which the guy ropes had when seen from a distance. It might remind him of the sea: the canvas billowing like sails in a slight breeze explained that. It might suggest gardens: there were ferns and vases of flowers on a table just inside the entrance. It might give an impression of leisure and well-being and abundance and freedom: the entrance gave a glimpse of groups of people chatting in easy postures, the interior was filled with cool brightness, the knobs outside which topped the invisible supporting poles were gilded. There was nothing startling about the marquee. It had none of the intensely exciting, apocalyptic quality of the steam-roller. It did not make the tutor feel that some tremendous, almost terrible revolution was taking place in the darkness of his soul. He felt calm and normal. The marquee, in spite of its variety and its bigness, was more ordinary than the steam-roller. He was no longer ecstatic or in tears. He was normally happy. The only abnormality – and this didn't bother him much now – was the ringing in his left ear, which was still rather loud.

Luckily this ringing became much fainter as soon as he escaped from the car. It probably had some connection with Mr Parkin or MacCreath or the boy or Stokes, was perhaps a kind of nervous protest against their presence. At any rate, it grew less and less audible the farther he walked away from the car. He was lucky to have escaped from the car as easily as he had. He had stepped out of it at the same moment that Mr Parkin had opened the door at the back, but Mr Parkin had suddenly seen someone in the crowd whom he wanted to avoid. The tutor hadn't been sure which of the figures in the crowd Mr Parkin wanted to avoid, but had thought it had been the tall young man with a girlish complexion who had stood beside a small two-seater talking to the car-park attendant.

'There's that young Heseltine again,' Mr Parkin had said.

The tutor hadn't heard very clearly the mild question which MacCreath had asked after this, but he had heard Mr Parkin's vigorous answer:

'He's as much right to be a curate at St Saviour's as I have to order a gin and Italian in Buckingham Palace. I don't care to meddle with religion as a rule – I've got no use for it – but I do know there are limits. I've only seen him officiate once and by God I could have strangled him – crossing himself, scratching with his foot like a cock, bowing before he lit the candles, and all manner of vagaries you'd have to see to believe. I could have strangled him with my own hands.'

'And yet,' the tutor thought, walking quickly away from the car, 'if I suggested that Donald should stop going to church, even for a single Sunday, the old swine would want to strangle me.'

The thought did not make the tutor indignant. He was too interested in getting away from the car. He wanted to be out of sight as quickly as he could, to put as many people between himself and the car as possible. Dodging among the crowd he felt slightly exhilarated, almost wanted to giggle. His escape became easier and easier. It was as though he were running down complicated alleys in a town, continually putting new corners, houses, obstructions, between himself and his pursuers. If Mr Parkin and MacCreath were following him they must almost certainly be thrown off the scent already.

Soon he would be out of danger altogether, an innocent walker in the open country. He was in the open country now. The crowd around him had thinned to a few strollers and the car park was well behind him. In front of him, about five hundred yards off, was the tall white marquee. But in area at least the marquee was quite dwarfed by the far larger crowd of racegoers. Above their heads it was no more formidable than a half-inflated toy balloon. And the crowd itself was in turn dwarfed by the extremely long racecourse, the distant end of which was dotted with not more than two or three solitary people. And the racecourse too was dwarfed, was completely dwarfed by the panorama visible from the table-land – by the variously coloured rectilinear fields, the ivy-grown church, the corrugated farm buildings, the mining town, the power house, the stone-armed harbour, the coast road, the dead-blue sea. And the sky was so penetrated with brilliance that it seemed to have absorbed most of the small molten sun. Brilliance hung in the blue air like millions of evenly distributed diamond particles. The tutor had never felt more serene.

In the equable morning, alone among so many unhurried people, he felt as though he had just woken up on the first day of a long-deserved holiday. He was absolutely calm. What did it matter that the ringing in his ear, very faint indeed now, was still going on? Perhaps it was a good thing that the ringing did go on. Perhaps it acted as a stimulant, preventing him from becoming too much at ease in his new serenity, reminding him of the stingy self-loving life he had so happily escaped from, the three months' life of petty miseries, comforts, spites, apathies, heroics, smudged vision, woolly hearing, hours telescoping into hours. Or perhaps the far-away mosquito voice was tempting him, saying plausibly: 'Yes, that life had its unpleasant features, but it had pleasant features, too. It was a mixture, as all life in this world of ours must be. It was thoroughly human – but is your present mood quite human? Isn't it rather strained and saintly? Will it last, do you think?' The tutor easily repulsed this suggestion. He was absolutely confident that the new serenity would last. It would last for ever. For ever and ever. Or was this absolute confidence of his rather dangerous?

The idea of danger didn't occur to him by chance or as a mere link in the chain of his thinking. The idea had an external cause. For a moment the tutor didn't realize what the cause was, but then he remembered the expression on the face of one of the racegoers whom he had just passed. A very big man, who had been wearing a bowler hat and a dark blue belted raincoat. The expression on his face was difficult to remember clearly, because it had been an unusually complex expression. Not just an ordinary poisonous, vicious, threatening look – it had been far more than that. It had been suspicious and at the same time tumescent with contempt, blackly menacing and at the same time designed to be impressive rather than to threaten an injury. And though quite uncalled for, it had had none of the conscious insolence of the look of a man who takes a dislike to a stranger's clothes or manner: it had been authoritative, firm, profoundly sure of its own rightness – as though this man had caught the tutor committing some elementary offence against common decency. What had the tutor done to evoke it? He felt he must turn round and see it again and make certain that he hadn't been mistaken. Walking very slowly, he turned his head. The man still had the same venomous look and was still staring at him. He was a broad, rather fat-shouldered man with prominent ears and with conspicuously large hands. He scraped on the ground with one of his feet, like a fat-shouldered bull which is going to charge. But he didn't move towards the tutor: his object seemed to be solely to make an unpleasant impression on him, to inject a feeling of uneasiness into him. The tutor thought that he might be a detective. He had flat feet and his gross hands were big enough to push down a door or suffocate someone. The tutor turned quickly round and walked on. He certainly did feel uneasy – not so much because of the man's loutish hostility as because he half suspected that the man might have some justification for staring like that. Perhaps the tutor was behaving queerly. What cowardly rot! Had a police spy any right to pass judgement on his behaviour? Of course, his serenity, his private smile, the skip in his walk, his obvious pleasure in his surroundings, would seem queer to a dullard like that. Only dullness, lack of zest, model behaviour, would be understandable to a dullard. Yet think what a weight of legality, what centuries of stupidity such a dullard had behind him. Think how hopeless the position of the solitary must be against him. Men like that have done to death the best spirits in all the ages. And this made the tutor so passionately angry that he immediately stopped walking and turned round to outstare the detective. The same poisonous face as before looked back at him. The tutor might have persisted in his stare, but something distracted his attention. Behind the detective another man, with a face startlingly different from the detective's, was approaching. Lively and pleased, the new face glanced to left and to right, liked everything it saw, finally looked with approval even at the detective, who was still glaring at the tutor. It might have been smelling a rosebush. It was the face of MacCreath.

Jauntily, perkily, walking rather quickly, MacCreath passed the detective and came on directly towards the tutor. He did not look at the tutor yet. Very interested he peered aside at the chalked-up names and figures on a bookmaker's blackboard, seemed on the point of changing the course of his walk. Delighted, he inclined to the left, saluted an acquaintance, then inclined to the right and resumed his advance towards the tutor. At last he looked at him, dared to give him a restrained smile of recognition. Evidently he had been on the tutor's track for some time, had perhaps followed him all the way from the car. With a certain meekness, as though he was conscious of doing himself an honour, still smiling, he came up to him. For a moment MacCreath's sandy-coloured very short eyelashes were shyly lowered, then he said a little too heartily:

'So this is where you've absconded to.'

'Yes.'

'I came away soon after you did. I remembered I'd promised to go and find my daughters.'

There was nothing in MacCreath's smile to suggest that he had noticed the detective's behaviour. His friendly voice gave no hint of complicity. Nor did he seem to be aware of what the detective was doing now, though without moving his head he could easily have seen him. It was true that the man was no longer blatantly staring at the tutor. He had walked away to the left and was standing with his back towards MacCreath. The thick-fleshed reddish nape of his neck bulged above his coat collar. His hands were behind his back and the thumb of one hand fidgeted between the thumb and forefinger of the other. His face in semi-profile appeared to be watching a bookmaker, but the tutor felt that his interest was really elsewhere.

'Well, what's your fancy for the two-thirty?' MacCreath asked. 'Or don't you go in for that sort of thing?'

The tutor didn't answer, but MacCreath was not at all abashed. On the contrary he seemed to be recovering from the shyness he had at first shown. Lively and pleased he once again looked around him, sniffed the gay air of the races. At the same time the detective turned a full profile towards them and squinted at the tutor out of the corner of his eye. Either Mac-

Creath was stupidly, idiotically unobservant or else he deliberately refused to see what was happening.

'I dare say you're not sorry to be relieved of your pupil for a while.'

A sympathetic note had crept into MacCreath's voice. His understanding face, softly ruddy and unevenly discoloured by confused surface ruptures of slight blue veins, looked directly at the detective. Its expression did not change.

'That household must be rather a trial at times.'

He could see, did see. Had seen from the beginning, had fully approved. Thought no doubt that the tutor was making an exhibition of himself. Had come to control him, to soothe him with smarmy pretended friendliness.

The detective turned his head for a moment and faced the tutor fully. His expression was no longer threatening but frigid and boorishly superior. It seemed to say: 'The incident is closed; no need to explain your conduct now.' The tutor was in respectable company and could be let off with a warning. He was in the company of a well-to-do ally of the detective, a disguised ally who used greasier, hypocritical methods. Irritably he broke through MacCreath's friendliness, asked:

'Can't you see that man?'

'Which man?'

'That man. Wearing a bowler. The man you were looking at. You passed right in front of him just now.'

MacCreath was puzzled, but he did not immediately attempt to follow the direction of the tutor's stare. When he did follow it he pretended not to be looking for anyone in particular. He saw the detective, then glanced elsewhere. He waited for some seconds before speaking.

'I don't remember him.'

'He's a detective, isn't he?'

MacCreath gave a respectful little laugh, became aware of the tutor's frown, said diplomatically:

'Is he? How does one detect a detective?'

'There wasn't much doubt about it just now. He might have been going to arrest me.'

'What?'

'I said he might have been going to arrest me. He was extraordinarily offensive.'

The shadow of an amazed suspicion, of a respectable alarm, momentarily clouded MacCreath's good humour. It was as though he were about to ask theatrically: 'Why, what have you done?' Almost at once he recovered himself, said:

'But it's ridiculous. What possible reason could he have for wanting to arrest you?'

'None. I suppose I didn't look rich and seemed to be enjoying myself.'

MacCreath laughed, uncomprehending.

'He can't have meant to be offensive to you. Probably what you saw was just his normal expression – for professional purposes.'

'He did mean to be offensive.'

'But what makes you think he's a detective?'

'His offensiveness.' The tutor, aware of MacCreath's confident incredulity, went on angrily: 'A police spy isn't bound to be always in the right. As a matter of fact he's bound to be in the wrong. A man like that gets to think he can make his own narrow-minded stupidity into a law for everyone else. He thinks he's above the ordinary law. But actually there's nothing to choose between his methods and the methods of so-called criminals. He is a criminal.'

MacCreath laid a gentle hand on the tutor's arm, made him execute an about turn, soothingly urged him into a walk.

'I see what you mean.'

He didn't see, refused to see. The tutor jabbed at him:

'He is the worst type of criminal. Far worse than mere pickpockets or housebreakers. They are only trying to get back what's due to them. They've been cheated out of a decent life, made to live in filthy conditions. He helps to maintain the swindle by criminal force.'

MacCreath said nothing. They were walking towards the marquee. The tutor looked at it with disgust. Its billowing luxuriousness seemed vulgar, flatulently ostentatious. Beyond it and in front of it crowds of people moved towards and along-side the white wooden railing which marked out the course. He no longer saw their diversity, only their dreary cheated same-ness. All preoccupied wholly with the thought of the races, swindled by a corrupt circus. MacCreath's face was benignant. He had the admiring look of a worldly-wise grandmother who has been listening to the extravagant talk of a brilliant grand-son. But evidently he found the tutor's remarks sufficiently plau-sible to require a mild rebuff:

'What you say about conditions. ... They are very much better now than they were before the war. I know, because I've seen the change in this part of the country with my own eyes.'

MacCreath slid his arm beneath the tutor's. His expensive oatmeal-coloured sleeve showed up against the tutor's dingy black overcoat. He had deliberately refused to see the detec-tive's offensiveness. He had refused because if he had allowed himself to see it he would have been forced either to condone it or to condemn it. And if he had condemned it he would have condemned himself. After all, the tutor thought, the detective was really no more than a servant acting in the interests of well-to-do, subtler, gentlemanly twisters like MacCreath.

The tutor said aloud:

'I was exaggerating when I said the detective was the worst type of criminal. He's only a hired subordinate. I don't suppose he's very highly paid, either.' The tutor tried to disengage his arm from MacCreath's. Controlling his hatred, he went on: 'The real criminals are his employers. People who get rich by cheating millions of others out of their right to a decent life. Who are all honey and bogus culture. Profess to believe that the working class they've swindled is very well off. And when any-one retaliates he is arrested and they loftily pretend not to notice.'

MacCreath allowed his arm to fall away from the tutor's. A little less crudely the tutor added:

'People like the M.F.H.'

'But the M.F.H. is about the most harmless and unassuming

man I know. He's the last person one would suspect of being mixed up in high finance or anything of that sort. He'd be perfectly content to spend the rest of his life hunting and shooting and racing.'

MacCreath was more startled than hurt by the tutor's attack.

'Besides, he hasn't the business ability to swindle a child.'

'That's just the point,' the tutor said. 'He's got no ability, and yet he's a millionaire. The fact that he isn't capable of doing his own thieving makes him even less excusable. He poses as an amiable country gentleman, and lets his paid agents do the dirty work of collecting his rents and squeezing profits out of his mines.'

Once again MacCreath slid his arm beneath the tutor's. But this time the movement was less comfortable, more hesitant.

'Surely someone must provide the money to keep industry going and to give employment.'

'The M.F.H. provides nothing. His father stole a fortune from the miners and now his agents are using the money as a means of stealing another fortune from them. The only people who really provide anything are the miners themselves.'

MacCreath's arm was quite nerveless, might have been made of cork. His friendliness had lost all its earlier exuberance. At the same time the tutor, as though new blood had been transfused from MacCreath into him, felt invigorated. His hostility was tinged with pleasure. Even MacCreath's walk had become listless. However, this might not have been due to the tutor. They had arrived in front of the marquee and they were approaching its entrance. Perhaps MacCreath wanted to go in. 'Let him,' the tutor thought. Without decreasing his pace he walked on. MacCreath kept up with him. They had passed the entrance. The tutor had very briefly, contemptuously glanced into the interior of the marquee. But the impression that remained with him after they had passed could not be treated with contempt. When he tried to remember in detail what he had seen he could remember almost nothing except his general feeling that the interior of the marquee was very luxurious. But when he dwelt on this feeling, allowed it to develop in him, certain details emerged from it. A mounted buffalo head jutting from high up on the canvas wall, with a thin rope of dark blue chenille hanging from its horns. A tall panel of glass engraved at its corners with big frosted monograms. On a green baize tablecloth a soda siphon encased in silver tracery. Turkey carpets on the grass. Palms planted in brass-bound mahogany barrels. Cutlery on white table surfaces and above the tables pink and white faces like the faces of waxworks. Flowers seen through the glass of decanters, deceptive as orchids in a conjurer's stage greenhouse. Veering of tobacco breath in subdued sunlight. A black statue of a big-breasted Nubian carrying a basket of gilded pomegranates on her head. Trying to focus these things in his memory the tutor finally lost sight of them altogether. But the impression of luxury remained. The very incongruity of this luxury – whatever its real nature in detail might be – the fact that it had its basis not in some super hotel or clubhouse, but in a marquee on the racecourse, served to intensify his impression. And his disgust at the luxury was tempered by a certain regret, a half-ashamed desire.

MacCreath was speaking again:

'It's a good thing to have ideals.'

The tutor roused himself.

'Who has ideals?'

'To be young and to be without them is not to be young at all. Mind you, I'm not sneering at ideals. I do honestly admire you for them.'

'I loathe ideals. They're a smoke screen for hypocrites. We are told that an ideal can never be realized in practice. Its genuineness can never be tested by mere material standards. Bishops who get their income from armament shares and from slum property are usually idealists.'

MacCreath didn't understand what the tutor meant, but he was discouraged by his tone of voice. Almost plaintively he said:

'You know, you are rather a mystery man.'

'Why?'

'Well, because you are. And the biggest mystery of all to me is how you came to take that job with the Parkins.'

'There was nothing else to take.'

MacCreath was incredulous, ignored the explanation.

'When I heard that they'd engaged a tutor I expected to find someone quite different. Someone of the huntin' and shootin' type, not very strong on the intellectual side. My curiosity was distinctly roused when I met you.' He hesitated for some seconds before he added:

'I've often wanted to have a talk with you.'

Then, as though he knew in advance that the tutor's reply would be unfavourable, he said despondently:

'I could get you a good job tomorrow. You only have to say the word.'

The tutor's first impulse was to answer with an insult. But something checked him. He stared sideways at MacCreath's face. Beneath its tilted trilby hat it had an air of disillusioned jauntiness, of puzzled desolation. To have answered Mac-Creath with an insult would have been like injuring an uncomprehending animal. Instead, the tutor asked:

'Why do you want to get me a job?'

'I suppose I feel it's your due. You ought not to be allowed to throw yourself away.' MacCreath's voice was embarrassed. 'With your ideas — I call them that because you don't like the word ideals — you ought to be doing something better than private tutoring. You ought to be in a position to mix with really interesting people.'

Interesting people. In other words, moneyed people. Twisters. With elegant voices. With delightfully easy manners. Dressed casually or carefully but always in harmony with the occasion. Posed idly in sunlight on the steps of hotels. Speeding in sports cars. Photographed by flashlight at hunt balls. Talking fashionably and indifferently about art. Owning aeroplanes. Buying themselves on to the stage. Saying a few words at the launching of a submarine. Presented at Court. Playing roulette for charity. Wearing bishop's gaiters and delivering an oily oration in memory of a titled murderer of Indian tribesmen. All that such people said and thought and were and did owed its existence to the poverty and suffering of the working class. Without the workers to feed and house and fetch and carry for them these people wouldn't have the time to be so charming. And were they so charming? Even in itself their charm was suspect, fraudulent. It smelt of carrion. Stank of starvation and murder, the tutor thought. Or did he say this out loud? He became aware that while he had been thinking he also had been speaking. He had felt so angry that he hadn't clearly realized it before. How much he had said aloud he didn't know.

MacCreath had stopped walking. The tutor mechanically stopped walking, too, heard him say:

'I ought to go and look for my daughters. I expect they are waiting for me in the marquee.'

The prospect of getting rid of MacCreath may have made the tutor look a little more friendly. MacCreath added:

'Why not come along, too?' Seeing a change in the tutor's look he corrected himself: 'Or perhaps you would rather come along later – after you've had a stroll round the course. The girls would like to see you. Especially Ann.' He was shyly sly: 'You seem to have made a conquest there. She's become quite a socialist since she's known you.'

The tutor could afford to say with perfunctory grace:

'I expect I'll come along.'

He wouldn't.

'I hope you'll think over what I suggested just now,' MacCreath said. 'I should be glad of the chance to do something for you.'

He turned and walked away.

His parting look had been queer, full of pathos. It had been injured and at the same time forgiving. Gently appealing yet infinitely hopeless. He had seemed on the verge of tears. This behaviour hardly accorded with the offer he had made to the tutor a few minutes before. The offer of a corrupt job. A job which would lift the tutor into the ranks of the hypocrites and twisters, the starvers and the murderers. The tutor would never stain his hands with that vileness. Urged by his hatred he began to walk. To walk where? In a negative direction, well away from MacCreath and the marquee. He was carried vigorously forward by the movement of his hatred. But quite soon he came to feel that the vigour was leaking out of the movement. He was walking more slowly. He began to look about him. Other walkers passed by him, crossed in front of him, receded from him, approached him. A white wooden railing formed a broad semicircular curve to the right of him. Big striped umbrellas rose at intervals in front of the railing. To the left five or six policemen stood in a group, affably chatting, their black chin-straps wagging. He vaguely read the horse names on a book-maker's blackboard. Fritillary; Willie Winkle; Shalimar; Ichneumon; Furbisher; Easter Egg; Pantechnicon; Waterhole; Bagshaw; The Gaffer. His lapsing hatred could find no point of support in what he saw around him. The racecourse was ordinary and complex, and it was alien to what he had been feeling. It contradicted the simplicity of his hatred, intruded coldly upon him, aroused a new feeling – undefined at first but unpleasant and disturbing.

He tried to revive his hatred by thinking of MacCreath. Walking rather more quickly he mumbled to himself again and again: 'That twister.' The incantation did not satisfy him. He pictured MacCreath's face, wanted to see it twisted with hypocrisy and cunning. But the picture, once evoked, could not be so simply interpreted. It took on a life of its own, independent of the tutor's wishes, faced him once more with MacCreath's queer parting look. The look was inescapably sincere. MacCreath in his limited way meant well by the tutor. He might not understand the tutor's ideas, but he genuinely admired him for having ideas. Saw in him perhaps an integrity and an ability such as he himself had possessed as a young man. Wanted him to prosper, not to be frustrated. Had himself been frustrated, had hoped for and been denied a university education. Had made money instead and betrayed his 'ideals'. Believed that by offering the tutor material help he would save him from the necessity of a similar betrayal. Regarded him as an ally, a champion of his own thwarted aspirations. As a descendant. As an unhoped-for heir who would perpetuate all that had been best in himself. Yet knew in his bones that the tutor would never accept his offer. Knew that he was right not to accept it, that the offer was inevitably corrupt. MacCreath's face confessed it. He understood that he could never have an heir, a son. He would be lastingly frustrated. The tutor might be imagining all this, but he could no longer hope to revive his hatred by thinking of MacCreath. His hatred seemed artificial. A puffed-up religious fake designed to hide something he didn't want to see.

There was something connected with the racecourse that he didn't want to see. The crowd he was walking among had become denser. It was true that none of the people round him showed any hostility to him. Nor were they friendly. They were ordinary and indifferent. Normal. That was the unpleasant and disturbing thing. The ordinary racecourse was a part of the ordinary landscape, and the landscape extended to the place he had come from this morning. The house with four lawns. His futile job as a tutor. That was the sordid actuality which his high-falutin hatred had tried to conceal. And that actuality was winning against him, had already begun to make him feel depressed and afraid.

The crowd was becoming much denser. He could no longer move forward through it. He had arrived at the outer fringe of a close-packed circle of people. They were mostly men, and they were watching something. A clear space in the middle of the circle was occupied by some kind of performer. He was wearing a maroon-coloured silk dressing-gown, and a marmoset was perched on his right shoulder. His face seemed familiar. It was sardonic, pug-nosed and bulging-eyed. It was the face of Stokes, but his hair was the wrong colour. He was not Stokes. He was someone extraordinarily like him. In his left hand he held a green apple. His fingers twirled it, tossed it into the air, caught it. From his busily-working mouth came a continuous patter. His words were not clearly articulated, but the tutor could distinguish now and again, or thought he could distinguish, what the man was saying.

'... Step on the juice, Archibald. ... Shakespeare, strato-sphere, bottled beer. .... You're smiling at my monkey, madam? Poor little fellow.'

He carefully raised his right arm and tickled the marmoset with the tip of his finger. The animal turned and pressed its face into his ear. Its almost transparent tail hung down over his brilliant silk shoulder. All the time he was twirling and tossing the apple with his left hand.

'That's a secret between us, that was. Archie was just telling me what a fine-looking lot of folks he could see hanging around. All the best people are heeah today. You're here. I'm here. We're all heeah. ... Bogey, bogey. ... Have you seen the girl with the dreamy eyes? ...'

The tutor was still on the fringe of the crowd, but the man's voice was becoming more distinct.

'Couldn't get along without my Archibald. Fetches my breakfast for me every morning. First met him out in South America. An old sailor sold him to me for luck. Banana-bugs they call 'em out there. It's a grand country. All the flowers and the birds, grand birds. Pick and choose. With her ding-dongs dangling in the dust. You needn't look at me like that – I didn't say nothink. Hoojahbifibliah.'

The movements of the man's lips curiously failed to synchronize with the sound of his words. He was like a talking-film that had gone slightly wrong, the tutor thought.

'Yes, I've seen a bit of the world in my day. And, touch wood' – he touched his head – 'I'll live to see some more. Had my ups and my downs. You mightn't think I'd been at Oxford University with the Prince of Wales. It's a fact. At Worcester College he was. Under the same roof. Now I'm here. Horses, geegees – that's my trouble. Don't think I'm blaming my luck. Do you know why I've got you folks together here today? Because my luck's going to change, and I want you to share it with me. In another minute I'm going to give you the winner of the big race. Luck doesn't run one way for ever and mine's just about due to turn. Trust to luck and never say die. There's nothing else you can trust. I'm not being irreverent. All of us heeah know the etymolololological derivation of the word 'clergy'. It comes from an old Greek word meaning 'to gamble'. You see, the first parsons were all chosen by lot, because luck is really the will of the Almighty, and there was no better way of finding out which ones He didn't want. Gambling is the ruling passion of mankind and the Lord God Himself put it in us. All over the world you'll find it – in Asia, in Africa, in New Zealand and the Fiji Islands. Every single human being is a gambler, not only the lazy-good-for-nothing fellows. Who could work harder than a Chinaman? Yet in his leisure moments John will think nothing of hazarding a week's wages on such games as fan-tan, pak-a-pu, and chuk-luk.'

He paused to take a bite out of the green apple.

'Hullo,' he exclaimed in mock surprise. 'Something's been at this before me. The strangest apple I ever ... Will some lady or gentleman be kind enough to lend me a silver fruit knife?'

The audience laughed. He dexterously spun the apple between the first fingers of his two hands. The part of it he had bitten formed a rotating band of white. The marmoset was shivering.

'I believe we are on the threshold of a secret. I have a feeling that at any moment now we may be told something important. Something we are all of us itching to know.'

A little hunchback, very obviously an accomplice, stepped out of the crowd and handed him what looked like a large hunting-knife.

'Thank you, sir. Just what I wanted.'

He began to peel the apple.

'Who can tell me the winner of the two-thirty? I can, said the sour old fruit.'

He dug the point of the knife into the apple, pretended suddenly to notice a face in the crowd.

'Oh, no, sir, not you, sir. This old fruit in my hand, I meant.'

He split the apple into halves.

'Me-he, me-hi, me-soomp-soomp-soomper-diddle, whip-bang periwinkle, nip-coom, nipcaht. . . . Hullo, what's this?'

He delicately drew out a small piece of folded paper from the core of the apple.

'A love-letter from a maggot. What wouldn't you give to hear me read it?'

The crowd began to throw coppers towards him. He smiled his thanks, but he did not try to catch the coppers, nor was he in any hurry to pick them up from the ground. He fingered the folded paper:

'It's getting hot. ... *Shake*speare, *strato*sphere, *bott*led beer. ... *Hor*ses, *gee*gees, thoroughbreds, gingerbreads, screwlegs, bandylegs, spindlelegs, featherbeds. ... Bogey, bogey, Archibald. ... And the lucky winner is ... Is ... Is ... Have you seen the girl with the dreamy eyes? ... Is, is, is, is, is ...'

He unfolded the paper.

'Easter Egg.'

He glanced impressively round the crowd.

'At fifteen to one, boys. A real gold-mine.'

He suddenly saw the tutor. His expression changed. Perhaps the tutor, without knowing it, had looked sceptical and superior. The man was vigorously angry, shouted:

'Break into your cash-box, you bounder.'

No one in the crowd turned to look at the tutor.

'Show your face, you maggot. You can't hide from me. I can see you trying to cringe behind the ladies' backs. And well you may, you ...'

The tutor was horribly embarrassed, but the crowd still showed no sign of interest in what the man was saying.

'I know you. I know your type. I've got you taped all right.'

As before, the sound of the man's voice failed to correspond with the movements of his mouth. But there was nothing ambiguous or unconvincing about the words which the tutor heard.

'Yes, you. You with the face like an out-of-work chapel minister. You're the sort that makes good luck turn sour. You'll never gamble. You wouldn't stoop to anything so petty, eh? You care for higher things. If you were offered a thousand pounds tomorrow you wouldn't take it, eh? So you think. Nor you wouldn't either, not if there was any risk attached. I know you and your *principles*, my lad. I could turn you inside out with my little finger. You suppose I haven't ever heard of Socrates? I was studying him before you were born. And I'm not saying that in his day there wasn't a lot of sense in him. What year of grace do you think you're living in, you glum-faced ninny? Don't tell me you don't know? I shouldn't be surprised to find you a couple of months out in your dates. But not as much as one thousand nine hundred and ninety-nine years. I'll tell you straight what I think of your principles. You don't believe in 'em any more than I do. You only pretend to. Because you are in a bad funk. You're as keen to lay your hands on the goods of this world as the worst of us. But you're afraid you might put your fingers round a stinging nettle instead of a five-pound note. So you kid yourself that your principles are finer than gold. In other words, you're a sop, you're a weakling, you're a sissy.'

The man was not even looking at the tutor now. He was bending down and had begun to pick up coins from the grass. The voice went on:

'I'm telling you for your own good. Wake up and be a man. Be human. You're British, aren't you? Then learn to take reasonable risks and don't always be worrying for the safety of your own skin. Know what you want, and don't be afraid to go right ahead and get it. All the good things of life can be yours, if only you'll make up your mind to take them. The really good things, I mean, not just the cheap and flashy makeshifts. Don't you want to be in love with a really beautiful woman? Aren't you ashamed when you think of your present condition – without any woman at all? Don't you want to travel, to see the world? Don't you want a home of your own? Don't you want a good job and plenty of friends? Yes, you want all these things. Why be afraid to admit it?'

The man had finished picking up the coppers. As he dropped the last of them into his pocket he said with a wink at the crowd:

'Win it and wear it, like the wooden leg at the battle of Balaclava.'

The show was over. The man's face relaxed, disburdened itself of its artificial animation. He did not walk away, did not

133

even take off his dressing-gown, but the people round him no longer gave him their undivided attention. He had retired into himself, was becoming one of the crowd. In a moment the circle would disintegrate and everyone would walk away. The tutor must speak now. He must get even with this nauseous charlatan. Speak, denounce, vomit out words of boundless disgust. British. Luck. Sissy. Be a man. Spew those words back at him, clotted with bilious loathing. You degenerate, muck-brained, syphilitic, superstitious swine. Then the man would retort more violently. Suppose there was a fight and the tutor won, would that prove that he did believe in his principles? Already the crowd was beginning to move away. Or could he say with perfect calm – 'I am not a weakling. I believe in intellectual and emotional integrity. I do not want to be a vulgar success or to make my mark in the material world. I know I am right, and this man's would-be insults mean nothing to me'? ... It would be a lie, and the crowd would roar with laughter. The tutor knew he did not believe in his principles. He was not a monk, he did not believe in self-abnegation, he did want to live. Flabby with misery he began to walk away. He did want to live, but not to live like that charlatan, not like the crowd on the race-course, not like MacCreath or the Parkins. He was afraid that if he tried to live he might become like other people. But other people did try. Even though they had made a mess of their lives they were not cowards. They were better than he was.

They were more than better – they were admirable. These people among whom he was walking had lived through horrible difficulties, had not surrendered. Poverty, ignorance, diseases – his woes were a luxurious fad compared with theirs. Yet most of them looked cheerful. They did not smell out vileness everywhere, as he did. They were not negative, did not draw back in disgust from life. His job with the Parkins would seem a happy sinecure to them. And with very little effort he could get a better job than that. He could accept MacCreath's offer. 'It is not too late,' he thought. He had stopped walking. A few yards in front of him a narrow sandy road cut across his path at right angles, and along this road from the left two cars were approaching. Sunlight glittered on the chromium-plated radiator of the first car. 'Why not accept?' he thought. The joy and the splendour of life. Success. The chance might never come again. The first car, moving slowly, was passing in front of him. It was an open touring car, very big but not big enough for the number of people in it. Yet they did not give the impression of being uncomfortably huddled together. They luxuriated; some reclining, some gracefully leaning, others as easily upright as flowers. They were all young. Only one of the men wore a hat, and none of the girls was fashionably dolled-up for the races. All – men and girls – seemed good-looking. One of the men, the tutor thought, was playing a mandolin. A girl was dressed in mauve gauze. Another man was holding a butterfly-net. A girl had a large slim book beneath her bare arm. The tutor thought he recognized Humphrey Silcox at the driving wheel. The car had passed. From the dickey of the second car a girl waved to the tutor. She was Ann MacCreath. The second car stopped. Ann called to him:

'Come with us for a drive round the course.'

Dorothy MacCreath, sitting at the wheel, smiled at him. From behind her head the dark red face of a young man peered keenly, with virile friendliness. The tutor ran across the grass and climbed into the dickey.

This car, unlike the first, was not crowded. Before the tutor had arrived there had been only three people in it. He wondered whether Ann had intentionally reserved a place for him, had been looking out for him. Dorothy was driving slowly, because of the crowds. The first car was about thirty yards ahead. To the right extended the white wooden railing which marked out the course. The narrow sandy road ran parallel with the course, and in the distance both road and railing curved sharply. The car would eventually arrive back at the marquee, the tutor thought. To the left the table-land ended in an abrupt invisible slope, defined only by the steeply descending tops of a few fir trees. Beyond the slope stretched a huge plain of variegated green. Smooth isolated hills broke up the line of the horizon. The sun was brilliant. Travel, love, joy, creation — nothing would be impossible for the tutor. 'All the worlds of nature and of art,' he said to himself. What wouldn't he do, what sights, odours, feelings he would savour. Don't wait a moment longer. Oh, begin, begin. But he had already begun. He was saying aloud to Ann:

'Come to Reykjavik.'

She looked at him with sober friendliness, unsurprised, but she did not answer. He went on vehemently:

'Anywhere. Ecuador. London. Now. Just as we are. With no preparations. Without even a toothbrush. Clear of all impedimenta. Nothing. Everything.'

Still she was not startled, did not speak.

'Why not? What's to stop us?'

She grinned pleasantly.

'Say something,' he insisted.

'You don't really mean it.'

'I do. Provided we start at once.'

She laughed.

'The fact is you don't want to come,' he said.

She was slightly annoyed for a moment:

'How could we start at once without any preparations? It just isn't practical.'

'That's the whole point. If it were practical it wouldn't be worth doing. If we had to collect toothbrushes and make all kinds of plans for the journey we might as well stay where we are. We can get as much practicality as we like here and now without travelling for it.'

'But we should have to take *some* kind of practical action. Get out of this car, for instance.'

'No. If both of us really wanted to go we should *find* ourselves out of the car. We shouldn't have to *get* out. We shouldn't have to make a cheap conscious effort of will.'

She was grinning again. He added:

'You wouldn't come even if I did agree to be practical.'

'Yes, I would.'

'I don't somehow see us getting married.'

136

'Who suggested marriage? Two people can go away together for a few weeks without binding themselves for life. *I* am in no hurry to get married.'

'A few weeks is a long time. We might get more involved with each other than we meant.'

'A few days then.'

'I don't know.'

'Or a single night.'

She was quite serious. But he no longer felt any enthusiasm for her. He looked into her face. It was well-proportioned and healthily coloured. It had no make-up on it. It was soberly intelligent. There was nothing enigmatic or disturbed about it. Perhaps there was a hint of pique in her voice as, realizing his change of feeling, she said:

'How long will you go on allowing the Parkins to decide what you do?'

'Not much longer.'

'You said that before.'

'Yes.' He was mysterious: 'But now I know I can get another job as soon as I want it.'

'What sort of job?'

'A better one.'

'You will find it just the same. Until you begin to act up to your opinions you will find any job the same.'

He wanted to say: 'I have changed my opinions,' but he could not. He became angry:

'I haven't particularly noticed *you* acting up to your opinions. Or perhaps you merely pretended to have the same ideas as I did, from ulterior motives.'

'You know that's rubbish. I didn't agree with you at first, and I didn't pretend to. But I became convinced you were right. And I *have* tried to do something about it.'

'Oh? What? Been manufacturing bombs in the attic?'

'You are just being childish. Anarchists and fascists manufacture bombs. We are opposed to assassination.'

'Well, what exactly have you done?'

'I have been selling pamphlets down at the docks.'

'Have you?'

'Yes. Tomorrow evening I am going to speak in public for the first time. In the street.'

Aware that he might think her boastful or romantic, she added:

'Of course, my main work will be among the middle class. You have to be a docker yourself if you hope to have real influence with dockers. But I want to get experience among the working class first.'

'What sort of experience do you think you're getting up here at the races? Or is this your first attempt to work among the middle class?'

She had a moment of honest awkwardness.

'No, I admit I didn't come here to work.' She recovered her assurance: 'But it won't do. I wouldn't go away with you even if you were practical. I have been deluding myself that I could live with a foot in both worlds. No one can be a socialist half the time and go for romantic pleasure jaunts the other half.'

Unreasonably he felt disappointed. She went on:

'It might be different if you were a socialist. Then there would be no question of our relation becoming a mere pleasure jaunt. The strange thing about you is that you see quite clearly what is wrong with the system under which we are living. More clearly than I do. But you take no action. You are content to hate and despise your life.'

'No.'

'Then what action do you take?'

How could he explain? He couldn't say: 'I have done nothing yet, but I intend to accept a good job which your father has offered me. I intend to be a success.' That would be hopelessly crude, not at all what he really meant. He meant to live a happy and splendid life. He meant to live it at once, to win a whole world of poetry and love. That was the action he would take. Now, in the slowly moving car, with Ann beside him. But her serious face checked him, and she said:

'You think you can get a better job. Perhaps you can. A

better-paid job, with fewer petty restrictions on your leisure. You may even have a liberal-minded employer. But unless you fight against capitalism you will feel just as servile as you do now. You will never be free in your mind and heart so long as all your actions, your real life, are still wholly in the service of the rich.'

He recognized phrases which he himself had used in an earlier conversation with her. He did not answer, stared out of the car at the racecourse.

'Or have you changed your mind about capitalism? Perhaps you think now that there is nothing seriously wrong with it and that it has a brilliant future. Or that it doesn't exist.'

Still he would not speak. He looked at the first car, saw the girl in mauve.

'Suppose you get a good job and make money. Suppose you become a capitalist. I can hardly imagine it, but if it did happen do you think you would be able to live the sort of life you want to? Your time would be mostly taken up in trying to squeeze profits out of the workers and in helping your friends to pre-pare for war. That's what capitalism increasingly leads to – not to a new world of poetry, love and science. You would have no option – unless you were ready to destroy yourself as a capitalist.'

The sandy road, keeping parallel with the white railing, had straightened out after a wide semicircular bend. It extended for-ward in the direction of the car park, then curved away again to the right. The girl in the first car looked back at him. Ann went on :

'Fascist war has already begun, and it will spread. How far it will spread will depend on how soon the workers' movement can become strong enough to stop it. We need all the allies we can get. We need them now.'

He felt a slight awkwardness, but he refused to argue.

'Why not come down to the docks with me tomorrow?'

He would have to say something soon. He looked at the girl in the first car, at the white railing curving away to the right. at the shifting crowds ahead. He was reassured.

'No,' he said. 'Anyway, not tomorrow.'

It was necessary to take action, but not Ann's sort of action. It was necessary for him to stop indulging in passive fantasies which left his real situation unchanged, but this did not mean that he must at once begin to lead the life of a militant socialist. There was no war here on the racecourse, and the capitalists who had come here had not come in order to prepare for war. Nor were the crowds of workers visibly being sweated or oppressed. Her ideas seemed abstract, irrelevant to the concrete reality which was before his eyes. What he must do was to recognize that reality and try from now on to act in accordance with it.

Ann's voice continued, but he no longer heard what she was saying. As the car curved along the curving road to the right the marquee came into view again. The girl who had returned his look was not, as he had at first imagined, dressed in mauve gauze. Nor did one of the men hold a butterfly-net, and the large slim book under the bare arm of another girl was also an illusion. These extravagances had been a trick played on him by his excitement. He was normal again now. He would be objective and practical. His view of the marquee was normal, was not influenced in any way by the different kind of excitement which he was now beginning to feel and which he must carefully control. On the contrary his new feeling was due to, was influenced by the objectively real marquee. Just to prove the efficiency of his control he stopped looking at the marquee for a moment, glanced once again at the people in the first car. There was nothing fantastic about them. They were ordinary upper-middle-class young men and women. Most of the men did in fact wear hats, no one was playing a mandolin, and the girl who had looked at him was dressed not in mauve gauze but in a fur coat – though it was true she did wear also a blue silk scarf. The tall man leaning against the side of the car, half sitting on the door, had a pallid puffy face like the face of an unhealthy boy. The tutor's earlier impression that everyone in the group was splendidly beautiful and unconstrained was a sickly make-believe. Yet he would have been equally deceived if he had regarded them as vile twisters smelling of carrion. He must try to see the actuality which was before his eyes. The fur coat might or might not be expensive or fashionable — that was a matter for abstract speculation. But its smoothness, its neat straightness descending from the fur-buttoned waist, its delicate fullness gathered into folds on either side of the open neck — were in *fact* difficult not to admire. The girl might or might not use cold cream or spend hours at the dressing-table — but the sun's warmth glowed in the frosty pendants of her earrings and illuminated the human warmth of her face with a cool bloom as of ice. She looked at him again and he looked away. The tall man was talking to someone. His puffy face was transformed with a new whimsical vigour. Suddenly the tutor understood the truth about these people. They were better, more beautiful, less constrained, more intelligent than most other people. They were not twisters like the charlatan with the apple, nor did they cringe away from life like the tutor. They dared to live in the world, and they lived better, more sanely, more happily than others.

Why shouldn't he become one of them? But he *was* one of them. He was after all not an ugly duckling, not a coward, not a failure. He had seen the swans flying. A queer cry of recognition and of freedom rose in his throat and he wanted to shout to the people in the first car: 'At last I am here.' But he restrained himself. He must be practical and objective. He looked again at the marquee.

His sense of control was becoming in itself an excitement. He felt as though he was in solitary command of some huge unexplored power-house. Or as though he was very ingeniously, with consummate mastery, concealing the fact that he was drunk or mad. But was this control natural? Wasn't it a new form of mysticism, of self-abnegation? Why shouldn't he dare to give free play, within sane limits, to a happiness which was based no longer on fantasies but on the actual possibilities of his real surroundings? He relaxed his control. The marquee looked the same as before. Only his feelings had changed, had expanded their power, risen at last to the level of the actuality which was before his eyes. The marquee was not like a racing-yacht in full sail, it was not like a white-walled aerodrome from which he could instantly fly to any part of the world, it was not like a crowded flutter of girls' frocks along the esplanade, was not like a mansion with circular mansard windows and broad white pillars and porticoes and gilded urns, not like a cool place for the protection of art and learning, not like a white balcony from which he could look at mountains through a powerful brass telescope. It was like an ordinary marquee, white and rather large. It was like the actual destination towards which a slowly moving car was taking the tutor. It was like a real place where the people in the first car would soon arrive, where he, too, would arrive, and where he would be able to meet some of them; was like an opportunity for beginning to make friends with them, or at least for striking up an acquaintance with them which later, after he had accepted MacCreath's offer, he would be in a position to develop further; was like a first step towards not an ideally happy future but a life much happier than he had lived in the past, a life in which travel, yacht-racing, flying, views of mountains, art and learning, girls, visits to mansions, would be practical possibilities. The marquee was like the headquarters from which he would begin his practical campaign to get what he knew he wanted.

'Travel,' he thought. Almost at once – or did the event precede the thought? – the car stopped. The first car, which was now only a few yards away and was directly in front of the main entrance of the marquee, had also stopped. The tall man and the girl in the fur coat and all the others except the driver, Humphrey Silcox, had got out. Someone who had not been in the car had come forward out of the shadow of the marquee entrance and was speaking to Silcox. The others turned to look at the newcomer. He wore a dark blue belted raincoat. Without alarm or revulsion the tutor recognized him as the detective.

Ann leant forward to ask Dorothy:

'What's happened?'

'Tod's going to find out.'

Dorothy's red-faced young man had jumped from the car and was striding over towards Silcox and the detective. He was broad-backed, stocky and powerful, and his long arms swung heavily from his shoulders. Dorothy and Ann got out of the car. Tod listened for a moment to what the detective was telling Silcox, then said curtly and loudly:

'We'll take them round to the side.'

The detective shook his head. His look was agreeable and regretful, suggested that he knew he was making an absurd demand but that no other course was open to him. Tod turned away from him with contempt, walked back towards the second car.

'What is it?' Dorothy asked.

'We've got to take the cars round to the car park.'

'Why?'

'Just darned officiousness.'

The tutor was climbing out of the dickey. Dorothy moved to regain her seat at the driving-wheel, but Tod intercepted her.

'I'll drive it round for you,' he said definitely. 'You go and enjoy yourself in the marquee with the others.'

Without waiting for her assent he stepped into the car. Then, as though he at last felt free to concern himself with something that really interested him, he looked at the tutor, asked confidently:

'You coming?'

His unhesitating grin overpowered the tutor's disinclination. 'Yes.'

In any case the tutor would be able to return to the marquee later. He found himself in the act of sitting down on the front seat of the car. Tod was pushing the gear lever into reverse. The car bounded backwards, curved with a jump from road to grass, struck the canvas wall of the marquee. The brakes squeaked, Tod changed gear, the car moved forward with an accelerating swerve and jerked on to the road again. People were crossing the road, but Tod did not slow down for them.

'There's a type that makes me feel sick,' he said.

'Where?'

'That meddling sod we've just left. I can't think why Silcox wastes time talking to him.'

The tutor realized with sudden pleasure that Tod was speaking of the detective.

'He reminds me of some of the specimens the government sends out to Nigeria. Just because they are officials, my God, they think they know your business better than you do yourself. It's getting worse every year.'

The tutor began to be glad that he had not stayed behind at the marquee. Here was someone who spoke his language, felt as he did. He asked with admiration:

'What's it like out there?'

'Not so good as it was. Too much government interference. And plenty of damned hard work. Still, I don't mind that. The pay's good enough.'

The tutor was eager to be sympathetic:

'What sort of job do you do?'

'Tin-mining. Not underground, you know – alluvial. I'd stick it for another year or two, but I doubt whether the life out there would suit Dorothy. Climate's the main snag.'

In spite of the speed at which Tod drove, the tutor did not feel there was any risk that he might knock someone down. People stood aside for him, and showed no resentment. And if someone had suddenly stepped out on to the road the tutor knew that Tod would have been able to pull up without the least difficulty. His driving was as controlled yet vigorous as his voice.

'But there are advantages. Besides the pay. I've a large house and servants to do all the odd jobs and a garden very nearly as big as an English estate.'

Ignoring the road for a moment, he turned to the tutor with a frank grin:

'Guess what breed of watch-dog I keep in my garden.'

'Well, what sorts of dogs are there in Nigeria?'

'It isn't a dog,' Tod almost crowed. 'It's a mandrill. You know – with a crimson and blue bottom. That's a fact. Better than any dog. No risk of burglars – it could fetch 'em down as quick as a tiger.'

His face had turned again to glance ahead. It was big-nosed and heavy-eyebrowed beneath a severe backward sweep of sleek black hair. Normally it would have seemed aggressive, but now its grimness of feature was broken by a look of happy friendliness. Evidently he liked the tutor.

'You're tutoring that Parkin boy aren't you?' he asked.

'Yes.'

'How do you like the job?'

'I don't.'

The tutor had a moment's uneasiness. But Tod, far from thinking him a muff or a grouser, was very pleased.

'There aren't many decent jobs going at home now.' His tone changed: 'Unless you happen to be the son of a company director. Like a fellow I knew at the mining school. No brains, and hadn't the guts of a louse. But he's fallen on his feet in one of the few mining jobs left in Cornwall.'

Tod's anger soon cleared.

'Anyway I've no intention of sticking in Nigeria for the rest of my days. I'm going to take up fruit farming. Down south, near Jo-burg.'

'Where's that?'

'Johannesburg. Out there we always call it Jo'burg.'

Once again Tod glanced away from the road, looked full at the tutor.

'Why don't you come out too? You could get a good job as lecturer at the university. Decent pay – enough to marry on.'

In an instant the tutor knew what he would do – he would go out to South Africa. Not to stay there permanently, not even to stay there for a whole year, but as a beginning of his travels. He wanted to explain this to Tod, to confide in him and at the same time to use words which would convey not too fulsomely how much he admired him. 'You are the real traveller, the pioneer, the genuine man of action,' he thought. He did not say this, or anything like it. For the moment he said nothing at all. Tod, for the first time since they had left the marquee, was concentrating his whole attention on driving the car. They were arriving at the car park.

The attendant came towards them. Tod steered the car into a narrow gap between two other cars. The engine stopped. He paid the attendant a shilling for a ticket. The attendant walked away. Tod stepped out on to the running-board, suddenly stumbled. Perhaps he fell against the door handle of the adjacent car. The tutor at first saw only the crouching curve of his back, then with a shock noticed his face. Its expression suggested fear rather than pain. It was like the face of a man who knows he has been hit by a poisoned arrow. The tutor hurried towards him round the back of the car.

'Have you hurt yourself?'

'No. I'm all right. Let's get out of here.'

Tod straightened himself. Staring in front of him he began to walk. The tutor kept up with him.

'I don't want to run into Silcox just at present,' Tod said.

With an almost savage effort he increased his pace.

'I couldn't stand his chatter.'

They arrived back at the entrance of the car park. Outside Tod turned to the left, away from the road and on to the grass. He began to walk more easily. There was no sign that Silcox's car had yet started from the marquee.

'I get these attacks now and again.'

'What are they?'

'My malaria. A dose of quinine will put me right.'

Tod was gloomy.

'I can't even play a game of tennis now without wondering all the time whether I'll be in bed for days afterwards.'

He was walking faster again. The tutor asked sympathetically:

'I suppose almost everyone gets it out in Nigeria?'

'Yes. Or something worse. You need a first-class physique if you're to stand up to the life out there even for a couple of months.'

'I can see that.'

The tutor sounded more impressed than he really felt now. Tod was flattered.

'And diseases aren't the only thing you're up against.'

His voice mysteriously stopped.

'What else?' the tutor asked.

'I expect you've wondered whether there is any truth in the stories about Englishmen who go native.'

'Yes.'

'Well, there is. It's more common than you'd think. I had to go and see a fellow on business who had been out there seven years. He was living with a black woman, and when I went to bed I found he'd provided me with one too. That was his idea of hospitality. I kicked her out.'

Tod was beginning to enjoy himself. His attack of malaria couldn't have been very severe.

'And the natives think nothing of offering you their wives. One evening my cook-boy brought me in a couple of black mams. He couldn't understand why I knocked him down.'

The tutor found it more and more difficult to maintain his enthusiasm for Tod. Even travel seemed less attractive now – though not because of the black mams.

'Drink's another thing. If you don't drink the climate gets you down, and if you do you have to know when to stop. You can't afford to be weak-willed. There was an Englishwoman in the lounge of an hotel at Lagos who was so doped that she allowed the Pekinese on her lap to bite away most of her left bub. The rest of it had to be amputated afterwards.'

The marquee was about a hundred yards in front of them. Perhaps less, but their route towards it across the grass was not as direct as the road would have been. Miles beyond it and far below it rose the rectilinear fields, the long coast road, the dead-blue sea. Without regret the tutor suddenly gave up the idea of travel, at any rate of Empire travel. Tod went on :

'I wouldn't care to introduce Dorothy to the life out there. Mind you, I'm not questioning her pluck – she'd face up to it all right. But Nigeria's no place for a white woman.'

147

His malaria seemed to affect him again. He stumbled against the tutor, recovered, said sourly:

'Someone's given her the idea that she won't like Jo'burg.'

His tone at once became milder, almost sad. He confided in the tutor:

'When I first suggested fruit-farming she was very keen about it. Then she changed her mind. Yesterday she told me she didn't want to leave England. She'll change her mind again, of course. She would never have had any doubts in the first place if it hadn't been for her sister's influence.'

He added with manful tact:

'I'm not saying a word against Ann. She's a fine girl, and I wish you the very best of luck. But I think you ought to know something about the sort of people she's been mixing with lately. If anyone can get her out of their hands you should be able to.'

The tutor looked with relief at the marquee. It was not much more than fifty yards off now.

'I don't know whether you know it, but they are socialists of the worst type. Not just the weak-kneed parlour sort — real scum from the gutter. Most of them Jews.'

Tod's voice had become strangely like Mr Parkin's. It had the same vicious jerkiness, but it was more dangerous, less easy to ignore than Mr Parkin's.

'There's only one thing to do with that sort of muck.'

The tutor tried to concentrate his attention on the marquee. How white it was, and how near. Soon he would be inside it, talking to someone else. But Tod's voice could not be evaded.

'Knock'm down before they guess what's coming to them. I shot a nigger in Nigeria for far less than some of the things they've done. I had to — or sooner or later he'd have murdered me.'

Tod was deliberately walking more slowly.

'God knows why you people at home have allowed them to get away with it for so long. They've practically smashed the army and navy and left us with the weakest air-force in Europe.

And it isn't as though you'd have had any trouble in stopping them.'

The absurdity of his words made his voice sound unreal. It was less like a voice than a nasty sultriness in the air, an apprehensive heaviness closing in upon the tutor. The marquee no longer seemed pleasant, the sky was a dull vacancy. The voice became crudely savage.

'Deal with one or two of them and the rest would scuttle like rats. They may be well paid by the Soviet for undermining our defences, but they'd soon drop it if they thought they might get hurt.'

The voice came closer to the tutor's ear.

'Do you know what they did down here at the Election?'

'No,' he said weakly.

'They slashed all the tyres on the M.F.H.'s car. I saw it myself soon afterwards. But the next night we were ready for them. I don't think they'll try that trick again.'

Tod abruptly stopped walking.

'I wonder whether they're up to something today?' he said.

A stimulating idea had occurred to him.

'That fellow who told us to take away the cars may not be such a fool after all. Perhaps he thinks there's going to be trouble. He may need our help. Those scum are always on the look-out for the M.F.H., and they know he'll be up here today.'

The idea was so patently ridiculous that the tutor mechanically received it as a joke.

He tittered, then became conscious that Tod was glaring at him. He tried to justify himself.

'It's hardly likely they'd think of attacking the M.F.H. on the racecourse.'

'They won't get the chance to think. We'll see to that. We'll do all the thinking, and we'll do it first.'

Tod's look was aggressively suspicious.

'I wasn't blind at the Election and I know most of them by sight, and even if I didn't I could spot them from a mile off by their noses.'

His face came nearer to the tutor's, grew bigger. Its red was minutely dotted with points of black, and from its forehead the greased hair went backwards in blackly shining strips. The tutor hadn't the energy to move his own face away from it.

'Hit them before they've got a chance to hit you — that's the way to deal with them.'

Not only Tod's face but his body also grew bigger. He was taller, and his shoulders were broader, than before. The heaviness had gone from the air, had become concentrated in the swelling bulk of his chest. There was very little air. The marquee, not more than ten yards off now, seemed as fragile and as dull as burnt-up paper. The tutor was not afraid, was even able to think of Tod with contempt, but he could not move or speak.

'Hit them good and hard — and to do that you've got to organize. Some of us have made a start already. After the Election we decided to form our first Storm detachment down here. Now we've got three detachments. We take our orders from G.H.Q. in London. The party is developing at the rate of about ten thousand new members per week. That isn't generally known, but it soon will be. Before long we shall have the whole country with us — at least all the Englishmen. And we shan't tolerate any passengers in the boat : everyone will have to pull his weight.'

The tutor could not have lifted a finger to protect himself if Tod had decided to hit him, could not have muttered the slightest protest if Tod had commanded him to report at once for Storm duty to the detective. The monstrous bulk of Tod's body dazed him, made him as helpless and lethargic as a frog squatting in the shadow of the expanded hood of a cobra. He could not even find the energy to look once more at the marquee. And now he could see nothing except Tod's face, and he no longer saw that clearly. A huge dim impatience convulsed it, then suddenly it turned away from him. The body became visible again, but this time the tutor was looking at Tod's back. The legs moved with an unnatural, military jerkiness. Tod had abandoned him, was striding towards the detective.

The tutor felt, not relief, but an extreme weakness — as

though his last support had been withdrawn from him. He watched Tod approach the detective, saw the two of them walk away together towards the front of the marquee, lost sight of them. He fell forward, it seemed; had the sensation of crawling on his hands and knees. He found himself standing before the side entrance of the marquee. Actually he had walked there, not crawled. He went into the marquee.

He at once felt stronger. He stood still, persuaded himself to focus what was before his eyes, saw a big canvas-vaulted space, faintly smoky, at the far end of which groups of people stood talking. The scene was reassuringly normal. Small tables covered with white cloths and surrounded by green iron chairs occupied the central area of uncarpeted grass, and he saw no Nubian statue, no chenille-hung buffalo head. The mild daylight, canvas-enclosed and warmer than it had been outside the marquee, hinted at springtime. But a voice spoke to him, asked him with surprising curtness to show his ticket. He noticed a man sitting at a baize-covered table to the right of the entrance.

'I haven't got one. Can I pay now?'

'Ten shillings.'

The tutor paid without thinking, would have paid ten times as much if he had been asked to and had had the money on him. He refused to allow the man's tone to disturb him. The essential thing now was to avoid over-emphasizing minor impressions. He advanced into the marquee. The grass he walked over was darker and seemed thicker than the grass outside, but that was natural because the light in here was more subdued. On the tables were cut-glass vases filled with daffodils, but slanting iron legs jutting from beneath the borders of the white cloths revealed that the tables were of the ordinary collapsible kind often used in popular tea-gardens. What luxury there was here was only an improvisation. The green iron chairs were collapsible also: a few of them not yet in use were stacked in a pile against the left-hand canvas wall of the marquee. A long and high table, covered from top to base with glossy marble-patterned American cloth, was near the stacked chairs, and from behind it rose receding tiers of bottles – golden, ruby, crème de menthe and glinting. But the bottles stood upon a terraced structure of upturned hampers, and he saw a frayed black overcoat hanging from a corner of one of the hampers. Or did he see it? When he looked more carefully the overcoat was not there.

Perhaps the bar-tender had removed it. For the moment, however, no bar-tender was visible, and the tutor did not try to discover one. A little uneasy, he looked away. He quickened his walk, nearly bumped into a small table. A heavy silver bowl, shaped like the head of a lion with a ring through its mouth, was on the table. But he must avoid over-emphasizing his impressions: the bowl was really tin, not silver. And on other tables there were other bowls, also shaped like, no, not like lions' heads but like the heads of other animals – foxes, elephants, stoats. And the tables were laid with white silk cloths, with brilliant knives, spoons and forks, with intricately folded napkins expanding like white roses from shining tumblers. He reasoned with himself that he must be imagining most of this, that the tables were really quite ordinary. But his reasoning was not convincing. The animal-headed bowls were still there, and they looked more and more like silver. He began to suspect even that he was under-emphasizing his impressions. Perhaps the luxury here was quite solid and real, and the frayed black overcoat had been a delusion, had been wilfully imagined by him in his desire to find everything here ordinary. Looking out of the corner of his right eye, he became aware again of the terraced bottles. He did not turn to look fully at them, because he suspected now that if he were to do so he would see that the long table was covered not with American cloth but with real marble. And this suspicion disturbed him.

The luxury of the marquee was real, not a mere impression, and in itself it was not unpleasant. True, it was a little remote and superior, made him feel as though he was attending a social function to which he was not quite sure he had been invited. What was disturbing, however, was that the luxury began to remind him of something which had happened just before he had come into the marquee. Something not luxurious but nasty, quite distinct from the silver bowls and the marble and yet having a queer affinity with them – as though the same basic materials had been made up into a different pattern. He refused to be reminded of what had happened. He shut his eyes, opened them, stared straight ahead towards the far end of the marquee. Groups of well-dressed men and women stood easily chatting. He advanced towards them.

'You know what you have to do,' he told himself. Make contact. Find someone whom he recognized, or failing that attach himself unobtrusively to one of the groups. He mustn't expect too much. This was only a beginning. Later there might be yachts and mountains, not today. But he saw no one whom he recognized. Faces comfortably talkative or smilingly rigid, various yet having a queer affinity. Hundreds, some of them sipping drinks. There must be a bar at this end of the marquee also. Clothes various, tweed or formal grey or brilliant, yet having some quality in common. Which group to approach? The nearest. Three well-preserved middle-aged men and one woman. Words, sentences flew out obliquely towards him, made him hesitate.

'And then the old girl crashed down on me from an altitude. ... "Oh, Mr Bover!"'

'While all the time Larry was laughing up his sleeve.'

'Excuse me, no.'

'She's a character. ... Born and bred at Southend.'

'Luckily the M.F.H. popped out of his library just at that moment.'

'Otherwise I'd have been down on my hands and knees – gathering up the fragments that remained.'

'She keeps him in order too.'

'She does.'

What could the tutor contribute to this conversation? Even if he had understood its meaning he would have been quite unable to imitate its tone. So airy it seemed, so detached and musical. The speakers might have been rehearsing for a play. Nevertheless the tutor could not afford to stand still and say nothing. Either he must go forward or he would find himself sliding back. Back to where? He refused to remember, forced himself to open his mouth. But, strain as he might, he could not make a sound. One of the men – Mr Bover? – big-handed and big-hipped, wearing a signet ring, loosely clothed and having the figure of an ex-rugby player, stared him lightly in the face and did not see him. The tutor remembered Tod. At all costs he must make himself heard. Give up trying to articulate words; to mumble or laugh would be sufficient. Not attempt to assert himself or add anything of his own to their intercourse, but to echo however inefficiently their latest tone. Merge himself in their ritual. They might accept him as an eccentric. Tod must not come back and find him isolated. He smiled, coughed out a laugh. They took no notice. His smile ached horribly. He could not maintain it much longer. But now, from behind them, appeared someone he recognized – the tall man with the puffy face who had been in the first car. The tutor turned the smile on to him.

At first the newcomer, like the others, took no notice. Then he saw the tutor and was embarrassed. Suddenly he mastered himself, smiled back. The ache subsided from the tutor's face. The tall man smiled more easily. Eagerly grateful the tutor laughed. The tall man laughed back. They stood facing one another, and the tutor found himself saying without difficulty:

'I saw you in the first car.'

'You were with Ann MacCreath, weren't you?'

'Yes. They picked me up.'

'My name's Gregory Mavors.'

The tutor said quickly:

'I'm the Parkins' tutor.'

Mavors looked keenly at him, but without disapproval; then asked:

'What about a drink?'

'A very good idea.'

They began to walk towards the long marble-patterned table.

'What will you have?'

'I don't know,' the tutor said. 'A stout.'

They approached the table. Its covering, if not of marble, was indisputably of some more solid material than American cloth. And an unlabelled bottle standing on the table contained an opaque golden liquid.

'A stout and a sidecar,' Mavors told the now visible and white-jacketed bar-tender. He said to the tutor: 'How long have you been with the Parkins?'

'About three months.'

'What are they like?'

'Pretty poisonous.'

The tutor immediately wished that he had not said this. Mavors showed no sign of knowing anything about the Parkins, but he seemed to take unfavourable note of the tutor's attitude. He had the interested look of a viva voce examiner who has discovered a gap in a candidate's knowledge. The tutor tried to rehabilitate himself:

'Of course, that's only my own personal view. Anyone who genuinely liked country life, fishing and shooting, might get on very well with them.'

Mavors still had the same look. The tutor picked up a glass of stout which had appeared on the table in front of him. He must not say anything more. But Mavors would not speak either, continued to watch him with the mild waiting stare of a questioner. Awkwardly fascinated the tutor had a sudden wish to commit himself, to confess. He said:

'I suppose I ought never to have taken the job. I'm not suited for it. That's why I called the Parkins poisonous, but I dare say they are quite decent people really.'

Mavors nodded. The tutor felt humiliated, wanted to assert himself again:

'Anyone would seem decent compared with the man I'd just been talking to.'

'Who's he?'

'Tod. I didn't hear his first name. He murdered someone out in Nigeria.'

'Tod Ewan. I know him.'

The inquisitorial look had faded from Mavors's face, was replaced by an interested thoughtfulness. The tutor said with heat:

'He may be lying, of course. Probably he thinks a reputation for murder will make people admire him. But I suspect he wasn't lying when he said he had formed a Storm Troop down here. I saw him talking to a police spy.'

Aware that Mavors was not much impressed, the tutor added more violently:

'He's loathsomely diseased.'

Quietly, and almost as though he was beginning to recite a poem, Mavors said:

'Tod Ewan is very ill. He is suffering from malaria and neurosis and on top of these he has had an attack of mob politics. But we have no right yet to describe his condition as loathsome. It may become so in the future, or on the other hand, if he knows how to take it, it may be the prelude of real health such as he has never before experienced.'

'How?' the tutor asked.

'Every disease is a cure if we know the right way to take it. Disease is a result of disobedience to the inner law of our own nature, which works by telling us what we want to do and has no use for "don'ts". From childhood up we are taught that our natural desires are evil, that we must control them, deny them room to grow. But they will not be denied. Twisted, clogged with moralizings, driven back from all normal avenues of development, they nevertheless find a way of asserting themselves, appear in disguise, take on unexpected and abnormal forms – malaria, murder, neurosis, joining a Storm Troop, and whatnot. Yet, even at this stage, there is hope for the sufferer. If only he will abandon Conscious Control. The difficulty for him is to discover which of all the conflicting things within him is Conscious Control and which is Desire, but he will have one sure rule to help him: Desire appears *always* unreasonable.'

'Why?'

The tutor couldn't help being attracted by Mavors. He felt that at last he was listening to someone who was genuinely interested in ideas. Perhaps Mavors was some kind of psychologist. In the same passionately quiet voice Mavors went on:

'Because Desire has been put in prison and driven wild. Consider the case of boys in a preparatory school dormitory, one of whom – Desire – is regarded as queer or bumptious by the rest. They object to his beautiful voice, to the clear ruddy skin of his face, to his dandy pyjamas. They conspire against him, make a combined attack on him, tie him up in a sheet. At first he craftily offers no resistance. Disappointed and a little uneasy they prod and pinch him, and still he does not respond. Then, just as they are about to leave him, he rises up from his bed. Muffled in the sheet he looks like a ghost. They are alarmed, fling themselves on him, try to suffocate him. But somehow he eludes them. Like a competitor in a sack race he goes bounding up the main aisle of the dormitory, makes for the door. They are terrified, plead with him not to be an idiot, tell him they were only joking and that it's all in the day's work. He takes no notice. He comes bounding back towards them. Some of them rush for their beds, try to hide beneath the clothes. But one of them, desperate, clutches at the ghost, tears off the muffling sheet. Desire stands revealed. So great is their relief that they are filled with gratitude towards him. The ringleader even goes up to him and shakes him by the hand, says emotionally – "It was jolly fine the way you took it." And, after that evening, Desire is respected and his queerness taken for granted.'

Mavors sipped his sidecar, gazed hypnotically into the tutor's eyes.

'There is only one sin,' he said, 'and that is disobedience to our desires. It is not our fault, in the first place, that we commit this sin – it is the fault of our early environment and education. The results of disobedience show themselves in disease and crime – and in hatred, and in regarding the people we live with as "poisonous".'

Mavors made no attempt to pretend that he wasn't thinking of the tutor's attitude towards the Parkins. He went on:

'Disease and hatred are warning symptoms of a sickness of the soul. They come to bring the offenders to their senses. They

157

are Desire in disguise. They are God. And the people who tell us we can "cure" ourselves of them by the exercise of reason and Conscious Control are the Devil. If you cut out a cancer or repress a hatred you will soon develop other symptoms, become a moralist or a dipsomaniac.'

Had the tutor shown a suspicious eagerness in drinking his stout?

'To the sufferer,' Mavors said, 'Conscious Control must always appear noble and right, because the whole natural system has been inverted for him in childhood. He cannot regard Desire otherwise than as something ignoble and wrong. Therefore his salvation lies in being "unreasonable", in rejecting what is "right", and doing what is "wrong". This can never be easy for him. But if once he succeeds in restoring the natural order he will never turn back. Desire carries its own conviction with it. Life gives nothing richer or lovelier than the moment when, after years of torturing self-control, we at last do what we want to do. When we do, not what we think we ought to do or ought to want to do, but what our nature really wants to do.'

Half amused, half exhilarated, the tutor smiled. He had a moment's misgiving, wondered whether Mavors would be offended, but the misgiving must have been due to Conscious Control. Mavors was frankly pleased, smiled back. He continued to gaze into the tutor's eyes. Intimately, cheekily, his look seemed to ask: 'Do *you* know what you really want to do?' But he said nothing, showed no sign of expecting the tutor to say anything. His inquiring eyes were very close together on either side of his thinly bridged nose. They appeared to move closer together, as though they were merging their separated gaze into a single mildly searching beam. And this beam penetrated into the tutor's brain, set some mechanism to work there, made him say to himself:

'I know now what I want to do. Since childhood I have deceived myself and been deceived. Even today I have allowed reason to falsify my desires. I have told myself that I wanted a good job and a woman and plenty of upper-middle-class friends, that I wanted to travel, to see mountains, to sail in a yacht. But these things were not what my nature really desired. They were the things that I believed I *ought* to desire. My nature has other, deeper needs. You, Gregory Mavors, have shown me what I want to do. Your love of ideas is my love also. When you speak I am filled with admiration and with envy. You are living the life that I have always wanted to live. You are living the truly intellectual life, the life which in my perverse "reasonableness" I have always despised, which I have regarded as a form of affectation and even of prostitution. I was a coward, and I bolstered up my cowardice with the conventional maxims of reason. But you have brought me to my senses. I know now what I shall do. At last, after years of frustration and sloth, I shall begin to use my brain. How dazzling, how lovely my Desire is now that it stands revealed. To study, to become aware of the detail of the world. Better than piloting an airship, more free than the physical abandon of childhood. And, having opened my eyes and viewed some part of the detail, to retire for a time into thought and there to transform and systematize what I have seen. And then to return to the world, give back to the world the finished product of my thought. And be acclaimed, be welcomed. For they *will* welcome me, even these people here in the marquee, perhaps these more than others. If I have hitherto found them distant, cliquish, superior, that was because my eyesight has been dimmed by the amblyopia of repressed desire. They are better than others, more intelligent, more beautiful. Their smoothness, their comfortable elegance, their musical voices, are signs of culture and goodwill. I shall bring them the dazzling products of my thought, a new, a startling view of history and of anthropology and geology and art, and they will acclaim me. And I know now that I *want* to be acclaimed.'

Mavors seemed to guess what the tutor had been thinking. He said gravely:

'Beware of dabbling in Science.'

'Why?'

'It will lead you back to reason and to Conscious Control. I know that Science looks innocent enough when you first approach it. You will begin by observing a few harmless "facts" about starfish or flowers or domestic animals. Or by picking up a flint arrow-head in a field, or going for a ramble with members of a geological society. But you will not be satisfied with these beginnings. I fancy you are not the type that can patiently spend a lifetime in the collection of facts or specimens. Soon you will turn your attention to human beings. You will learn to regard your body as a mechanism. Even now no irreparable harm will have been done, unless you become interested in medicine or surgery. I need not stress the terrible results which would follow if you were to become convinced that the "irregularities" of the human body can be cured by drugs or by the knife. Let us suppose that you avoid this pitfall, that for the moment you do not follow your mechanistic conception of the body to its logical conclusion. Before long you will find yourself applying this same conception to the human situation in general – to the "body politic", as no doubt you will call it. You will examine social conditions and discover that they are morbid. You will diagnose poverty, malnutrition, overcrowding, injustice and crime. And now reason will come into its own. It will show you a future black with horror, will prove beyond dispute that there can be no escape, that conditions must steadily worsen, unrest grow, starvation and tyranny advance, and finally that war will deluge the whole world with blood. Poisoned inwardly by these ideas you will become shifty and timid in your outward behaviour. The people you most want to make friends with, the beautiful, the cultured, the happy and the free, will intuitively recoil from you. And in the end you will not even be allowed the consolation of exercising your brain. So grim a picture of the future will reason have painted for you that thought itself will begin to appear futile to you. The disease of reason will have run its course, and you will sink into a final coma. Or if, by a last effort, you continue to think, your thinking will be a mere echo of the shrill and sterile slogans of one of the new mob-militant political movements.'

The tutor, in spite of his exhilaration and his admiration for Mavors, couldn't help raising an objection:

'But if the world situation is in actual fact getting worse every day I don't see how I could save myself from it merely by rejecting reason. War would still maim or kill me, however promptly I obeyed the voice of Desire. Or do you believe that war and starvation and tyranny are only figments of reason and that they don't really exist?'

Mavors was surprised at the tutor's stupidity.

'Of course they exist,' he said. 'But not as reason makes them appear to us. And if you apply Conscious Control to them you will make them even worse than they are already. If you demolish a slum in one part of a city you will create a far larger slum in another part. If you try to stop a war in Asia you will give a fillip to civil war in Europe. If you introduce measures of "reasonable" reform into a Crown colony you will evoke an orgy of blind assassination. Because poverty and war and slavery and all the social evils of our time are themselves the result of disobedience to Desire. In our hearts we *want* to be well off and free and to live at peace with our neighbours, but we *reason* with ourselves that our bank accounts or our employers or our neighbours will prevent us from getting what we want. So we throttle our desires within us and consciously try to adapt ourselves to the outer world as reason views it. But Desire will not be throttled, returns to us in sinister disguises, drives us to acts of degradation and violence. Starvation and war begin to advance across the world. And at this stage, if you try to "cure" the world with further doses of reason and Control, the result will be universal Death.'

Mavors stared into the tutor's eyes, added:

'Give your Desire room to grow. Don't tell yourself — "I can't". You can — and all these obstacles which reason has conjured up before you will fall away like straw.'

The tutor still had his doubts:

'If I have got to reject reason how am I going to use my brain? That is what I really want to do.'

'Put the question to yourself in another way: "If I cling to reason how am I going to use my brain?" Reason is death, destroys the mind as well as the body. Unreason is life, is the life of the mind as well as of the body. Without unreason there can be no thought.'

'But what is the nature of unreason? I mean, if it just seems a blank to me I can't very well use my brain on it.'

'Unreason is the language of Desire. Years of patient study would not help even the most brilliant linguist to understand a single word of it. If you are to master it you must first of all release your Desire from prison. As soon as you have done that you will find yourself speaking it like a native. You want to make friends with these people here in the marquee, to admire them and be admired by them. Very well: go up to them and introduce yourself. Don't let reason persuade you that you will be snubbed or that you will not be able to add anything of interest to their conversation. Speak. Don't be put out when reason warns you that what you are saying to them is fantastic and impertinent. Remember that whatever seems "wrong" to your conscious mind is, according to the inner law of your nature, right. And though at first they, too, may be deceived by reason and may try to ignore you, their Desire will recognize the authentic voice of yours and in the end they will respond to you with deepest gratitude.'

The tutor said:

'I know what my Desire is; and I think I know now what unreason is, but I doubt whether it would give me any intellectual satisfaction. It seems negative, the mere contradiction of reason. What concrete data has unreason to work on?'

Mavors may or may not have answered this question. The tutor did not listen. Before he had finished speaking he had himself found an answer. His attention, possibly because Mavors was no longer staring into his eyes, had strayed to the unlabelled bottle on the marble-patterned table. Mavors may or may not have been looking at it too. The tutor wasn't sure. The opaque liquid in the bottle had all the brightness of solid brass. An excitement surged up like a rocket within the tutor. He understood now what concrete materials unreason would work on. This bottle and this table and the animal-headed bowls and the white silk table-cloths – these were the data of unreason. These he would study, would know in their every detail, would analyse and develop and transform within his mind, would give back in startling images to the world from which he had taken them. He would give them back to the people in the marquee, and he would be acclaimed. These were the things he would speak of when he introduced himself. But mightn't it be dangerous to speak of them, dangerous even to think of them? He looked at a silver bowl on one of the small tables, saw that it was moulded to represent a squirrel. No, not moulded; its detail was far too clear-cut and intricate. Every hair of the curving tail must have been modelled separately. The figure as a whole had nothing impressionistic about it, did not suggest that more was meant by it than had been visibly expressed. It was unambiguously pleasant, was what he desired it to be. Certainly if he were to look at it now through the eyes of reason it would soon become ambiguous and disturbing, would begin to remind him of Tod. But never again would he allow reason to stultify his Desire. He had wanted Tod to be friendly, to be a hero and a pioneer, but his reason had argued that Tod could not really be like this, and consequently his Desire, driven wild by the opposition of reason, had made Tod someone dangerous, a reactionary and an enemy. He had wanted the people in the marquee to welcome him, but he had reasoned that they would not do so, and therefore his Desire, poisoned by reason, had made them aloof and superior. He had wanted the bowls on the tables to be silver, and his Desire, freed at last from reason, had made them silver. Now, having learnt his lesson, he would look again at the people in the marquee, would see them this time through the eyes of unreason, and they would become what he desired them to become.

He looked boldly at the group which had ignored him a few minutes before. He saw no immediate change in them: their postures, their gestures were much the same now as then. The ex-rugby player was still elegantly talking, chin in air, elbow bent outwards and forward and fingers resting with artificial ease on a tweed-clothed thigh. The woman, permanently smiling, blinked her eyelids in rapid little signals of amazed assent. The faces of the two male listeners, less demonstratively amused, were turned towards the woman and at right angles to each other, had an almost identical expression of pleased inquiry – as though one had been an oblique mirror-reflection of the other. But as the tutor stared at them the two men began to lose confidence in their pose, to grow restive. The woman also – in spite of her ever-increasing effort to appear remote and theatrical, of her flickering eyelashes imitating the waving antennae of an insect – was becoming more genuinely animated, more human. An uncontrollable tremor – perhaps of alarm, perhaps of delighted expectancy – disturbed her posing face and rippled down her body. And then the ex-rugby player, in the middle of achieving an exquisitely superior airy gesture with his cocktail glass, turned his head and looked at the tutor. The look was one of entire surrender, of friendly awe. The tutor had come to power. In a moment he would be among them, would begin to deliver the message they were waiting for. Words, colours, tunes, all he knew and felt about the decorations here, about the squirrel, the bright brass bottle, the tablecloths. What words? Already he imagined himself saying: 'A gilded cinema organ might I think embellish.' He would not say that, perhaps: unreason would furnish him, when the moment came for him to speak, with words far richer than any he could now imagine. How he would dazzle, charm, bewilder these people; and then he would leave them. He would advance, win other and fuller recognition, would extend his power to the farthest limits of the marquee. He would extend it even to the people now standing by the main entrance of the marquee, though that might be less easy.

Tod had just come in through the main entrance. He was no longer in the company of the detective, and his serious red face did not appear in any way alarming. Nevertheless, his presence had introduced a casual doubt into the tutor's enthusiastic train of thought. Unreason might have, certainly did have, power to change inanimate objects, but would it always succeed with human beings, with conscious objects who might themselves choose to reason and to ignore the voice of his Desire?

The tutor must have expressed this doubt aloud, for Mavors said:

'The man who has released his Desire will always prevail over the man who tries to keep his Desire in chains. And the explanation of this is simple: the man who reasons is divided against himself, and the more vital part of him, his Desire, must take the side of his unreasoning opponent, of the man whose Desire is free. Therefore your power to change human beings will be no less than your power to change inanimate objects.'

The tutor was ready to believe it. However, before he could be quite sure that Mavors was right, he must look once again at Tod. But Tod was no longer standing by the main entrance, was not to be seen anywhere, must have mixed with the crowd in the marquee. His disappearance somehow suggested a new doubt to the tutor, who said aloud:

'But suppose one man converts another to unreason – might not the other's released Desire come into conflict with the Desire of the converter?'

'No. Conflict is a product of reason. Unrepressed Desire is always gay and friendly. What's good for you – good in the profoundest sense – can never be bad for another person.'

The tutor thought: 'But does it follow that what's good for another person will be good for me?' He said:

'Was it good for the Nigerian native when Tod Ewan shot him?'

Mavors had a look of impatience. Controlling himself he said slowly, like a schoolmaster to a very stupid boy:

'Of course not. Nor was it good for Tod. Think – why did he do it? Because he *desired* to bring about a death? Is that the answer? No. Desire creates life; only reason brings death. He listened to reason, and reason told him that he was in a foreign country, that he was there not as a guest but as a usurper, as an exploiter whom the Hausa natives must wish to be rid of; and so his Desire to be happy and friendly was distorted by reason into a suspicion, a distrust, and finally into a certainty that the native in question had designs against his life. Even now murder might have been avoided — if only the native had been unreasonable. But he, too, was affected by the same virus; he, too, reasoned that Tod was an intruder, and so his natural Desire to be friendly and happy became —'

Mavors stopped, apparently in order to sip his cocktail. The tutor said:

'I understand what you mean. Conflict can only arise when *both* parties to it are poisoned by reason. I suppose you would say the same about international war: if one side behaved unreasonably then war could never break out. Or if one country behaved unreasonably war couldn't break out. Of even if a few individuals in one country. ... But how many individuals? Ten or eleven wouldn't be enough. They couldn't influence the decisive mass of reasonable people, because they would come in contact with too few of them. What's the minimum number of unreasonable people required if Desire is to be effective in the world as a whole? And can we get them — shall we get them in time?'

Mavors sipped his cocktail, said nothing, did not appear to have been paying much attention to what the tutor had said. But the tutor had found his own solution to the problem he had raised. With conviction, with enthusiasm he went on:

'We may not get them in time. But we can and must try to get them. It is the only hope. You have taught me that, Gregory Mavors. I shall remember it. And already I have succeeded in winning over some of the people here. I shall go on, and I shall win over others.'

Mavors looked pleased. But he was not looking at the tutor. He waved his cocktail glass and grinned. And now the tutor understood why Mavors had stopped speaking. Tod had reappeared out of the crowd and was walking towards them. Making his way between the tables in the middle of the marquee — a short cut which involved him in clumsily pushing chairs out of his way — he called out to Mavors:

'Looking for you all over the place.'

Mavors called back:

'When in doubt try the bar.'

Tod came up to them, his face beaming, and Mavors asked him:

'What are you having?'

'No, thanks. There isn't time. I wanted a word with you. Something you ought to know.'

His face beamed, gleamed like a varnished mask, but his eyes were serious.

He ignored the tutor.

'What is it?' Mavors asked.

Tod took him by the elbow, urged him away from the bar. Mavors hesitated, glanced back for a moment at the tutor, said indecisively:

'Why not here?'

Tod answered with an abrupt shake of the head. He led Mavors away.

The tutor tried not to feel insulted. 'Be unreasonable,' he told himself. He thought of the unlabelled bottle and the silver squirrel. He stared at the bottle. The liquid inside it was still as bright as brass. Reassured, he turned his head and looked at the squirrel. It was silver, in no way changed. But why did it give him the feeling that he must not take his eyes off it? Wrong: this feeling came from another source, from something that he suspected was happening at the far end of the marquee. The squirrel, properly regarded, was a guarantee that what was now happening beyond it would also be amenable to unreason, could also be made pleasant. Danger lay only in refusing to look beyond.

He looked.

Near the main entrance Humphrey Silcox stood facing a group of about twenty young men. A few girls, apart from the main group, were watching. The men, bunched closely together, were not talking. They were waiting. Silcox signalled to them with a casual wave of his hand. They moved smartly into line, formed two ranks, stood at attention. He numbered them. Their behaviour caused no visible surprise among the other people near them. On the contrary, there seemed a tendency for the men elsewhere in the marquee to imitate them, to stand more stiffly. And now Silcox had raised his arm in the fascist salute. His men saluted also. Tod, arriving with Mavors, returned the salute. He said something to Silcox, and Mavors then walked over to the group, attached himself to the end of the rear rank, stood at attention. Mavors had not saluted, and he did not look altogether sure of himself now. The tutor regarded the scene as wholly ridiculous, a comic game. But he was unable to sustain his amusement for long; against his will he began to feel bored. These antics weren't even really funny. His gaze shifted back again to the unlabelled bottle. That at least was interesting. He noticed that there were other people standing quite near him at the bar. They were drinking and talking: there was nothing unnatural about them. They weren't on parade. But why had the parade at the far end of the marquee seemed boring? Because he had allowed himself to think of it reasonably. Boredom was bad, should not be tolerated. Tod and Silcox and the young men were behaving unreasonably, and therefore they were in fact interesting. It was up to the tutor to view them unreasonably, and then they would seem interesting. He must try again.

Tod was making a speech. Broad-backed and stiff, fists on hips, elbows jutting sideways like the heavy handles of a fat earthenware jug. The rigidity of his body gave additional emphasis to the violent activity of his face. His chin prodded out towards the listening young men, reached so far that the tutor wondered why his body didn't bend or overbalance. His lips gobbled, pouted to a pause, flapped open again, and moved even faster than before. The young men listened with expressionless faces. At intervals they mechanically clapped. Mavors clapped, too, but his face was not expressionless. He looked uncomfortable. The tutor noticed that people elsewhere in the marquee were listening also. The speech was having its effect even on the group of four who had just previously been ready to welcome him. There were signs that they were becoming aloof and superior once again. He was losing his influence over them. Quick, reassert himself, back to the attack, plunge deeper still into unreason.

He began to hear what Tod was saying.

'... Our observers have kept us well supplied with information. The first report to come in this morning left us in no doubt as to what was afoot ... Number five noticed suspicious activity on the part of a steam-roller driver. Also, a hostile demonstration by women in a motor-coach. ... A large section of the crowd, carrying rucksacks and armed with sticks, was seen to cut across the road and to climb towards the racecourse under cover of the trees. We are in possession of the names of the leaders. As was to have been expected, all of them came from outside the district and the majority from abroad. I have received photographs of them and these will be passed round before we leave the marquee. ... The position is serious, but less so than it was two months ago. We recognize that this plot is a sign of desperation. ... Having failed to ruin the M.F.H. by financial trickery, they are resorting to criminal violence. ... International Jewry –'

Tod was interrupted by a burst of jeering laughter. But the young men were not, as the tutor momentarily hoped, laughing at Tod: they were applauding him. They believed every word he had said. Or, at least, their negative devitalized faces showed no glimmer of disbelief. Tod went on:

'... They'll be looking pretty yellow by the time we've finished with them. ... It won't take us long. ... Just a spot of bother. ... The police will co-operate. ... This plot is a signal we have long been waiting for. At last the criminal forces have come into the open. They have thrown off the humanitarian, peace-loving, progressive disguises with which they hoped to fool the more sentimental and woolly-minded of our fellow-countrymen. ... It is our privilege today to strike a blow for all that is best in the national heritage. For honour, for romance, for the spirit, for idealism, for everything that makes life worth while. Against the cowardly hypocrisy of politicians, against dis-loyalty, against money-grubbing materialism, against the selfish-ness of the profiteering employer, against the whining discon-tent of the socialistic trade unionist. ... To restore the moral fibre of our nation. ... We shall not falter. ...'

The young men clapped and cheered. The girls cheered also, but less loudly – as though they were afraid of appearing unladylike. Mr Bover clapped, and the woman, and the other two men. Even the people standing near the tutor at the bar seemed to approve of the speech. For an instant the tutor felt that he, too, if he tried hard enough, might be able to approve, or at least to prevent himself from disapproving. He must try to remember that this parade was only a game, a charade of unreason. It was a game, and he, too, could play it. But did he want to play it? Would it enable him to realize his profoundest desire, give him scope to use his brain? He might continue to *think* about the silver squirrel and the unlabelled bottle, but he would have to *talk* about abstract colourless words like 'romance', and 'the spirit'. Or worse, he would have to stand at attention and listen carefully while Tod gave orders. He wouldn't be able to think for himself at all, not even unreasonably. And suppose he refused to play Tod's game, suppose he attached himself to some other group in the marquee – would he be any less restricted? The other people here – even those who had not applauded Tod's speech – were every moment becoming more interested in the parade of the young men. There was no scope anywhere here for the tutor. He would never be able to use his brain, would never be acclaimed.

It was futile, dangerous to allow himself to become alarmed. He knew he would never be a poet or a prophet, but that didn't mean he was done for, a hopeless failure. There were other, humbler ways of living a happy life. What ways? Where? Not outside the marquee, not by going back to the house he had come from this morning. The happier life must be here or nowhere, must be among these people here. But they were becoming more and more aloof, even those who stood nearest to the tutor and who had been least impressed by Tod. They looked colder and older, devitalized: their sociable movements, head-noddings and hand gesturings, were weary and sluggish, seemed to arise no longer from their own volition but to be compelled by some external influence. Even their expensive clothes had begun to look dowdy and colourless. And the flesh of their faces, in the faintly green light reflected from the grass, was dusty grey, like the flesh of dead goldfish. The tutor knew that he would never succeed in making contact with these people. They were as inaccessible to the language of his wishes as the dead in a cemetery or the imagined inhabitants of Mars. He was isolated, lost, perhaps for ever.

He was no longer able to control his alarm. 'Perhaps I am done for,' he thought. But as he thought this someone stared at him. A girl standing quite near him at the bar. At first he dared not return the stare, because he was afraid he might discover that he had been mistaken. But the girl continued to stare. She moved towards him. Her fingers, holding a cocktail glass, slid along the marble edge of the bar. She was wearing a fur coat and a blue scarf. He looked up at her face and saw it animated with recognition and pleasure.

'You don't remember me,' she said.

'... Yes. I saw you in the first car.'

'You saw me at least six years before that.'

'I think. ... I'm not sure.'

'Think again.'

'One evening. At Cambridge.'

'In the street. You were wearing a black gown, but you looked like a faun. I pretended I wanted to escape. I hurried down a dark alley by one of the colleges. You followed me and I came to a stop on the grass against some railings. I was only nineteen and I was very excited. You talked about mountains.'

'Did I?'

Disturbed, he forced himself to add casually:

'What happened then?'

'You played with the fur of my gloves. It was rabbit's fur. There was frost on the railings and on the grass. You talked about pergolas and about fountains. I had never heard that sort of language spoken before, but I knew at once that I had always wanted to hear it. I remember one phrase especially: "Rubber statuary in gardens of ice-cream roses." It made me laugh — really laugh, not just giggle in the way I had always done when other men had made jokes for my benefit. I nearly cried. Your talk was like some marvellous poem, and you never hesitated for a word. I think you realized how much I appreciated what you were saying. You got better and better as you went on. And when you told me you had never been so lucky with any girl before, I believed you.'

Her eyes, bright white and dark brown, were warm with frank desire. But he refused to allow their warmth to invade him. He must see her quite dispassionately – a beautiful dummy with icy ear-rings and a face cool as a frozen peach. And her voice was warm:

'I agreed to meet you next evening outside a cinema. I've forgotten the name of the cinema but I remember exactly where it was.'

'The Rendezvous.'

Her face moved towards his, and he had an impulse to add: 'Why didn't you come?' But he warned himself that if he showed any interest in her she might begin to find him less attractive. She said:

'Then I asked you whether you had been drinking.'

'I had, of course.'

'I might never have noticed it if I hadn't kissed you. I suppose you guessed it would make a bad impression, and that's why you tried to keep your face away from mine. And when I'd found you out you told me that you hadn't drunk very much.'

'I'd seldom drunk more.'

'You tried to convince me that it made no difference and that your feeling for me would be just the same the next day. You pleaded with me to let you prove you were telling the truth. You made me promise twice that I wouldn't fail to meet you outside the cinema. I swore I would come, but you knew I was only humouring you. Then you told me you would give anything not to have been drinking, that in the morning you would realize to the full what I was and what you had lost.'

He heard himself say:

'That was quite true.'

'I know it was. I knew it then. But I had made up my mind

earlier in the evening that I would never again have anything to do with any man who got drunk. Oh, how can I have been such a fool? All because I had just had a quarrel with Humphrey. What a hateful little prig I must have been.'

He was surprised into asking anxiously:

'Do you mean Humphrey Silcox?'

'Yes.'

She controlled a smile, added quickly:

'I had decided never to see him again. His friends had always disgusted me, and that evening I felt there was nothing to choose between him and them. All they could do was to drink and tell dirty stories. They were terribly boring. I suddenly lost my temper and walked out of the room. Humphrey was doing a tap-dance on the fender. He ran after me, but I told him he made me sick. He didn't ask why – he just got frightfully angry. That was typical of him. I walked out into the street. Soon afterwards I met you.'

Her face moved nearer to his. Her lips were trembling.

'I realized at once that you were different from the others, but when I discovered that you had been drinking too I made up my mind I wouldn't meet you next day. I didn't turn up at the cinema. It was sheer obstinacy. I have never forgiven myself.'

She tilted her head backwards, took a deep breath, sighed with theatrical regret. Her half-closed eyelids fluttered. Her full, rouged lips pouted wooingly. Her face was very young. He knew that she was play-acting, but she acted with such confidence and vitality, with such whole-hearted indifference to the other people standing near her at the bar, that he couldn't help admiring her. He was no longer able to check the feeling of warmth that was increasing within him. Nevertheless he was determined that she should not see what he felt. He waited for her to speak again. She said:

'Afterwards I knew that you were the first person I'd met in my life who had made me really happy. You were the first, and there's been no one like you since then.'

She whispered, moaned. Her eyes were closed, her head

dropped backwards, surrendering, waiting for him to bend over her. He did not move. Her eyes slowly opened again, tried to discover what impression her behaviour had made on him, were puzzled. Displeasure or apprehension for a moment disturbed her deliberately yearning face. She had become aware of the possibility of defeat. But a new, a final tactic occurred to her. Still looking at him, she moved away from him, stepped quickly backwards, tense and agile as a dancer. Her hands rose towards her throat, gripping the edges of her fur coat. The coat fell open, exposing a silk-covered bosom. Her small blue scarf pointed downwards between her breasts. He was not deceived, knew without the least doubt that her action was a deliberate trick. But there was no trickery, nothing artificial, about what she had to show him. Slowly she arched her back, and her large rigid breasts swelled out towards him, seemed to force aside the heavy edges of her coat. With softness and yet with unhesitating strength they rose, like soft young plants pushing up through heavy soil. They burst into silky blossom, mauve shot with orange. Impudently they pointed sideways, their clearly defined nipples like ogling eyes. They were solid and hostile as fists, yet tender as fluff. Their brutal rigidity assaulted and wounded him, yet they were divided and meekly offered themselves to him. Warmth spurted up within him like the spurting of a hot spring. In an instant he decided to surrender. 'Let it gush out,' he thought. No matter how foolish or how dangerous. He would deliver himself over to her. He said:

'I waited more than an hour. Then I walked up and down the main streets, looking for you. I was in despair. And the next night I looked for you again. You were the first girl I had been genuinely attracted to, had admired without any reservations. I was in love with you. I still am.'

As he spoke he became more confident. He would conquer her, not sacrifice himself to her. He would penetrate her pretences, seize hold of her genuine beauty. She said mildly:

'I am in love with you, too. We were born for each other.'

Triumph deepened the colour of her face, and tears came into her eyes. Mildly she added:

'I have never been able to make Humphrey understand ...
how I felt towards you.'

Shock made him ask sharply:

'What's Humphrey got to do with it?'

'I'm engaged to him. Didn't I tell you?'

He was aware that he had lost control of the muscles of his
face. He tried to be angry, to show contempt, but his disappointment overpowered him, exhibited itself to her in wretched
nakedness. She made an effort not to laugh at him, said with
excessive sympathy:

'Oh, but darling, it will make no difference. You must believe
me. I could never feel the same about Humphrey as I do about
you.'

She had to laugh. Her voice rose in a trill of genuine delight.
Quickly, primly, she checked herself. Her small fist thumped
against her silk-covered collar-bone. Tragically she said:

'I ought not to have become engaged to him. I do feel such a
swine. What bitches women are. I don't know why I did it. You
are the only man I've ever really cared for.'

She had conquered her amusement. Her tone of tragic passion
became more assured:

'I cannot believe that it's too late. We will go away together.
We will live together. In a golden land. Among the pergolas and
the fountains. You will come with me, won't you, my sweet?'

He stared at her in an unhappy stupor. She jumped towards
him. Regardless of the other people at the bar she put her arm
round his neck, pushed her lips against his mouth. His lips responded; weakly at first, then with increasing pleasure. He began
to move to the attack, to kiss with vigour. Immediately she
withdrew her lips from his. Her arms slid slowly away from his
neck and across his shoulder, her body detached itself from him
with the precise ease of some potent perfectly controlled
machine. She stared calmly at his face, watched its new confidence lapse into protest, into dejection, into abasement. Then, as
though judging him finally tamed, she put her arm round his
neck once again, pressed softly against him, kissed. This time he
did not try to move to the attack, did not even try to defend.

His nerves, his body, responded to her slavishly. Her bosom crowded against his chest; her lips pressed, withdrew until their touch seemed as light as the touch of an insect's trembling feelers, pressed again, sucking and warm and heavy. He was in her power, wholly dependent on her, humbled with abject longing. After a while she released him, stepped back. She watched him, waited like some brilliant dangerous insect till the delicious poison she had injected should begin to take its full effect.

He began to speak:

'I can't do without you.'

'There's no need for you to do without me.'

'How soon can we live together?'

'As soon as you like. Tomorrow. Next week. What does time matter to us?'

She was entirely calm. He said:

'But time does matter to me. I can't help it. I don't know what I should do if I had to wait.'

She gave a flattered, superficial little laugh, said:

'Let's go now, at once.'

'Yes. I'm sick of this place. Let's get away. We can decide later where we'll go.' He hesitated. 'But I suppose I ought to find Mr Parkin and tell him I'm not coming back. Otherwise he might — no, why should I tell him? Serve him right.' He hesitated again. 'But you'll want to go home first and collect your things.'

She was laughing again.

'What a practical little man you are.'

'Am I? I only thought — I mean, if we're going away, you'll want to pack some clothes, won't you?'

Gaily she raised her arms from her sides, made a gesture of careless freedom.

'No. I don't want us to make any preparations. That would spoil it all. I want us to fly. I feel I could fly through the air now, like a swallow — or a swan.'

She waved her arms like wings.

'All right. Where shall we fly to?'

176

'Anywhere. Everywhere. Honolulu. London. Now. Just as we are. Cape Wrath. Better still – Reykjavik.'

Her words jerked him out of the satisfying trance into which he had begun to sink. He tried and failed to remember where he had heard them before. He looked at her face and was certain of one thing – that she was not jeering at him. She was waiting, without impatience, with confidence, for him to speak, for him to add something new to her daydream. She was unmistakably sincere. Her face had a genuine innocence, was like the face of a child who is preoccupied with playing an exciting imaginative game. If only he could discover what her words reminded him of, then perhaps he, too, would be able to enter wholeheartedly into the game, would be able to feel happy. But he found difficulty in concentrating his thoughts. He was becoming aware once again of the people at the far end of the marquee. He tried not to look at them, but they increasingly forced themselves upon his attention. The young men, as before, stood in ranks on either side of the main entrance. Now, however, their faces were not altogether expressionless, showed a stolid exaltation, were upturned towards the top half of the entrance as though they expected to see appear there at any moment the head of an abnormally tall man. A whisper arose from among them, faint and prolonged, like the hiss of water in a remote cistern. Tod glanced very briefly along the ranks, then turned again to stare towards the entrance. The whisper began to spread among the crowd. Slowly it approached the tutor, resolved itself into audible words:

'Scumming. Scumming. 'Scoming. He's coming. He's coming. He's coming.'

He looked at the girl in front of him, saw that she, too, had heard. With mild interest she said:

'I suppose it's the M.F.H.'

Her face gave no hint of uneasiness or enthusiasm. Soon she had ceased to pay any attention to the whisper. She was looking steadily at him, waiting for him to make the next move in her daydream game. Now, more than ever, she appeared to him childish and innocent. Her vices – her teasing and her posing –

no longer seemed important, were even charming. Against the dangerous background of the whispering crowd she had for him something of the pathos of a very young and good-looking woman naïvely exhibiting herself at a commercialized beauty competition. Afterwards the millionaire judges would auction her among themselves. Silcox would get her, Tod and the whisperers would crudely strip her of all her charm. She was weak and ignorant, without the least suspicion of what was being prepared for her behind her back. Yet she was strong, too. She stood looking at him, upright and without moving, her back towards the crowd and the ugly preparations, undisturbed, powerful with young dignity, with beauty no longer aphrodisiac, with simple joy. Silcox and Tod would never get her. She was stronger than they were. They had violence and conviction, but in the end they would destroy themselves, perish in their own ugliness. They would perish because they were fighting against nature and humanity, were fighting against themselves. She, or others like her, would survive, because she was on the side of the forces of life, and those forces would survive. But was the tutor himself on the side of life? Would he get her? That was the crucial uncertainty. He began to understand the meaning of what she had said about Reykjavik. He could not remember yet where he had heard her words before, but he knew now what they implied – uncertainty. They were words in the air, cloudy daydream words, nothing more than words. It was necessary for him to bring them down to earth, to make her define them in terms of real life; otherwise he would lose her. He could not afford to lose her. He knew that she was his last chance of joy. More, she was the only valid joy; all other pleasures – travel, using his brain, poetry, making new friends – were, even if they had still been possible for him, profoundly inferior. With love and amazement he looked at her, thought: 'She is a human being, has feelings like mine.' Yet in every feature she seemed his opposite, as foreign to him as though she were some lovely mythical animal. A minute chemical difference in the hormones, and this unique wonder had arisen. He was not going to lose her. The joy and splendour of life. No matter what she demanded of him. He would even wear a top hat, accompany her to social tea-parties, have the baby christened, live in a house with servants to wait on him, travel daily by car to the office. He would get her, bring her down to earth, make her declare herself – yes or no. Otherwise –

But she seemed to have a premonition of what he was going to tell her. And as though she wished to fend him off she said airily:

'Definitely we must go to Reykjavik.'

He said:

'I want to marry you.'

Her face changed with the abruptness of a lantern-slide. From dreaminess to business. She laughed slightly, but her laugh, for the first time since the beginning of their encounter, was forced.

'Oh, but darling, you are far too nice to marry.'

'Why?'

'I don't want to hurt your feelings, my sweet, but really' – her amusement became a little more genuine – 'I simply can't picture you as the earnest breadwinner supporting a wife and family.'

'I don't propose to be an earnest breadwinner. And I know that if I went on being a tutor I couldn't hope to support a wife and family. But this afternoon I've had the offer of a really good job.'

She was visibly startled, she hesitated, then said firmly:

'No, it's impossible. I only wish we could.'

'Why is it impossible?'

'Darling, you're not the marrying sort.'

'And I suppose Humphrey Silcox is the marrying sort.'

'Yes, he is. I wish you could understand. I feel quite differently towards him. I am much more, more *passive* with him than with you. With you I feel an extraordinary tenderness, my heart melts when I look at you. I feel all protective. I can't imagine you keeping a wife in order, darling. And women are such bitches. I do wish I could make Humphrey understand what I feel about you. He's so jealous. I adore you.'

'I love you.'

'I adore you. I know I ought to marry you and not him. What a fool I am. We were made for each other.'

Her face showed a genuine indecision, but he guessed that if he were to mention marriage again she would harden against him. He must wait for her to make the next move. It was not easy to wait. Apprehension, misery, were beginning to take hold of him. Soon he would lose control over them, she would see what he felt and his chances of getting her would be ruined finally. It was difficult to control them, because they gained impetus not only from her attitude towards him but also from the behaviour of the other people in the marquee. The whisper which the young men had started had deepened into a murmur. An ugly enthusiasm was spreading everywhere. He dared not wait any longer.

'We needn't be married. We can live together.' Her look made him add: 'I mean, we can go *away* together for a time.'.

'Yes.' Instantly she changed her mind: 'I don't know. A few minutes ago I shouldn't have hesitated. But I had no idea then that you took it so seriously.'

'I'll take it in whatever way you want me to take it.'

'No. It wouldn't work. You would feel even more wretched afterwards than you do now.'

'I don't feel wretched now.'

The murmur had become louder. He pleaded:

'We can't know that it wouldn't work until we've tried it. Come away with me for one night.'

'No. darling. I've been a swine enough already. I don't want to become even worse.'

He made a last attempt.

'Let's go to Reykjavik.'

But even that daydream pretence had ceased to appeal to her. She didn't bother to answer him. The murmur grew louder and louder. She turned her head away from him, looked towards the main entrance of the marquee. Suddenly, with a simple delighted laugh, she said:

'Well, I never, if that isn't Humphrey parading over there. How frightfully funny he looks.'

'I can't do without you.'

With an effort she brought her attention back to the tutor.

'You needn't do without me, darling. I wish you would understand. I adore you. We ought never to have made the mistake of getting our relationship mixed up with sex. You are really something much more to me than just a lover. I feel I can talk to you – about anything I like. I don't feel that when I'm with Humphrey. You are good for me.' She paused to find the right words. 'It's so difficult to explain. You see, I don't think of you exactly as a *man*. You are more like a girl friend. Or a faun. You are someone I can be really happy with.'

Abjectly he said:

'Promise at least that you won't abandon me.'

'Of course I won't abandon you.'

The noise in the marquee was no longer a murmur: it was almost a roar. Like the subdued roar of the draught in a newly lighted stove. She was again looking at Humphrey. Smiling, she said:

'I think I ought to go over and talk to him. He'll begin to get jealous if I don't. I'll come back to you later.' She gave the tutor a gay stare, then added earnestly: 'You mustn't look so miserable. I don't like it.'

He weakly tried to control his face.

'You poor little swine,' she said.

She turned and, with a hint of disapproval in her final glance at him, walked away.

He soon lost sight of her. The increasing noise confused him, blurred all his feelings, affected even his vision. Now he saw nothing distinctly – except the opaque golden bottle on the marble bar. The sight of it was his only support: if it disappeared anything might happen to him, he would fall down, lose consciousness altogether. But it did not disappear. Very gradually his field of vision began to expand, he saw again the nearer tables, the animal-headed silver bowls. The noise increased to a roar, vaulted into a bellow of cheering. The bowls had an evil look, like objects in a devil temple. They were something more than quaint ornaments: they had a definite connection with the nasty ritual which was being performed at the other end of the marquee. The cheering grew louder and louder. All at once – with the icy clearness which comes in instants of danger, which comes in the fraction of a second before a traffic accident or a blow from a baton – he saw exactly what was happening. The M.F.H. was walking into the marquee through the main entrance. He was abnormally short, and his face had an exhausted look, but there was nothing else unusual about him. Perfunctorily he raised his arm in reply to the rigid salutes of the young men. He stopped walking. Slowly the cheering subsided. He, or someone else – possibly Tod or Silcox – the tutor couldn't be sure – began to speak. Most of the words were inaudible, but now and again a phrase or a sentence reached the tutor so clearly and loudly that it might have come from an amplifier hanging within a few yards of his left ear.

'... Fritillary will run today. ...'

The cheering, which had not yet entirely ceased, now bellowed out once again. As it dwindled anew, the tutor heard:

'... The threatened strike has been called off. Not a moment too soon. ...'

Mad cheering. People were jumping about in their enthusiasm. Even the young men were agitated, were beginning to break out of their ranks. Among the enthusiasts the tutor noticed Mr Parkin. He was hysterically capering, prancing, thumping the backs of his neighbours in the crowd. The sight did not disgust the tutor, gave him no feelings at all. He was without feelings, and might have remained so if he had not suddenly seen Dorothy MacCreath. She was dancing a Highland fling. He had no sooner recognized her than he became aware, one by one, of the men and girls he had seen in the first car. Of all those who had seemed so admirable, so free and happy, only Ann was not here, was not cheering. And now, in retrospect, their freedom and their happiness had an odious fraudulence which made them appear far more ugly, more brutally stupid, than any of the other people in the marquee. The tutor felt a sick despair, began to be really afraid. The voice went on:

'... I am at liberty now to tell you the whole truth ... It has been a very close thing indeed ... Our untiring vigilance ... Their object was first of all to paralyse transport and the mines, and thus to cripple our munitions industry ... The docks ... Their agents ... The police were able to make a number of important arrests early this morning ... A mere question of hours before we get the others ... With your cooperation ... It is a very great victory ... No cause for complacency ... We have smashed the internal attack and now we may expect the external ... At any moment ... Yes ... Thank God we are in a better condition to face it than we were, than we should have been if ... But we are not yet out of the wood ... The common effort of a united nation ... Our defences have been criminally neglected ... I say it with shame ... Our responsibility too ... Happily there is yet time ...'

The cheering had reached its summit, could not conceivably become any louder. Or if it did become louder it would cease to be cheering, would cease even to be a noise. It would change into something else, might take on a tangible or visible form. And this in fact was what seemed to happen. The marquee became darker, as though it were slowly filling with a dark odourless smoke, and this smoke pressed upon the tutor's body, seemed to lift him slightly above the ground. For a moment he was falling, was absolutely without support, more helpless than an abandoned baby; then his feet came down on to the grass again. Noise reasserted itself – though now it had an entirely new quality. It was still cheering, was quite as loud as before, but it no longer arose from a visible source. The people in the marquee had grown calmer, were listening. The cheering came from outside the marquee – at first from immediately outside the main entrance. Gradually it decreased there, was taken up by remoter voices. However, the volume of noise did not dwindle – because now far more people were cheering. Thousands, tens of thousands. The sinister enthusiasm was spreading to the most distant parts of the racecourse. Hundreds of thousands were acclaiming the M.F.H. There were no dissentients; or if there were they would soon be lynched. A quarter of a million, perhaps more, were ready to believe whatever the M.F.H. or Tod or Silcox chose to tell them. Men and women of all social classes. The pest would spread far beyond the racecourse, had without doubt begun to spread already. A desert of limitless ignorance surrounded the tutor. A desert of danger. He knew that the M.F.H.'s story of a plot was a lie, the story of an immediate external threat was a lie; but he knew too that violence was much nearer him now than it had been before the cheering. War had been distant from him before; now it was rapidly approaching. It might break out at any moment – visibly, tangibly, in one form or another. Audibly – a noise of reconnoitring aeroplanes, the bawling of sergeants. But not yet. The noise at present was nothing more than cheering. Louder it grew, straining to mount beyond the highest peaks of sound.

Darkness pressed in upon him once again, lifted him. Horror of the future alone supported him, kept his consciousness alive. He would be gassed, bayoneted in the groin, slowly burned, his eyeballs punctured by wire barbs. Yet it was not the thought of these physical agonies that really horrified him. He was unable to imagine them vividly enough. And such extremes of torture could not last long, could not compare in persistence with the other slower horrors which he *was* able to imagine. The horror of isolation among a drilled herd of dehumanized murderers. The death of all poetry, of all love, of all happiness. Never more to be allowed to use his brain. Lucky the men who got killed at once, at the very beginning of the war, before the world had reached this stage of slavery. But perhaps this stage would come first, would precede the war; perhaps it had come already. It had come, it was here, was in the marquee. They were mobilizing. Gone for ever was his hope of making friends, of establishing contact with human beings. There were no human beings. He was isolated among brutal slaves. Nothing remained for him except to try to live in his imagination. But he would not even be allowed to do that. They would seize him, mobilize him. He would be drilled, given no rest, bawled at or kicked whenever he tried to begin to dream. They were coming for him now. The young men had broken their ranks, were dividing into groups. Darkly he saw them, some of them filing out through the main entrance, others moving forwards among the crowd inside the marquee. They were searching for someone. They were advancing towards him. All at once he lost sight of them completely. Strain his eyes as he might he could not locate them in the darkness. Nevertheless he knew with certainty that they were rapidly approaching him. At any moment one of them might touch him, might come up from behind and catch him by the elbows. In panic he swung round to look behind him, saw no one. Madly he began to run.

Nobody opposed him, no foot shot out to trip him up. He raced towards the side entrance. The ticket seller sitting at the table took no notice of him. The tutor plunged out into the sunlight. He stumbled over a tent peg, only just regained his balance. Darkness had disappeared. There was no noise out here, not a hint of a sound of cheering. He stopped running.

3

In a daze he began to walk. The sun was bright and there was no noise at all. There were no people. Wrong: there was someone walking away from him, on his left. Someone who might have come out of the marquee at the same time as he had. A man; short, hatless, wearing a black overcoat. Strangely, the tutor didn't feel in the least afraid, didn't suspect that he was being shadowed. On the contrary he had a feeling of security; and this wasn't merely because the man was walking *away* – it was because there was something sympathetic, almost friendly, about him. The tutor glanced towards him again, but he had gone. Where? How? The tutor felt cheated. He had badly wanted to have another glimpse of him. And now he knew why – because the man had had an extraordinary resemblance to himself, had worn exactly the same kind of clothes, had had the same kind of face and figure. But all this was simply a delusion. The events in the marquee must have affected his mental health.

He must be very careful; if he lost control of his thoughts, if he became really insane, he would be finished for ever. He must regain control, face what had happened to him during the last quarter of an hour. He remembered the marquee, and his new feeling of security was finally destroyed. Where was he going now?

He was going away. To escape from people, because people meant death for all that he wanted and admired. The happy, innocent, gentle, generous life – this could not exist among them. Perhaps it could not exist anywhere at all. Consider the possibility calmly: suppose that sort of life were an hallucination, a mirage. What would remain? Nothing. A gap. A huge crevasse. But feeling would not cease to exist; it would become gradually, agonizingly colder. And the colder it became the greater would be the agony. His heart walled round with ice. Walking seemed more of an effort than it had been before. But he must walk. Never give up. Fight to think out this problem. How, even now, to learn to live the desirable life. Never to abandon that hope, so lovely, so brilliantly convincing in its emotional power. It could not be a fraud. He had made the mistake of trying to realize it among people. Now he knew better. If that life was to be found at all it must be looked for in solitude and in imagination. He would go to live in a country cottage, by himself. How? Possibly he could induce MacCreath to offer him a cash allowance in lieu of a job. Don't consider the details. Imagine the cottage. He would arrive there. Then the life would begin – day after day after day. Innocent poetry. Walks, reading, contemplation. What about food? Don't consider that now. He would at any rate have the money to buy it. But tradesmen would call; or worse, he would have to go into shops in the village. He would have to deal with people. Don't consider – besides, he could grow his own food. Could he? No, he wasn't Thoreau. As a matter of fact he was exceptionally helpless, unpractical. He would have to go into shops, would have to make contact with one or two people. And those people would be in contact with other people who would be in contact with wider circles outside the village. News would come through to him, rumours, warnings. More; fashions, opinions, modes of behaviour, politics, would invade the village from outside. Ultimately he would be no better off than if he had chosen to live in town. He would be worse off – because he would be more conspicuous. War preparations, tyranny, bestiality, would invade the village, and he would have no more chance of escape than a rabbit who has been singled out by a weasel. There was no escape. The happy life was a fraud.

An icy vacancy remained. Walking was becoming more and more difficult. A freezing cramp tortured the movement of his legs and arms. He dared not stop. If he did he would freeze to death. No, not to death – he would not be as fortunate as that. His consciousness would continue to live, intolerably constricted, concentrated into an atom of agony, pricked and pressed upon from all sides by microscopic needles of ice. But there must be a way of escape. If only he could think of it in time. He thought of death. Deliberate death. Suicide. The idea made him feel a little better. He would not become insane, lose all control. He would destroy himself. How? Don't consider the details. But unless he considered them he would not be able to convince himself that he was really going to do it. He would shoot himself. That meant he would first of all have to buy a gun or a rifle or a revolver. Preferably a revolver. Then the licence. Would the police believe him when he told them he wanted to shoot rabbits? Very well – consider an air rifle. Too clumsy. An air pistol. It wouldn't be powerful enough. Suddenly he had solved the problem. He would buy an air pistol, travel down to the seaside, hire a boat, row well out to sea. He would stand facing the side of the boat, so that when he had shot himself he would fall forward into the water. He would shoot himself in the right temple, be stunned instantly, would be drowned without knowing what was happening. Painless as wishing. He would do it on his birthday. He felt almost exhilarated. The pain had gone from his arms and legs and he was walking now with hardly any effort. The problem was solved. Once again he began to believe that the desirable life was possible for him. But wasn't there a contradiction here? Death and life. If the prospect of living was no longer intolerable what was the point of killing himself? Suppose he didn't kill himself. Then sooner or later he would arrive back at the state of unbearable misery from which his idea of suicide had originated. On the other hand if he did kill himself the desirable life would be lost to him for ever. But he knew he wouldn't kill himself. When the time came he wouldn't dare, would be too weak. The idea was nothing more than a daydream, a consolation. It was already beginning to abandon him. He was slipping back into the crevasse.

Ice was closing in upon him. More painful than ever became the effort to walk. The freezing cramp renewed in his legs and arms, began to extend to his chest and to the small of his back. Soon he would lose all power of resistance, go mad. Horrible thoughts, diseased images, sickening sounds, would gain unrestricted mastery over him. But there was one last chance of escape. To turn back towards the marquee. To make a final effort to identify himself with those people. Surrender all his romantic demands, become a hopeless slave. He could not go on, go forward. Vacancy, a huge crevasse, was in front of him. He could see nothing, not even the ground that was directly beneath his feet. An icy-cold mountain mist confronted him. He turned. He saw the grass. Then he saw the marquee – quite clearly. But as soon as he tried to move towards it he realized that his legs were dead, devoid of feeling. Life, an agonized life, existed somewhere – not down there. Feeling had been driven up into the middle of his body, into his bowels, his stomach. If he wanted to move at all the movement would have to begin from the muscles here, from the agony here. He made a terrible effort, looked down and saw that he had lifted his right foot a few inches above the grass. He looked ahead: the marquee was at least fifty yards away. He shut his eyes. Terror suggested a device to him: he would imagine a line drawn on the grass in front of him and would try to step over that. He opened his eyes, imagined a straight line of grass blades. He exerted his muscles to the utmost. With aching, horrifying labour – as though he was lifting some huge external weight – he moved his right foot a few inches forward. Now it was directly above the imagined line. The descent should be easier. He foolishly looked up for a moment at the marquee. It was at least a hundred yards away. And after his right foot had descended he would have to lift his left foot. But at the same moment he saw something else which prevented these thoughts from developing to their conclusion. A man was passing quite close to him, walking easily and in the opposite direction. The tutor's double, the man whom he had seen soon after he had come out of the marquee. The meaning of this reappearance was plain. The tutor was on the point of going mad. At all costs he must persist in trying to move forward. No matter if he never got anywhere near the marquee. The effort, however agonizing, would at least give him a sense of control, of power to put up some kind of resistance against the forces of boundless horror. He saw that his right foot had descended, had reached the ground. Now to begin to try to raise his left foot. But first he must imagine another line. No; the line was already there – a clearly defined ridge of thick dark grass, crossing his intended path at right angles. He fought to lift his left foot. He looked down and saw that he had not shifted it an inch. He was slowly freezing. Particles of ice were whirling brilliantly through the air. The marquee – though he did not seem to have moved his gaze from the grass – became visible to him. It had a flat and brittle look, as though it had been painted on a screen of glass or of ice. And the row of black fir trees on the slope behind it could have been shattered to fragments by the touch of a finger. But he could not shift his left foot an inch. A glacial panic tightened round his heart. He could not do anything at all, could not even move his eyelids. He was done for, paralysed, a hopeless failure. He had become insane. Suddenly he surrendered, gave up trying to move. An infinite relief, a blissful vacancy, expanded within him. Like a patient on an operating table who has been struggling frantically against the suffocating ether, he was at last anaesthetized. No need to worry about anything any more.

Now nothing existed. But out of nothing something was

born. A noise, a voice. Ghostly and distinct, it came from high up among the fir trees. It spoke into his left ear. It said:

'... But you *are* walking. You have not failed.'

He answered it:

'I am standing still. I am frozen. I am paralysed.'

'... You are walking away from the marquee. You are going down towards the racecourse.'

'That's only an hallucination. I am frozen stiff and I have become insane.'

'... No. If you really believed you were standing still – that would be an hallucination. But you don't believe it. You can see with your eyes that you are walking towards the white railing of the racecourse.'

'That's what I seem to see.'

'... You do see it. You can't pretend you have forgotten your double, the man who came out of the marquee at the same time as you did. You know well enough who he was. He was you. He is you. He was never a delusion; but the frozen paralytic with whom you tried to identify yourself was a delusion. Actually you haven't stopped walking since you left the marquee.'

'Then I am certainly insane.'

'... No, not now. You are slowly getting better.'

'But if I am not insane how is it that I can hear this voice speaking out of the trees?'

'... Listen more carefully. The voice is not coming from the trees. It isn't really a voice at all. It is nothing more than a noise. A noise in your left ear.'

'It might be.'

'... Cast you mind back to what happened before you set out for the races this morning. Don't you remember following Mr Parkin and MacCreath out of the hall? Don't you remember the ringing in your left ear as you went towards the car?'

'Yes. But even supposing the voice is a continuation of that ringing, how am I to explain the words I can hear?'

'... They are nothing more than your own thoughts. They have confused themselves with the noise in your ear. You are carrying on a dialogue with yourself. But that is far from being a proof of insanity: on the contrary, it is a very effective method for arriving at a solution of intellectual problems. You are much less excited than you were. You can see your surroundings perfectly clearly. You know that you are on an ordinary racecourse, that you arrived here in the car with Mr Parkin and MacCreath and Stokes and the boy, that you have temporarily given them the slip. You know that the marquee which you have just left is really nothing other than a small grey tent, that the animal-headed bowls and the opaque golden bottle don't exist, that all your experiences for the last half-hour or so have been due to morbid make-believe on your part.'

'I am not quite sure yet.'

'... You ought to be. Remember the silk table-cloths and the marble bar and the fantastic behaviour of the young men. Ask yourself: Are these things probable? Are they what a sane observer would expect to find on an ordinary racecourse? You know they are not. They are the wildest nonsense.'

'Yes. That's how I am beginning to regard them now. I am sane now. But they didn't seem nonsense to me a few minutes ago. Doesn't this mean that I *was* insane then?'

'... You can call your condition insanity if you like. An alienist might be less sure about it. There is room for doubt. Between sanity and insanity there is a sort of no-man's-land. The opposing forces in the deep trenches on either side wear conspicuous uniforms and can be easily distinguished from one another, but no responsible psychologist would be prepared to state categorically to which side belonged an individual crawling in the intervening mud among shell-holes and wire-snags. Your condition could be best described, in clinical language, as "on the border".'

'Then I was very nearly insane?'

'... Put it that way if you choose. But you would be equally justified in saying that you had been very nearly sane. Perhaps rather more justified – in view of the fact that you have subsequently become sane.'

'Am I out of danger now?'

'... You are. Provided you have the ability and the good sense to learn from your recent experiences. Don't begin to persuade yourself that because you are safe now you have never been in danger. You have been in very great danger. Perhaps if you had persisted in your attempt to get back to the marquee, if, in spite of the pain and the freezing, you had forced yourself to cross the line – then you might have become definitely insane.'

'What ought I to learn from my recent experiences?'

'... You ought to learn first of all that your problems cannot be solved in the mind alone. Nor can they be solved in the heart, in the emotions. They must be dealt with in the external world, because they have their origin in that world. You must take action – living practical action. Remember once more the circumstances of your first evasion, of the evasion which led you finally to the edge of madness. Think back to the beginning. You were standing in the dining-room, looking out of the window, and you did not want to go to the races. You decided to tell Mr Parkin that you would not go, but when the time came you failed to tell him. This cowardice was the source of all your subsequent delusions. They began as a consolation, as a substitute for action.'

'Suppose I had refused to go, would such a trivial act of defiance have been worth while? Next day my life would have been just as dull, just as vile as before. I should still have been the Parkins' tutor. But my fantasies, in their beginning at least, did offer me something worth thinking about. Besides, they were not mere irresponsible daydreams. They were deliberate. I created them and I had control over them.'

'... Had you control over them when you were in the marquee?'

'I don't know. Yes, I remember now: even in the marquee, even when I felt most afraid, I knew at the back of my mind that I was deliberately faking the things that alarmed me.'

'... You are mistaken. There was something which you were not faking, which you could not control. You had lost sight of it from the very beginning of your delusions, but it was always there, influencing you. It was the real external world. Your sense of control was merely another of your delusions. You could do nothing against the horror, the freezing madness, which advanced upon you; because these feelings were disguises assumed by the real world outside you.'

'Horror and madness were not my only feelings. There was something else, far more important. Something worth living and dying for. A sense of beauty and of joy.'

'... What good has it done you? You are back again to where you started from. You are the Parkins' tutor. Your sense of beauty and joy cannot help you to change that fact. It cannot help you, because it has no basis in reality.'

'Oh, but it has, it must have a basis. It came to me with such conviction. And that's not the only reason why I believe in it. I trust in it because I know that sheer imagination is an impossibility. Even the maddest fantasies must fetch their materials from real life. Where else could they fetch them from?'

'... You are partly right. There must always be some sort of correspondence between your thinking and your real situation, even if it's no more than a correspondence between thought processes and brain processes. But the significant question is: what's the *degree* of correspondence? How far do your thoughts give a true picture of the relations actually existing among things? You might think of a man with wings. The man might be real, a friend of yours, and the wings might have belonged to a real swan you had seen in a public park, but the combination in your mind would be nothing more than a contemptible whimsy, a myth.'

'I did not see a man with wings. I saw ordinary people, many of whom I had met before. And their behaviour – with certain momentary exceptions – was normally probable. I admit that the silver bowls and the marble bar and the parade of the young men were improbable. I invented them because I thought they would be interesting and exciting. And they weren't mere myths, they weren't absolutely impossible. They had a basis in reality. They have taught me something that I might never have learnt if I had gone on living in the old normal unimaginative way.'

'. . . What have they taught you?'

'They have given me an insight into my real situation. They have shown me my life in its relation to the larger life of human society. They have taught me something about the future.'

'. . . They have deceived you. It is true perhaps that they were not mere myths. You had seen some of them before in real life: they were bric-à-brac from the box-room of your memory. And most of the experiences which you imagined to be happening to you on the racecourse have actually happened to you at one time and another during your normal life. But they have had very little relation, perhaps none at all, to the events which have in fact taken place on the racecourse since your arrival here. There may have been some slight connection between these events and your recent experiences – you may, for instance, actually have met and have had a few casual words with MacCreath or Ann or Tod or Mavors, and you may have walked into the refreshment tent – but how close or how remote the connection has been you will never know.'

'Nevertheless, I do at least know that there was a connection. I may not be able to discover the real origin of my feeling of joy, but I know that there was a real origin.'

'. . . You won't get much comfort out of that argument. If your joy had a real origin, so had your horror. Both came to you from the external world. But both, luckily for you, were false, were sickly distortions of that world. Tyranny and war are in fact approaching, but they are not hopelessly inevitable. And the slave mentality will never become, as your horror pictured it, universal. The desirable life, also, can be found in actuality, but you will not find it in the society and in the surroundings where your joy led you to look for it.'

'Then what am I to do now?'

'. . . Look round you. Become aware of your real situation.'

'I am looking.'

'. . . What do you see?'

'I see people standing in front of the white railing of the racecourse. There are not very many people. The racecourse itself is much smaller than I thought it was. I see a bookmaker standing on some kind of platform. A woman is showing him a ticket. Perhaps the first race is finished already.'

'... Good. You are getting down to the facts at last. You are quite normal again.'

'It doesn't interest me.'

'... It ought to. Examine the facts a little further. What do you think you will see next?'

'There will be other races.'

'... And after that?'

'The races will come to an end. People will begin to disperse. Some of them will go towards the car park. That's where I shall go. I shall see the car which brought me here. I shall see Mr Parkin and the boy.'

'... Fine. Now you're facing it. And next?'

'The return. The house with the four lawns. Bed. Tomorrow. The window and the treetops. Rooks. Beer. Latin and Scripture. The day after tomorrow and the days after that.'

'... There's your real situation.'

'No, no, I can't stand it. Anything would be better. So slavish, so mean. Such a contemptible apathy. It isn't life at all.'

'... What can you do?'

'Escape. Anything. Go back to delusions. Back to the marquee. Risk the horror. That at least would be an act of courage. There's no other chance of life.'

'... There is another chance.'

'Only in delusions.'

'... No. You are wrong. Horror is a certainty, not just a risk, if you go back to delusions. By turning your head away from the world you will not immunize yourself from the world. On the contrary, if you fail to deal with reality your external problems will become more pressing. There will be nothing to check the impetus of their attack. And they will make themselves known to you not in their normal, comparatively unalarming forms, but in nightmare masks. Another thing: don't fool yourself with the popular belief that the insane are often happy. It is doubtful whether they are ever really happy. Possibly even cases of mania, in their most ecstatic moments, are aware that there's something gravely wrong. And you would not become a case of mania. Dementia would be far more likely for your type. Gradually sinking deeper into apprehensive dullness.'

'There's nothing I can do.'

'. . . Yes, there is. Consider the practical possibilities of your situation.'

'I have, I have considered them.'

'. . . What are they?'

'To go on living in the same way as before. To be a tutor. To serve the Parkins. Or perhaps to leave them and to serve someone else. There is no other way. Except to live in delusions.'

'. . . There is another way.'

'I suppose I might get a different kind of job. My conversation with MacCreath may not have been altogether imaginary. He may in fact feel well disposed towards me, want to do me a good turn. If I cultivated him he might eventually put me in touch with someone who might introduce me to someone who might offer me quite a good job.'

'. . . It isn't impossible.'

'I might even make money, become a success. Retire at forty, have a house in the country, travel round the world, collect a library, marry an actress.'

'. . . It's very unlikely. However, let us consider what would happen if you did become a rich man. In the first place the world situation, when the time came for you to retire, would be very different from what it is now. War might have reached England by then. You would have materially improved your own situation, but you would have done nothing to improve the general situation outside you. You would, to a greater or less degree, have helped to worsen it, brought it nearer to that nightmare extremity of tyranny and murder which you imagined in the marquee. You would, whether you liked it or not, have made your money indirectly or directly out of armaments and out of swindling the working class. And don't comfort yourself with the notion that when you retired you would be able to enjoy yourself. The builders might construct a gas-proof shelter with a ten-foot concrete roof in the basement of your country mansion, and it might save you from being murdered by air-craft, but it wouldn't help you to do anything worth while with your leisure. Your whole life, your thoughts, your actions, your feelings, would be poisoned by the life outside you.'

'Someone else told me almost the same thing earlier this morning.'

'. . . That doesn't make it any less true.'

'I remember: I imagined it. I imagined that Ann told me. And I had talked to her about Reykjavik. Now I understand why I had the feeling later on that I had heard about Reykjavik somewhere before.'

'. . . Be careful. You are trying to evade the issue again. The fundamental issue, the issue you ought to have faced long ago. Let us admit that your conversation with Ann was largely imaginary. She may or may not actually hold the opinions which you imagined she said she had got from you. The point is that you do hold them, have held them for some time. The ideas she seemed to express are yours.'

'What good have they done me?'

'. . . You have never tried to put them into practice.'

'I suppose I have always thought that, for me, they were impracticable. I am a tutor in a reactionary household. I am isolated. There is no way out.'

'. . . There is a way.'

'Where?'

'. . . You know where.'

'Yes, I know where.'

'. . . The way of the workers. You must get in touch with the workers' movement.'

'The way of the workers. But will they accept me into their movement?'

'. . . They will accept you.'

'But my upbringing, my education, my social origin – won't these tell against me?'

'. . . Others from your social class have been accepted before you, have become loyal and exemplary fighters for the cause.'

'I should never become an exemplary fighter. I haven't the

will-power, the tenacity. Sooner or later I should cease to carry on the fight.'

'... Even the strongest, the most heroic, must sooner or later cease to carry on the fight. The man or woman who holds out against prison and torture cannot hold out against the firing-squad. Death, no matter in what form it comes, must always put an end to the individual fight.'

'Nothing so extreme would be required to put an end to my fight. A mere fit of depression might do it.'

'... Possibly. But before your surrender you would at least have achieved something.'

'Very little.'

'... You would have achieved something, however little, for the cause. Your life would not have been altogether wasted and worthless, as it would have been if you made no effort at all to help the movement.'

'I cannot believe that I should be accepted. My insanity would tell against me.'

'... You are deliberately exaggerating the seriousness of your recent condition. Call it auto-hypnosis – that would be a more correct description. However, let us suppose that you actually have been insane: you can be sure that, if your disease is curable, you could not find a better way of curing it than by joining the workers' movement. Because there is no other way of dealing *successfully* with the real external problems which confront you – and which, incidentally, confront the whole of humanity at the present time.'

'The fact that I had been insane would hardly recommend me to the workers. I shouldn't be regarded as a very reliable recruit.'

'... No, you wouldn't. You couldn't expect them to elect you to a leading position or to entrust you with important information. On the other hand, they wouldn't treat you as a pariah, as a soul deaf to all righteous communication and therefore damned beyond reprieve. The workers' movement isn't a religion – though your perverted education may have led you to regard it as such. It is an organized fight to bring about certain major improvements in the external world.'

'What use could I be to the movement? What should I be asked to do for it?'

'... You would be asked to do whatever you are most capable of doing. Whatever work you are most suited for. No one, however weak, however injured, is useless to the movement – provided he is genuinely willing to help and to carry out, in a disciplined way, the collective decisions of the movement. There is something, no matter how small, that each individual member can do, and something that as an individual he can do better than anyone else could do it.'

'Discipline – the word has nasty associations.'

'... Self-discipline. The workers' movement is not a tyranny, does not issue orders from above, does not require unreasoning obedience. It requires individual initiative, active and intelligent co-operation. It demands that each of its members shall actively participate in the formation of its decisions. And when those decisions have been formed it demands that each member shall do his best to implement them in practice. You can understand that this is necessary: otherwise there would be chaos, the organized fight would be an impossibility. But if you refuse to carry out the collective decisions you will not be coerced, will not be forcibly disciplined into carrying them out. You will merely cease to be a member of the movement. It will have no further use for you. That is the full extent of its discipline. The initiative, the activity, must come from you – or you will be of no use to the workers at all.'

'But have I the courage to take the first step? To knock on the door, introduce myself to the group secretary, ask what work I can do?'

'... It wouldn't require much courage. At worst they might tell you politely that they didn't need you. However, you know they won't do that.'

'I know. Nevertheless for me it would require courage. It would be such a plunge in the dark.'

'... Not in the dark. You would not be ignorant of where you were going.'

'I should not be ignorant. But I should be aware that my life was about to undergo a complete change. Yes, there's the crux, there's the root of all my remaining misgivings. I should be aware that joining the workers' movement would teach me to fight against the things in my life that I have helplessly loathed and feared; but might it not also destroy the things I have valued and loved?'

'... What things?'

'I cannot easily explain. Poetic dreams. The splendour and the joy.'

'... Dreams of escape. Twisted fantasies. Unhealthy substitutes for the action you ought to have taken.'

'Quite true. But they were something more than that. They may have been a substitute for action, but at the same time they were themselves a form of action. They may have been fantastic but at the same time they contained within them elements of something other than fantasy. Unreality was not their essence: it was foreign to their essence, a taint, a disease that had invaded them. I can explain now what they were. They were my attempts to find a significance in the life I was leading, to build up my experiences into a coherent, a satisfying pattern.'

'... They failed. They failed because the life you were leading could never be satisfying, and consequently any attempt to build up your experiences into a coherent pattern must have resulted in a lie, a fantasy.'

'But surely my attempt was better than nothing, was a sign of life, a form of action, was better than allowing myself to sink into apathy. The effort to understand the world, to arrive at the intellectual and emotional truth about real happenings, can never, even if it fails entirely, be worthless.'

'... In your circumstances it was almost worthless.'

'But if I am not allowed to dream or to think at all I do not want to live.'

'... You will be allowed to dream and to think.'

'Joining the workers' movement will mean hard practical work in addition to my work as a tutor. It will mean keeping my nose down to a hundred minor jobs which in themselves and by themselves would have very little interest for me. It will leave me no time for thinking or feeling.'

'... You are quite wrong. Though it's true that you will temporarily have to make a complete break with your former thoughts and feelings. You will have to move out of the region of thinking and feeling altogether, to cross over the frontier into effective action. For a short time you will be in an unfamiliar country. You will have taken your so-called "plunge in the dark"; but it will not be in the dark for very long. Out of action your thinking and your feeling will be born again. A new thinking and a new feeling.'

'What will they be like in their new form? I may find them unpleasant.'

'... They will bear a certain hereditary resemblance to the earlier thoughts and feelings from which they were descended. But at the same time they will be different, entirely new. Just as a son resembles yet differs from his parents. They will be more vigorous, more normally human, less tortured and introspective. They will be concerned more with the world outside you than with yourself.'

'They will be grim and crude and cold. They will be disfigured with the scars of bitter struggle. I have no illusions about the probable outcome of the action I am preparing to take. It may mean that I shall eventually have to fight in a war. A war of defence, a war for liberty, no doubt – not just a senseless war for tyranny's sake. But it will be a war all the same. And it will hustle and brutalize my dreams, even if it doesn't totally destroy them.'

'... A world war is not yet inevitable. And the action you are preparing to take is the only kind of action that can help to prevent its becoming inevitable. But you are right not to shut your eyes to the worst possibilities of the future. You may have to fight. You are wrong, however, in supposing that a war for liberty would mean the death of all beauty and of all poetry. Even in the vile imperialist war of 1914 there were poets. You have always felt a high admiration for the work of Wilfrid Owen.'

'But the sunniness, the subtle happiness, the passionate and gentle study of the intricate detail of the real world which I have admired in Shakespeare and in Keats – these will perish.'

'... They will suffer, yes, but they will not perish. And the action you are preparing to take will help them to survive in you. No other action can help them. You have tried to justify your imaginary experiences in the marquee by claiming that they have taught you something which otherwise you might never have discovered. They should have taught you that in capitalist society there is no future for poetry or for anything worth while. There is no future for anything except tyranny and death.'

'Yes, I have learnt that.'

'... Only the workers can save the things you value and love. All that is gentle, generous, lovely, innocent, free, they will fight to save. And in the end they will win. There will be a time of harshness and of bitter struggle, but out of it will come flowers; splendour and joy will come back to the world. And life will be better than it has ever been yet in the world's history.'

'How soon can I join the workers' movement?'

'... You can join some time within the next few days.'

'I don't want to wait.'

'... It's true that you are late, but you needn't be in quite such a desperate hurry. You don't imagine you'll find the workers' movement here on the racecourse, do you?'

'I shall find workers here.'

'... Of course.'

'I must get in touch with them.'

'... If you catch yourself beginning to think you've found the movement you'll know what that means. You will have had a relapse, gone back to delusions.'

'No. I shall not do it again. I have learnt my lesson.'

'... Where are you walking?'

'I am walking towards the white railing of the racecourse. People are standing in front of it. There must be workers among them.'

'... Very well. You know the risk.'

'I do.'

Here and there the crowd stood three- or four-deep in front of
the railing. At rarer intervals they were bunched into dense
groups, or were diffused so that gaps appeared among them.
Not many people were here; but there were more than the tutor,
comparing their numbers with the multitudes he had pictured
in his delusions, was immediately willing to suppose. However, now that he had recovered his sanity he must be careful
not to fall into the error of belittling the actuality which surrounded him. The huge white marquee had been a fake, but
the reality upon which the fake had been based was something
more than a small grey tent. It was an ordinary medium-sized
refreshment tent. And the crowd was an ordinary crowd of
racegoers, neither small nor immensely large. Neither fashionably elegant nor dirty. Normal people, sane and unpretentious.
A few were walking, going perhaps towards or away from the
bookmakers or looking for a better position from which to
watch the races. The majority showed no movement, except
of hands and faces. They were chatting, peering, nodding, call-
ing. He walked on towards them. He was sane, had entirely
recovered. He had even put a stop to his harmless internal
dialogue. He must avoid any kind of thinking or feeling which
was in the remotest degree abnormal. He must move out of
the region of thinking and feeling altogether. He must act,
must go among the people.

He found himself among them. Three- or four-deep the
crowd lined the white railing. He had walked among them. He
stood still. No one peered at him. He was neither welcomed
nor treated as an intruder. The people round him went on chatting as before. Nevertheless he was not ignored. He had the impression that they knew he was here and were pleased. There
was a feeling of easy friendliness in the air. He warned himself
that feelings ought not to be allowed to invade him quite so
soon after he had moved out into the region of action. There
should be an intermediate period, a dreamless and fallow period.
But he could not resist the happiness he was beginning to feel.

He knew that at last he was among people who were really human, who did not try to appear remote and superior, who had known life at its hardest and were generous and considerate, whom he could love. He knew that he was among the workers.

Why not dare to be glad? No; not yet, not for some time yet. He had learned his lesson. First he must get in touch with the workers' movement. Workers were here, but not the movement. He was on a racecourse. He had walked across the grass, joined the crowd in front of the white railing. He had taken no other action, was not justified in beginning to feel glad. Quick, check the feeling. Be austere. Otherwise, back to delusions. But it was difficult for him to be austere. The sun, the friendliness in the air, the knowledge that he was among the workers, all urged him to be glad. And there was another difficulty: he had become aware that he wanted to speak to a young man who was standing near him, who was looking at him. Don't speak. Don't return the look. Why not? Because it might lead to delusions. Already the tutor had begun to feel interested and a little excited. A worker was looking at him. The tutor was pleasantly uneasy. Stop it at once. Try to feel indifferent. But this was ridiculous. The tutor must and would avoid delusions, but there was no need for him to shut his eyes to what was actually going on around him. To shut his eyes, to be an ostrich, would be to indulge in a new and perhaps more dangerous kind of make-believe. Very well, then, look at him. But remember where you are, and keep a hold over your imagination.

The young man was hatless, wore baggy plus-four breeches and a dark suède-type jacket with a zip-fastener at the neck. There were diamond-shaped canary-coloured checks on his stockings. However, his style of dress did not give an impression of showiness or of bad taste. The loud colours and the assertive bagginess were mellowed by wear and weather, though not to the point of dinginess or shabbiness. Fashions which in the places of their origin – Oxford and Cambridge and the golf-club – would have appeared cranky and pretentious, had now become sober and mild. They had been democratized. His face too was mild. He had close-cut auburn hair, and his complexion was evenly and palely red — with a redness which slightly resembled the colour of brick-dust. His eyes were light blue, and they looked at the tutor with friendly interest. Suddenly, easily, he spoke to the tutor.

'You've been lucky.'

'How?'

'My mistake, perhaps. I thought you looked as though you'd just picked a winner.'

'A horse? No. I haven't. As a matter of fact I didn't put anything on.'

The tutor at once wished he hadn't said this. It might give the impression that he disapproved of betting. But the young man wasn't repelled, said:

'I don't bet much myself. Only now and again, for amusement, and nearly always on the wrong horse. I haven't had any luck yet today. That's what comes of reading the papers. Best way is to shut your eyes and have a dab at the names with a pin. It's a mug's game any way.'

The tutor non-committally grinned, and the young man went on:

'I didn't know the day before yesterday that I'd be up here today. I usually go cycling on Saturdays, but a pal of mine persuaded me to come to the races instead. He works with me for the same firm. Now he's gone off somewhere — after some skirt, I expect — and I can't find him. I shall have something to say to him on Monday.'

The words 'He works with me' excited the tutor. He wanted to ask what the work was, but he dared not. He was afraid of appearing inquisitive. However, the young man seemed very ready to talk about himself. The tutor risked an indirect approach:

'Do you find you get much time for cycling?'

'Week-ends. In the winter it's not so good, of course. But in the summer we often do a hundred miles or so. We take our tent with us. I'm very fond of camping.'

Smiling, the young man added:

'There's only one snag in it — knowing you'll have to get

back and start work in the factory again on Monday morning.'

'The factory' – the tutor began. He checked himself. This was almost too interesting to be true. Perhaps he had allowed himself to fall back into delusions. No; he knew he was perfectly sane. Calming himself he almost dared to ask:

'What sort of factory is it?'

'We turn out electrical equipment. Switch-gear and insulators and such-like.'

The tutor became bolder:

'What do you have to do – I mean, what's your particular job there?'

'I work at a lathe. My pal's at the same bench. We work from drawings.'

'Do you find it monotonous?'

'It might be worse. The work's pretty easy once you've learnt how to do it, and there's a fair amount of variety.'

'Are the hours long?'

'Just about the usual. But a lot of us live out of the district, and what with the journey there and back every morning and evening we don't get much time to amuse ourselves.'

'Is the pay good?'

'Not bad – it's slightly above the average rate.'

The young man showed no surprise at the tutor's questions, did not think him impertinent. And now an even more audacious line of inquiry suggested itself to the tutor. He did not try to hide his eagerness as he asked:

'Do most of the workers in your factory belong to a union?'

'No. We're quite unorganized. You see, the trade's a comparatively new one, and most of the workers are young fellows who haven't much industrial experience and who don't see the need for a union. They'll tell you that the pay they're getting is a bit above the union rate, and that it would be lowered if they started to organize.'

Eagerly and almost didactically the tutor said:

'That's bad. There may be a boom now – owing to rearmament – but a slump is bound to follow. And when it comes it will be worse than anything the workers have yet experienced.

That's why the unions must at all costs be built up and strengthened now – while the conditions are fairly favourable.'

'I guess I know it as well as you do. A few of us are doing what we can. I guess there's no other way out for the workers.'

The Americanism sounded quite natural and unaffected, though it had probably been picked up from the cinema. There was no hint of parody in the young man's tone of voice. And he understood the meaning of what he was saying; he was not posing or mechanically repeating second-hand phrases. He understood very much better than the tutor. Because he was a worker, and he knew the real problems which faced the workers. He had fought for the workers' movement in practice, with intelligence and with daily unromantic courage, was perhaps one of the workers' leaders. Whereas the tutor was no more than a hypersensitive little daydreamer. A superficial social-theorist of very recent growth, emotionally unstable, who had had the naïve impudence to try to tell this militant worker what to do. The tutor was worthless compared with him. Humbled before the young man's friendly light blue gaze, he hesitantly said:

'I wondered – could you put me in touch with the local workers' movement? If you think I'd be suitable. I suppose you do a good deal of work for them.'

'I don't do much. My pal and I have been trying to get something going in the factory – that's all. I haven't the time to attend political meetings. Or perhaps it would be truer to say I'm not prepared to sacrifice the time. Now and again in the winter I drop in and listen – if there's a good speaker. My brother-in-law's very active in the movement, and he takes me along with him. I could introduce you to him if you like. Provided I can get hold of him – he's nearly always out. But it wouldn't be necessary: all you have to do is to walk into one of their meetings. I'm sure they'd be glad to have you.'

'Thanks. That's what I'll do, I think.'

The tutor's initial disappointment at discovering that he wasn't speaking to a militant socialist was offset by the thought that he ought not to expect to meet one on the racecourse. If he had met one he could not have been certain that he wasn't up to his old fantasy tricks again. And there was another thing which blunted, which entirely neutralized his disappointment. An interesting face, a face that he recognized, had appeared among the crowd. It was about twenty yards away from him. It was the face of Ann. She too was talking with a young man, and he looked like a worker. As the tutor watched her the young engineer beside him said:

'I can give you my brother-in-law's address, if you like.' He paused, asked: 'Have you got a pencil?'

The tutor undid the top button of his overcoat and ran his hand over the outside of the breast pocket of his jacket.

'I'm afraid I haven't. It doesn't matter. I can go to one of their meetings. Thanks very much, all the same.'

He was still looking at Ann. Perhaps his conversation with her in the car had not been altogether a delusion. She might in actual fact have become interested in the workers' movement. He remembered that she had discussed it with him once when she and MacCreath had come to tea with the Parkins. Certainly, he didn't intend to let himself imagine now that she had become really active, a militant; but perhaps she had made a beginning, got in touch. Perhaps she had gone farther than he had.

'They're beginning to line up for the next race,' the young engineer said. There was pleasure in his voice. He added:

'Just time to go and put a little something on. Are you coming?'

'Well, I don't think I will.'

'All right.' He looked mildly into the tutor's eyes. 'See you again later perhaps. So long.'

As he turned and began to walk away his face seemed to show that he had already forgotten all about the tutor. His interest had turned wholly in another direction – but the change did not suggest unfriendliness. His new and final look had nothing in common with the aloofness and superiority of the people in the marquee. Potentially he was still well-disposed towards the tutor. Just as the crowd along the railing were well-disposed, though their friendliness had not yet actively shown itself. He must do something to deserve their friendliness, to bring it out into the open. He must do something to help the cause of the people. Ann had already begun. He would go and speak to her. He would tell her that at last he had decided to act up to his opinions. Perhaps he and she would be able to work for socialism together. What an abysmal little fool he had been with the girl in the marquee — even if he hadn't actually said and done a quarter of the things he'd imagined himself saying and doing. Love could never come first, could never be sufficient in itself. The fight for the cause must always come first. Afterwards there might or might not be love, but he would never find it if he went out deliberately hunting for it. Nevertheless, he must not turn his back on it, like a monk. If love was denied to him he would not whine — because he would not have made it his goal — but if it presented itself to him he would gratefully take it.

The crowd on his right had begun to move closer to the railing. Ann's head was still visible, but he would have to stand on his toes now if he wanted to see her face. He stretched, almost jumped, caught a glimpse that showed her earnestly talking. More people were coming towards the railing. Quickly he began to move. He must at least get somewhere where he wouldn't lose sight of her. He moved forward behind the backs of the crowd. A pre-occupied walker, gazing towards the course, obstructed him. The tutor dodged, lightly bumped into someone else. He apologized. He looked up and saw MacCreath.

'Hullo,' MacCreath said. 'Don't let me stop you if you're in search of a bookie.'

'No, I'm not,' the tutor stupidly admitted.

'Anyway, I doubt whether you would have got to him in time. The race is just about due to start. Yes; look. My word, I believe they're off. Yes, they are.'

He caught the tutor by the elbow and hurried him back in the direction of the railing. The crowd completely blocked the tutor's view. A rhythmical thudding grew rapidly louder, and for a moment the ground under his feet seemed to be shaken. He saw nothing of the race except the dark blue passing top of a jockey's cap. The thudding dwindled. MacCreath somehow had seen everything.

'Won by less than half a head,' he asserted. 'Easter Egg was leading him all the way. Right up to the finish. Won't Jim Parkin be pleased.'

'What won?'

'Fritillary, of course. But I was unlucky. I listened to Stokes. Won't Jim be delighted. Nothing pleases him better than to score off Stokes. He doesn't often succeed in doing that.'

MacCreath smiled significantly at the tutor, added:

'He'll hardly be able to contain himself. Which reminds me – he'll be wondering where I've got to.' Again the significant smile. 'Between you and me I was not altogether sorry to be able to tell him – quite truthfully, mind you – that I'd promised to go and look for my daughters. I'm very fond of Jim, but there are times when – well, you know what I'm referring to. Perhaps better than I do.'

The tutor said nothing. A little less intimately MacCreath added:

'You haven't by any chance seen Ann, have you?'

The tutor didn't answer. He was surprised that MacCreath had mentioned only Ann and not Dorothy. Fortunately Mac-Creath took his silence to mean that he hadn't seen her.

'I can't imagine where she's got to. I hope she hasn't taken it into her head to go off home. I wouldn't put it beyond her to decide at the last moment that the races weren't interesting. And I badly wanted to have a talk with her about arrangements for this evening.'

MacCreath gave the tutor a shy look, asked:

'Have you changed your mind yet about my suggestion?'

The tutor became alarmed. What suggestion? The offer to get him a good job. MacCreath was referring to their earlier conversation, to a conversation which in actual fact had never occurred. The tutor must be losing his grip, beginning to slide back into hallucinations. The offer had been wholly improbable, fantastic, would never have been made to him on an ordinary racecourse or by a man so little acquainted with him as

MacCreath was. And there were other indications that the tutor had had a relapse. Something queer was beginning to happen among the crowd. Away to his right there was suddenly a violent stirring among them. It was spreading, and other people were hurrying from all directions towards the centre of this interesting convulsion. A passionate shout went up into the bright air.

MacCreath, observing the tutor's bewilderment, added:

'I mean my suggestion about going to the dance.'

'What dance?'

'The dance in the Town Hall this evening.'

The tutor remembered. So he was all right, had not had a relapse. MacCreath was referring to a real conversation, and was actually saying what the tutor heard him say. There was no hallucination. But this meant that the commotion among the crowd must also be actual, not an hallucination. Then what was it about? What were they going to do?

'Quite an informal affair,' MacCreath said. 'No need to dress yourself up. I shan't, anyway.'

He had seen what was happening, but he deliberately, genially ignored it. His look implied that it was insignificant and not quite nice; it was beneath the notice of a gentleman. The tutor's curiosity increased. Something very interesting must be happening. What? It probably had some connection with the race that had just finished. Fritillary had won. Perhaps the crowd disputed the decision. MacCreath had said the race was a very close thing. A new and exciting thought flashed on the tutor: Fritillary was owned by the M.F.H.

'I'm sure you would enjoy it,' MacCreath said patiently.

Perhaps the crowd were not questioning the decision, but were giving vent to an habitual resentment against the M.F.H. That wasn't altogether impossible. The M.F.H. was, indirectly, one of the biggest employers in the north of England, and the working conditions in his mines and docks and factories were notorious. Sooner or later the men and women who worked to enrich him would cease to tolerate him. Mightn't they have made a beginning now, spontaneously, confusedly, here on this ordinary racecourse?

'Well?' MacCreath said.

Why not? The tutor knew, as a general historical rule, that insurrections seldom began in the way that their leaders wished or expected them to begin. He did not suppose, however, that he was witnessing an insurrection now. The crowd were making a protest, demonstrating against the M.F.H. – nothing more. Their protest had not taken the usual form of a strike or a procession with banners: it had taken the form of a disturbance on the racecourse. Fritillary's win had unexpectedly been the last straw, had broken the people's patience.

'Are you coming?' MacCreath persisted.

Their passionate shout could have no other meaning. They had crudely, spontaneously begun to rebel, to hit back against their exploiters. They had begun to move to the attack against the forces of privilege and darkness, against everything in the world which the tutor hated most. Against war and tyranny and mystery, against the conditions which had made him, too, a slave. And he was standing here and passively watching them. He had allowed himself to listen to MacCreath. But he wouldn't listen any longer. He answered MacCreath:

'No, I'm not coming.'

He looked towards the crowd and noticed that they seemed to have become less active. He added briskly:

'And if you'll excuse me, I've something I want to attend to now.'

He rudely turned and walked away. He hurried behind the backs of the crowd towards the centre of the disturbance. But the centre had shifted, become more distant. About thirty yards in front of him, indistinctly beyond a screen of dodging heads, he saw something or someone that did not move. Whatever it was, the climax of its interest for the crowd had already passed. People no longer came running towards it from all directions, and even the dodging heads in front of him showed a decreasing eagerness to get a glimpse of it. Perhaps the police had arrived, the tutor thought. The protest had failed. And he had done nothing to help it. He had betrayed it, weakly shirked his first chance to join with the workers. But perhaps the protest had not yet failed, would soon rise again. Even now he might not be too late.

He ran. He swerved away from the crowd at the railing, peering among them as he ran, trying to locate some point of promising activity among them. There was none. Movement had distributed itself evenly again along their lines, had dwindled to a normal disturbance of heads and hands. Their faces were turned once more towards the course.

He, too, became normal, stopped running. The crowd had not demonstrated against the M.F.H. Or if they had they had very soon desisted, allowed themselves to be doped by a footling interest in the next race which was just about to begin. More likely, the disturbance had been due to an argument with a bookmaker. Or perhaps one of the spectators had quarrelled with another who had blocked his view. Or, at most, a pick-pocket had been caught. Demonstration, protest — nonsense. The tutor had expected too much.

The crowd cared only for the races. He walked on behind their backs. He walked without purpose. They would never protest, provided they got the chance of amusing themselves occasionally; and their rulers would always see that they did get it. The people would never raise a finger against injustice, against tyranny and war. They would ignorantly, willingly submit. He walked on, weak with depression.

He turned away from them. The ground in front of him sloped upwards slightly. He was going in the direction of the car-park. He looked once again at the crowd by the railing. The course curved in a semicircle away to the left. Without shock he saw, standing a few feet back from the crowd and at the point where the bend began, Mr Parkin and the boy. They were staring at the course. They did not see him. He felt no alarm or distaste — only a feeble grief, as though in a moment of utter defeat someone had laughed at him. He walked on.

The ground in front of him gently ascended, reached its un-remarkable green summit about twenty yards ahead, stretched level from that point onwards towards the car park. On the summit and away to the right there was a small green mound. A young man was standing on this mound. He wore a smart black hat and his complexion was pink and girlish. He was facing the course, but there was something about his posture and expression which suggested that he was not looking at the course. He was looking beyond it: and with such a bemused intensity that the tutor mechanically turned round to discover what the young man saw.

Nothing. At least, nothing that was new to the tutor. The table-land abuptly ending, vanishing downwards towards the broad afternoon countryside. The variously coloured rectilinear fields. Broken glimpses among hedges and trees of the road along which he had come this morning in the car. And far away to the left another, a dead-straight road, the coast road which led from the town. The white insulators on the telegraph poles. Pithead gear. The remote harbour. The sea — no longer dead-blue. Blue in part, and in part glittering. And the air, though still almost cloudless — except towards the south — showed a sharp contrast in its colours: where the sun was on the water the sky above the horizon appeared gloomy, and where the water was lustreless the sky was brilliant. Towards the south a single cloud was rising slowly above the line of the horizon. A cloud-bank or a fog-bank, with a straight edge — minutely jagged like the edge of a razor seen under a microscope. The sea was very calm. The land, too, was calm. Unstirring trees at the top of a steep grass slope cast distorted shadows downwards — like reflections in water. A small ivy-grown church, with golden Roman numerals on its clock-face, stood isolated among the nearer fields. The church that he had seen from the car this morning. It was just the same as it had been then. It was the same as it had always been. The countryside had not changed: in its essentials it had never changed and would never change. As it had been in the beginning, so it remained. Change was nothing more than an illusion. Men spent their lives in futile rebellion against nature, gave all their energies to the struggle for a few meagre material improvements, and they died in failure and in wretched discontent.

But, all the while, happiness and peace were theirs for the asking. If only they would realize that the material struggle, even when it was apparently successful, could never bring them contentment. Submission, resignation – these were the only happiness. 'His will is our peace.'

The tutor pulled himself up sharply. He recognized where his thoughts were leading. But what or who had caused them to take this religious direction? The ivy-grown church; and the young man in the black hat. The tutor suddenly remembered who this young man was: Everard Heseltine, the new curate at St Saviour's, whose high-church practices had so infuriated Mr Parkin. The fact that he was high-church perhaps explained why he had had no scruples about visiting the races. Everard Heseltine, wearer of the reversed collar – though he wasn't wearing it now; intransigent popularizer of a reversed, a twisted picture of the world. Once – a thousand, even two hundred years ago – he would have been in the right. Then there was no real opportunity for the mass of the people to better their material conditions. Magic had failed them, and they could no longer hope to establish by their own exertions a heaven on earth. Therefore, they tried to establish a heaven within themselves, within their minds and hearts, trusting that the other, the real heaven, would come in God's good time. It never came, neither did they establish it within themselves. They had submitted to poverty and to external oppression, and their submission had warped them through and through. They were not to be blamed, had had no valid alternative. The objective conditions for a successful revolt had not then even begun to exist. Heseltine's forerunners had been right to teach resignation. But he was wrong. England need no longer be a land of poverty and of tragedy. Men had mastered nature, and the requisite conditions now existed for creating – not a heaven on earth, but a society in which every man and woman would at least have the chance to be normally happy. The pleasures promised by the sunlight, by the sea, by the rectilinear fields, need no longer be a sinister mockery. The time had come when it was possible to make an end of poverty. Everyone, even the blindest, was becoming aware that it was possible. But there were men who resisted the necessary change. Either because they knew that it would be materially unprofitable for them, or because, like Heseltine, they were afraid to abandon their reversed picture of the world. They dared not abandon the wisdom of their forerunners, who, recognizing that satisfaction was not to be had from an external world as yet unmastered by men, turned for consolation to the fantastic world of the spirit. They dared not lose their distrust of human action, dared not relinquish their belief that materialism meant nothing more than the provision of toothpaste and greenhouses for everybody.

But Heseltine was not the only, was not the chief offender. The tutor, far less excusably, had allowed himself to fall back into the same kind of error. He had known the risk of setting out to look for workers on the racecourse, had warned himself that he must not expect to find the movement here. Yet, a few minutes after meeting the young engineer, he had been up to his old daydreaming tricks once again. It was true that he hadn't allowed himself to relapse into hallucinations, but he had been dangerously close to them. He had let his imagination fly, had almost believed that the crowd were demonstrating against the M.F.H. And, when he had discovered his mistake, he had at first become despondent and had then begun to dream comfortably about the abolition of poverty. The next stage, unless he pulled himself together quickly and stopped dreaming, would be an even deeper despondency – accompanied probably by thorough-going delusions. He must act at once, drag himself out of the quag of thinking and feeling. He would not find the workers' movement on the racecourse, but he must begin here and now to make his first practical move towards finding it elsewhere. The difficulty was – how would he begin? What reasonable action, if any, could he take here and now?

While his mind fumbled, his body seemed already to have solved the difficulty. He was walking down towards the section of the crowd which lined the bend in the white railing. He was walking towards Mr Parkin and the boy. The race must be over, because they were looking towards him and away from the course. They did not see him yet. He had no idea what he would say to them. His body walked unhesitatingly on. They saw him. He came up to them.

'Hullo,' Mr Parkin said. 'Where did you get to?'

'I've been walking round.'

Mr Parkin was neither angry nor suspicious. He comfortably accepted the tutor's explanation. Behind the points of his moustache his cheeks curved in a fixed but convincing smile. Yet he had probably lost on the last race – otherwise he would have been hurrying off to claim his money from the bookmaker.

'I won ten shillings,' the boy was saying.

'I put it on for him,' Mr Parkin explained. 'On Fritillary.'

'But, Daddy, I told you to. I told you Fritillary was going to win. And I gave you your ten shillings back. If I'd kept it I should have won a pound.'

'Yes, yes, you told me. You earned your ten shillings all right, every bit of it.'

Mr Parkin added a very audible aside to the tutor:

'I'd have let him keep the other ten, of course, but it's good for him to feel he's earned all his winnings himself.'

Mr Parkin's face had a look of calm pleasure. The tutor felt depressed. He had lost the unthinking confidence which his body had given him when he had been walking, and he could not make up his mind now about what he wanted to say. He had dimly expected that the encounter with Mr Parkin would be disagreeable and dramatic. But in fact it had turned out to be very ordinary. There was no opportunity here for heroics of any kind. He had come back to where he had started from, to the situation which had faced him in the dining-room this morning. Soon the races would be over, he would get back into the car, and next morning he would be standing in the dining-room once again.

'We kept your lunch for you,' Mr Parkin said agreeably.

The tutor looked down at the grass. Its green was dusty and stale, dulled by the tread of ordinary feet. He remembered his decision to make contact with the workers' movement, and the remembrance was stale and lifeless. He had no feelings. Why bother to try to get his own way with Mr Parkin? All forms of action were equally tasteless and unattractive to the tutor. He felt no urge, no genuine desire to assert himself. Nevertheless, out of sheer dull obstinacy, he would assert himself. He would do it on principle, without feeling, without satisfaction; he would do it merely because he had decided to do it. He said tonelessly:

'There's something I've been meaning to tell you. I shall be out this evening.'

He had not known that he was going to say this. Surprised at his own words, he was even more surprised to see that Mr Parkin was not at all astounded.

'So you've decided to go to the dance.' Mr Parkin added an explanation: 'Mac was telling me all about it.'

'I'm not going to the dance,' the tutor said.

Mr Parkin either did not hear him or did not believe him.

'I'll tell Stokes to take you in the car.'

'Thanks. But I shan't need the car.'

This time Mr Parkin did hear. Inexplicably, he grinned; and there was a queer suggestion of slyness in his grin.

'Just as you like,' he said.

The tutor firmly went on:

'And I shall not be coming back to the house tonight.'

Mr Parkin made a polite but reluctant objection:

'There's no need for you to stay out, you know. Even if you are late. We can leave the key under the mat.'

'No. I'd prefer to stay out.'

'Well, please yourself.'

Mr Parkin was relieved. The worst was over, he appeared to think. Probably MacCreath had persuaded him not to make a fuss if the tutor wanted to go to the dance, had succeeded after a long argument in calming all Mr Parkin's fears – except the fear that the tutor might arrive back late and forget to lock the front door. Now all was well. But the tutor would soon show Mr Parkin that it wasn't.

'I shall not be coming back with you in the car.'

The boy asked excitedly, aggrievedly:

'Why aren't you coming with us?'

The tutor ignored him. Mr Parkin looked sly. He seemed to wink at the tutor, who said:

'I think I had better be leaving you now.'

Mr Parkin, almost laughing, retorted:

'I can see you don't believe in letting the grass grow under your feet.'

Observing that the tutor was already beginning to move away, he became more serious:

'Don't forget your lunch. You'll find it in the hamper in the back of the car. If I knew where Stokes was I'd tell him to take it out for you. I've no idea where he's got to. Everyone seems to be wandering off today.'

The tutor, stimulated by the faint resentment in Mr Parkin's voice, turned and left him. Mr Parkin called out:

'Have a good time.'

Again the suggestion of slyness. The tutor, walking away, suddenly guessed what it meant. Mr Parkin thought that he was going off to look for the MacCreath girls, that he had been promised a lift in their car, was going with them to the dance this evening: thought that he was a bit of a dog. Tomorrow, when the tutor arrived back from the town, Mr Parkin would think differently. He would be hysterically angry.

Would he? The tutor walking towards the road which led downwards from the car-park, could not imagine it. Mr Parkin would be annoyed, perhaps, but not frantic. He would ask questions, and the tutor would avoid answering them. Mr Parkin would not scream or show his teeth or shake his fist in the tutor's face. He was not a maniac. He was not even the unspeakable swine that the tutor had formerly supposed him to be. That supposition had been due to the tutor's cowardice, to his failure to assert himself against Mr Parkin. Now, at last, he had asserted himself. He had done it rather too easily and partly by trickery, but nevertheless he had done it. He need no longer regard Mr Parkin with impotent loathing. He could afford to recognize his more amiable qualities as well as his offensiveness, to see him as a human being, to attribute his vices not to deliberate personal wickedness but to his social origin. But Mr Parkin was still a potential enemy. By birth and by sympathy he belonged to the class of the oppressors, and he would almost certainly refuse to tolerate a militant socialist in his household. The tutor had not settled with him yet. Mr Parkin, in so far as he tried to hinder the tutor from becoming politically active, would have to be fought.

The tutor was passing the refreshment tent, was approaching the downhill road which led away from the racecourse. He had made up his mind about what he would do. He would walk into the town. It was not more than five miles away, and he would arrive there within an hour and a half. He would visit the small newsagent's shop outside which, on the one occasion when he had been allowed to go with Mr Parkin to the town in the car, he had seen a poster advertising the workers' daily paper. He would ask the newsagent to put him in touch with the local workers' movement.

He would get in touch. What the workers would require him to do for the movement he did not know. They would certainly not advise him to run away from his job as a tutor. He would go back to the house on Sunday morning. He would begin tutoring again, but with a difference. Perhaps in the evenings he would be able to do propaganda work in the village, among the agricultural workers. He would make a point of meeting the village schoolmaster, would have a talk with Stokes. Perhaps he would be sacked from his job as a tutor. If so he could try to get another job – next time preferably in an industrial town. His decision to join the workers' movement would lead to difficulties. But he would at least have come down to earth, out of the cloud of his cowardly fantasies; would have begun to live. He had already begun. He had made a stand against Mr Parkin. Nothing, no subsequent danger, could cancel that.

The tutor reached the road and began to walk down the hill.

The Island

WHAT are you fond of? Is it the sun, is it the girls, is it mornings in rowing-boats, is it giving yourself wild primroses, or trickily nursing a frantic box-kite, or studying at first hand materials of history or of geology, or identifying distant liners, is it palaces on the screens of picture palaces, or the narrow strip of wheel racing beneath the silver-bright handle-bars of your cycle, or larking for hours with the kids, or walking for miles, or reading a serious book, dancing, wearing pink, just lying flat on the sands? Social, brainy, daft, lazy, athletic, whatever your warmest pleasure is, so long as it isn't stealing or anything else illegal, there should be scope for it here.

Look across the real water; look, this island can't be a flood-lit cloud, can't be a daydream through which you'll slip to find yourself back on the job and under the poisonous eye of a bullying foreman. One hundred and fifty square miles of it, and the sand is unarguably sand, the earth is earth, the limestone limestone, fluvio-marine and estuarial, and roundly the real downs descend to the town, and the houses and bright hotels are crowding towards the pier, and the pier a pavilion-headed millipede is toddling through the springtime waves towards your paddle-steamer, this holiday steamer loaded with the first visitors of the year.

Nevertheless some of you are not wholly convinced, your faces show a certain listlessness – though you may not feel it – or even a certain rigour, you look almost as if you were confronted with things you are not fond of, as if you had seen something on the island which makes you apprehensive about rates and rents, or about feeding and clothing your children, or holding your jobs down. But there is really nothing here to force such anxieties upon you and you know that the cost of your holiday won't ruin you. Step hard on this deck, it isn't made of wishes, and you can't suppose that you'll be ordered below to work in the engine-room, or that the terrace of the yacht club like a redoubt behind its semi-circular sea-wall hides enemy cannon, or that the pier pavilion will bite your head off. You know you are going to have a good time, you knew it, you planned it weeks or months ago, and now you can feel it in the air, the sea smells of it, the wooded shore promises it, the canoe lake, the midget golf course affirm it, your eyes tell you it is true. This place must be a fact, this life fit for men and women must be real. How could you have doubted it? What weary imposture, what ghost-life, what Devil's Island in the heart have you allowed yourself to be cheated with until now? Did you mistake for realities those vile feelings, those arid panics in face of the future, those creeping apprehensions about losing your job, those sweating calculations before foodstalls in the market, all those nightmares which have been coming at you more and more venomously for so many weeks and months? Did you compromise with them, did you kowtow to them, eat dirt for them, did you betray for them this only life, this real life, this sea, this sun, this air brighter than diamonds or happiest tears? The moment is near now when you will be able to adopt a new tone, less diplomatic, less accommodating, towards all those ghost-miseries. The moment is here already, in a flash, as though it had been signalled by the sun-flashing windows of the pavilion. To hell now with that slave-life, that life not fit for beasts, down with it, drown it, throw it casually away as the sailor boy, the sea-boy emerging from the iron galley beside you, flings the used contents of a teapot into the thoughtless water. A good time, your birthright, has come.

Families, couples, hikers, cyclists passed along the two gangways and on to the concrete landing-stage of the pier. Other steamers just as crowded would arrive after this one, and in two or three days the steamers would go back crowded to the mainland. The social composition of the mass of visitors was difficult to determine, since it was obviously a mixture and contained both working-class and middle-class elements, but the office workers probably out-numbered the industrial workers, and there were possibly a few professional men with their small families, very few if any clergymen because Easter means business for the churches, and almost certainly no unemployed – owing to the cost of the journey – except perhaps one or at most two rich unemployed returning to their houses of retirement in the middle of the island. All tramped on to the deck of the pier, some to catch the train at the pier-head, others to walk or cycle or take the motor-tram to the pier-gates, and on the whole it could be fairly said that though none of them looked really gay all of them looked pleased.

One hundred and fifty square miles. Where will you go? Do your wishes whirl in a merry-go-round of indecision, uncertain which stopping-place to choose? There's no need for alarm, because whichever place you choose – whether here for automatic-machines and entertainments, or the downs for air and view, or the eastern bay for sand-cricket and the well-known chine, or that sun-trap behind the highest downs where east and north winds are unheard-of – whichever the place and whatever your tastes you are sure to find satisfaction. But this may sound like an exaggeration. Perhaps you are being kidded for the benefit of the railway company or the local councils. To dispel any such suspicions let it be added frankly that not all parts of the island would be equally attractive to all types of visitor. Obviously these severe-looking people gathering outside the pier-gates, these keen cyclists wearing the badge of a workers' sports club on their leather jackets, might complain if they found themselves riding over sharp stones along a cliff path – though surely they could dismount and wheel their cycles, and the view would go far to compensate them for their disappointment. Or again, you might be fond of crowds and find yourselves in some dead-alive village where nothing happens in the evenings and where there's nothing to look at except marshes and the flat-bottomed boats of the fowlers and cormorants perching on weed-hung posts – though what would stop you moving on at once to somewhere more congenial? But perhaps people exist who would discover nothing anywhere on the island to please them. The Commander's widow, for instance – that lady, that powdered marine fossil with her hair in whorls, who sits stuck in the bay window of her large modern cottage at the top of the hill, who never tires of believing that you have ruined the island for her with your voices and your clothes and your hiking and cycling, your cinemas, your lodging-houses, your crowds, your faces – though there's no reason why she should go on living here if she doesn't want to, since her property would make an excellent site for an hotel and she would have no difficulty in selling it, so possibly after all the island has its attractions for her as she leans against her crazy-pattern cushions in the window-seat, as she sits on guard over the past amidst her antique furniture and her superior knick-knacks, her bureau with the brass handles, her bowl of lavender, her china dogs and her real terrier, her framed samplers, water-colours, pestles and mortars, candle-lamps, toasting forks, teacups hanging from nails. It doesn't matter who you are or what you are fond of, it doesn't matter how energetic or crippled or intelligent or old-fashioned or frivolous you may be, this island should be able to provide something out of its variety to satisfy you. No strength should be denied exercise here, no weakness exposed or tortured.

What do you most want to do? Think – don't rush for a motor-coach or a train or go dashing off at once on your cycle. Lean back against the esplanade railing with the island before you, the wooded coast dwindling away on either hand, the town steeply retreating, the downs, farms, villages, streams, other towns, miles of brilliance and of fields, stretching invisible now behind ascending housetops. Are you bewildered, are you shaken by the daring or the queerness of your keenest wishes, are you tempted to smother them as fantastic and to decide on doing something you are only mildly fond of or not really fond of at all? There's no need for such caution, because however fantastic your wishes may seem, however vulnerable or high-flying or naïve, you should be able to fulfil them now. Uncover them, off with their wrappings of prudence and diffidence, expose them to the sun in all their fragility, their too-shy warmth, their over-excited tenderness – let them learn to live. No long-ing, no ambition should be ridiculous or impossible here. Do you want to be an engineer, for instance? You might think such a wish would be out of place on this island where there are no factories worth mentioning and no great works of con-struction in progress, and certainly you will not be given the op-portunity here of slaving at a conveyor belt or of sitting astride girders hundreds of feet above the ground. But why should you want to bind yourself to physical labour when it is possible for you to study the most up-to-date achievements of engineering at ease and without any material limitations or interference from machinery or foremen? Look back across the water and examine at leisure the aircraft-carrier anchored there. That ela-borate weapon, which cost millions of pounds to construct, so trim and severe with its uninterrupted length of deck and fun-nels neatly on one side, with its barely visible guns, its concealed lifts and hangar, should teach you something. Though it may teach you more about destruction than about engineering.

But you may want to devote yourself to some more funda-mental study. Go deeper, look with your mind now, see be-neath this hill of houses, this pier, this broad concrete parking-place for motor-coaches at the end of the esplanade, beneath even this water, study the crust of the earth itself. And look with your eyes also: walk along the shore and see how the cliffs expose layer on layer of petrified ages, lucid almost as in a museum model, sediments of years on years when life struggled out of the warm oceans, life dying in millions, winning, grow-ing carapace and fibre and preserving moisture in lungs, starv-ing under frightful frost, luxuriating in the coal-measures, de-veloping through aeons and aeons whose ruins teach you that the existence of the island itself is no more than a passing in-cident. And this knowledge will not condemn you to humility or to impotent reverence; on the contrary, the wider your under-standing of nature becomes the less mystery will its laws have for you and the more confident you will be in your power to make it serve you. Though you won't get much chance of mak-ing it serve you here. And you won't be able to understand it very widely either, since two or three days' holiday will hardly give you time to gain anything but a smattering of geological knowledge. However you can walk under the cliffs and admire the strata without bothering whether they are called greensand, limestone, the grey Punfield shales, Blue Slipper or the Crackers, and if you are lucky you may pick up some beautiful jasper pebbles veined with dendritical figures.

But you may feel geology would be rather a sterile study, you may prefer to occupy yourself with something equally serious but more human. Look beyond this complex of seaside living, these workers on holiday and what is provided for them and the inhabitants who live by providing it and the residents who are always on holiday, beyond this esplanade bandstand, these leather-jacketed cyclists, that large modern cottage at the top of the hill, this departing motor-coach issuing blue exhaust as its driver changes gear – consider the many historic phases that human society had to go through before it could arrive at its present state on the island. Many evidences in valley, in village, in town, on the downs, Celtic, Roman, Saxon, Norman, remain to tell you of past struggles, of gradual developments and cataclysmic changes, of new forms of society successively arising and decaying and being violently superseded by more vigorous and better adapted forms, just as the present form of society must decay and be superseded. And this knowledge will not fill you with pessimism and self-distrust but with confidence in the power of men to make even greater changes in the future than any they have made in the past, and with the determination that you will help in the making of those changes. Though it's true you are unlikely to participate actively here in a great historical movement. But isn't the island good enough for you already without its being convulsed by further struggles? And you aren't likely either to make a very profound study of history in two or three days. However you will be able to look at historical remains – earthworks, a burial ground, a Roman villa with a hypocaust and well-preserved tessellated pavement, churches, a whipping-post and stocks, the houses where Garibaldi stayed as a guest, the castle where Charles I was imprisoned, the site on which John Wilkes, fighter for freedom of speech, built his *Villakin* and erected to the memory of the poet Churchill a Doric column with a receptacle at its base for the storing of bottles of old port.

But you may consider this kind of history superficial and sentimental, you may conclude that since the shortness of your holiday makes any thorough acquisition of knowledge impossible you will do better to devote yourself to livelier and healthier forms of activity, to living rather than to the dry study of life. Think what an island of promise is before you, what sunlight, what fields for athletic leisure, for sport free from all taint of professionalism, for that fulfilment of the body which was long ago the ambition of the Greeks, what paths for love, what satisfied evenings for discussion, for the arts, for literature, for music, what a chance to begin a new life of culture and vigour. Come, begin now. But begin where? This flat esplanade offers no foothold for such climbing excitement. You cannot be a Greek here. And you aren't likely to find anywhere else on the island where you can begin a new life in two or three days. Perhaps there is nothing worth while anywhere here, perhaps the island has nothing in store for you beyond these freshly painted hotel fronts, this stationer's window crammed with humorous postcards, worthless china souvenirs, poker-work mottoes on bits of wood. Perhaps you will do nothing here, perhaps you will never succeed in throwing off the exhaustion and worry of the past, you are too weak, too injured to recover, perhaps you are done for.

What morbid bunk! This is the result of indulging in freakish fantasies and getting above yourself. Who but a fool would want to be a Greek? Come out of that sickly dreamland, that paradisal island of culture and everlasting joy, come and see the island as it really is and make the best of the ordinary human pleasures it has to offer you. Stop thinking and start moving, jump into a train or a motor-coach or on to your cycle, rush, drive, ride through the bright countryside, through woods, over bridges, down lanes, away to a real destination.

Arrive at the eastern bay. Come down to the beach. Feel

your feet in the sun-warmed sand, every grain of it real. Walk on it, run on it, be free. Race, play cricket, fly a kite, dig ponds for the kids. Bathe, paddle in the real sea. Be lively. Be lazy, choose out a spot sheltered from the slight but chilly spring wind, lie in the sun beneath the esplanade steps or beneath the jutting sea-wall which surrounds the platform of the war memorial. Read a book or look at the other people. Make friends. Go to sleep if you feel like it; no traffic will disturb you here, and the forts on the cliff are taking a rest from gunnery practice for today. Be happy, be normal, make a joke of all pretentious fancies and morbid thoughts. Enjoy yourself like the other workers, the other clerks, other shop-employees. Like these men and girls playing rounders, those territorials in uniform strolling through the amusements arcade, this child scribbling with a coloured pencil on a piece of old newspaper. Like these leather-jacketed cyclists singing as they ride past the Cosy Café and down to the sea front.

But what's happened? Something seems to be wrong. It is as though everyone has for a split second stopped moving. Wooden groups with surprised faces are stolidly planted along the esplanade. Now everyone has become almost normal again. Very few people seem pleased, many are slightly embarrassed, most looked puzzled. Of three young men sitting together in the café one shouts out some hostile remark. The cyclists are singing of hunger and war and social revolution. They must be mad.

Could anything be more inappropriate on a holiday? And what have hunger and war and revolution to do with the island? There is every sign of prosperity here, people look contented, a new pier pavilion and swimming pool are being built, a section of the esplanade is completely blocked with temporary huts, sacks of cement, piles of steel rods, cranes, concrete mixers – there can't be much unemployment. And as for war – well, even the most unbalanced extremist would have to admit that the peaceful presence of a few territorials, forts, guns, is hardly the same thing as actual fighting. What right have these cyclists to try to spoil your enjoyment, to remind you of feelings which you wanted to destroy?

Vile feelings, feelings which you wanted to fling casually away, arid panics in face of the future, apprehensions about losing your job, sweating calculations before foodstalls, nightmares which you tried to drown for ever in the real sunny sea. Feelings which have been coming at you more and more venomously, which are coming at you even now. The sands will not cover them, the sun will not burn them out, you cannot exorcise them, they are not· ghosts, are not mere nightmares, not mere psychological ailments to be cured by playing lively games or by sunbathing on the beach. ·You know that they come to you from the real mainland, from the real life to which you will return in two or three days, the life which has cancelled in advance all the opportunities for culture offered by this pleasant island. And look more closely at this island: get up from the beach and walk to the back-streets of the town and see there some of the filthiest overcrowding that can be found anywhere in England. But you need not get up: look at this woman shuffling along in dirty canvas shoes, searching among the lines of rubbish left by the tide – seaweed, shavings from the construction work on the pier, dead crabs, straw, ice-cream cartons, blackened banana skins, a gouged-out hemisphere of grape-fruit filled with sand – hoping to find something that may be of value, perhaps as food. Or consider those forts on the cliff and see them not in their apparent stillness as grass-grown mounds beneath the mild sun, but in their real movement of preparation for a world-wide war. Or look with new eyes at the amusements arcade, the strings of coloured light-bulbs along the sea front, the soft-witted advertisements outside the picture houses – what are these but hypocritical decorations concealing danger and misery, fraudulent as vulgar icing on a celebration cake rotten inside with maggots, sugary poison to drug you into contentment?

The cyclists are not mad. You know they are right to sing here on this island about hunger and war. And yet there is something worthwhile here, something that is not poison, some freedom, some joy, some real leisure, something that you cannot easily abandon for a life of grim revolutionary struggle, some beauty that seems to invite your trust and your love. But while you trust in it enemies are attacking it, powers of destruction are undermining it, the powers of hunger and war, the powers that are driven to destroy because further construction means their ruin, because your life means their death, your awakening their disaster, the powers that would have you sit still and trust in dreams. Or would have you fight for dreams. No doubt the three young men sitting together in the café are aware of something rotten in the island and would explain it as due to the materialistic attitude of people like the worker cyclists, to your attitude, your desire for a decent life now and in this world, no doubt they feel there is too much liberty here, too much selfishness and indifference to the things of the spirit, they would gladly tighten their belts in the service of some great spiritual cause and would gallantly obey orders.

Your view of the island will be different from theirs. You will see rottenness not in the leisure and the opportunities for enjoyment, however meagre these may be, which the island offers you, but in the forces that are working for the destruction of all freedom and culture. You will remember that such inadequate liberties as you possess at present have been won by bitter struggle, and you will recognize that now more than ever it is necessary for you to fight to defend them, to fight to extend them, to fight till you have made them adequate and made them secure, till you have destroyed their destroyers. And if ever in the setbacks and the tortures of the final struggle you think of the island, let the thought bring to you not the weakness of regret, not nostalgia for a ghost-place dazzling with false promise in the spring weather, not remembrance of the island as you saw it from the steamer today, but the strength of the certainty of a real place, the island as it can be, a place fit for men and women, as it must be, as it will be.

New Order

THE invaders can march no farther. Post-office, power-house, banks, all have been occupied, and the traitor mayor sits at work in the town-hall. Smoke and the corpses have gone from the streets; the trailing telephone wires, the amputated tram standards and even a few windows, have been repaired. The oppressor's soldiers have offered soup from their field-kitchens to those among the inhabitants who are utterly destitute. The old night-life of the cabarets in the whorehouses has begun again for a new clientele. There are still men, women, boys, girls whom the invaders can shoot, starve, hang if they choose, but nothing further can be gained by that, and the sufferers have only their wretchedness to lose. Oppression has reached its limit, is mature and entire, can destroy no further without diminishing its own empire here; and now, out of its ripeness and out of the fullness of its own nature, an enemy is born. You, few at first, rebels, saboteurs, guerrillas, marked with the birthmark of oppression and of death, born merciless as your enemy and begetter is merciless, but with far to go now while he can go no farther, are born to be the death of death, the oppression of oppression. At night in private houses, and if possible never twice in the same house, you meet briefly, and always one of you is set to watch at the outer door.

From the gallows in the market-place, near the old stone horse-trough, a body hangs with bent head peering down. Broad-backed and with insolent faces the soldiers pass in twos and threes. But they are never more insolent than when they are amiable, when one of them stops to help a blind woman across the road. A man sells postcards in sight of the gallows. Shock and despair have shut out even the consciousness of oppression from the minds of many of the people. Though they suffer they do not dare to know why. You who are conscious, to whom hate has brought life, must begin your fight with little support. The drilled confidence of units in a huge, well-equipped, uniformed army is not for you. No hourly wireless, daily newspapers, will inject you with courage. Though you have friends and comrades in other countries they cannot easily or often get in touch with you. You are alone, and your strength is your own. You do not sit and ask one another – 'What is going to happen?' You do not anxiously consult your feelings as though they were prophetic oracles and find them one day exuberant with hope, the next day in the depths. You act to make things happen. And in the morning on the walls, under doors, in telephone kiosks, your leaflets announce: 'Inhabitants . . . On June the twenty-fifth at the government arsenal there occurred a terrible explosion. It was our work. Fires at the oil-refinery were also our work. Because we did not want this oil, those arms, to help to kill our brothers. Fellow-countrymen, the derailing of the ammunition train in the mountains was the work of true sons of our country. . . . Join with us, and together we shall destroy the invaders.'

They are watching; their agents are looking for you in the streets; at any hour you may hear the thudding on the door; when you sleep you must be light and fitful sleepers; it is possible that not one of you now active will escape them. You are aware and were aware from the start that there's no guarantee of success attached to your activities. It was not the certainty of victory that made you begin your enterprise. It was not your understanding of the irremediable weaknesses shaking the heart of the highest control-centres of the enemy, it was not even faith in the final coming to power here and everywhere of the people – though you have that faith. It was more, it was stronger than that. It was your nature, the nature of men and of women, the human nature which in every recorded century and in all places – and even when and where success was wholly impossible – has asserted itself in war against inhuman conditions. The workers walking or cycling here in the darkness of the morning to work in the factories where arms are manufactured for the use of their enemies, the people in uninvaded countries to whom knowledge of the horror here comes only from wireless and newspapers, the millions even in the invaders' country who have been bribed and drugged with promsies, these are of the same stock as you are, will not in the end submit to the rule of suffering, are capable of the same contempt of death. You are the evidence, the assurance that human beings have not lost their nature in these times. You, few at first, rebels, saboteurs, guerrillas, you yourselves are the guarantee that others over the whole world will strike with you to destroy the oppressors.

FOR THE BEST IN PAPERBACKS, LOOK FOR THE

In every corner of the world, on every subject under the sun, Penguin represents quality and variety – the very best in publishing today.

For complete information about books available from Penguin – including Pelicans, Puffins, Peregrines and Penguin Classics – and how to order them, write to us at the appropriate address below. Please note that for copyright reasons the selection of books varies from country to country.

In the United Kingdom: For a complete list of books available from Penguin in the U.K., please write to *Dept E.P., Penguin Books Ltd, Harmondsworth, Middlesex, UB7 0DA*

In the United States: For a complete list of books available from Penguin in the U.S., please write to *Dept BA, Penguin, 299 Murray Hill Parkway, East Rutherford, New Jersey 07073*

In Canada: For a complete list of books available from Penguin in Canada, please write to *Penguin Books Canada Ltd, 2801 John Street, Markham, Ontario L3R 1B4*

In Australia: For a complete list of books available from Penguin in Australia, please write to the *Marketing Department, Penguin Books Australia Ltd, P.O. Box 257, Ringwood, Victoria 3134*

In New Zealand: For a complete list of books available from Penguin in New Zealand, please write to the *Marketing Department, Penguin Books (NZ) Ltd, Private Bag, Takapuna, Auckland 9*

In India: For a complete list of books available from Penguin, please write to *Penguin Overseas Ltd, 706 Eros Apartments, 56 Nehru Place, New Delhi, 110019*

In Holland: For a complete list of books available from Penguin in Holland, please write to *Penguin Books Nederland B.V., Postbus 195, NL–1380 AD Weesp, Netherlands*

In Germany: For a complete list of books available from Penguin, please write to *Penguin Books Ltd, Friedrichstrasse 10 – 12, D–6000 Frankfurt Main 1, Federal Republic of Germany*

In Spain: For a complete list of books available from Penguin in Spain, please write to *Longman Penguin España, Calle San Nicolas 15, E–28013 Madrid, Spain*

PENGUIN MODERN CLASSICS

The Collected Stories of Elizabeth Bowen

Seventy-nine stories – love stories, ghost stories, stories of childhood and of London during the Blitz – which all prove that 'the instinctive artist is there at the very heart of her work' – Angus Wilson

Tarr Wyndham Lewis

A strange picture of a grotesque world where human relationships are just fodder for a master race of artists, Lewis's extraordinary book remains 'a masterpiece of the period' – V. S. Pritchett

Chéri and The Last of Chéri Colette

Two novels that 'form the classic analysis of a love-affair between a very young man and a middle-aged woman' – Raymond Mortimer

Selected Poems 1923–1967 Jorge Luis Borges

A magnificent bilingual edition of the poetry of one of the greatest writers of today, conjuring up a unique world of invisible roses, uncaught tigers . . .

Beware of Pity Stefan Zweig

A cavalry officer becomes involved in the suffering of a young girl; when he attempts to avoid the consequences of his behaviour, the results prove fatal . . .

Valmouth and Other Novels Ronald Firbank

The world of Ronald Firbank – vibrant, colourful and fantastic – is to be found beneath soft deeps of velvet sky dotted with cognac clouds.

FOR THE BEST IN PAPERBACKS, LOOK FOR THE

PENGUIN MODERN CLASSICS

Death of a Salesman Arthur Miller

One of the great American plays of the century, this classic study of failure brings to life an unforgettable character: Willy Loman, the shifting and inarticulate hero who is nonetheless a unique individual.

The Echoing Grove Rosamund Lehmann

'No English writer has told of the pains of women in love more truly or more movingly than Rosamund Lehmann' – Marghenita Laski. 'This novel is one of the most absorbing I have read for years' – Simon Raven, *Listener*

Pale Fire Vladimir Nabokov

This book contains the last poem by John Shade, together with a Preface, notes and Index by his posthumous editor. But is the eccentric editor more than just haughty and intolerant – mad, bad, perhaps even dangerous . . .?

The Man Who Was Thursday G. K. Chesterton

This hilarious extravaganza concerns a secret society of revolutionaries sworn to destroy the world. But when Thursday turns out to be not a poet but a Scotland Yard detective, one starts to wonder about the identity of the others . . .

The Rebel Albert Camus

Camus's attempt to understand 'the time I live in' tries to justify innocence in an age of atrocity. 'One of the vital works of our time, compassionate and disillusioned, intelligent but instructed by deeply felt experience' – *Observer*

Letters to Milena Franz Kafka

Perhaps the greatest collection of love letters written in the twentieth century, they are an orgy of bliss and despair, of ecstasy and desperation poured out by Kafka in his brief two-year relationship with Milena Jesenska.

FOR THE BEST IN PAPERBACKS, LOOK FOR THE

PENGUIN MODERN CLASSICS

The Second Sex Simone de Beauvoir

This great study of Woman is a landmark in feminist history, drawing together insights from biology, history and sociology as well as literature, psychoanalysis and mythology to produce one of the supreme classics of the twentieth century.

The Bridge of San Luis Rey Thornton Wilder

On 20 July 1714 the finest bridge in all Peru collapsed, killing 5 people. Why? Did it reveal a latent pattern in human life? In this beautiful, vivid and compassionate investigation, Wilder asks some searching questions in telling the story of the survivors.

Parents and Children Ivy Compton-Burnett

This richly entertaining introduction to the world of a unique novelist brings to light the deadly claustrophobia within a late-Victorian upper-middle-class family . . .

Vienna 1900 Arthur Schnitzler

These deceptively languid sketches, four 'games with love and death', lay bare an astonishing and disturbing world of sexual turmoil (which anticipates Freud's discoveries) beneath the smooth surface of manners and convention.

Confessions of Zeno Italo Svevo

Zeno, an innocent in a corrupt world, triumphs in the end through his stoic acceptance of his own failings in this extraordinary, experimental novel which fuses memory, obsession and desire.

The House of Mirth Edith Wharton

Lily Bart – beautiful, intelligent and charming – is trapped like a butterfly in the inverted jam jar of wealthy New York society . . . This tragic comedy of manners was one of Wharton's most shocking and innovative books.

The Glass Bead Game Hermann Hesse

In a perfect world where passions are tamed by meditation, where academic discipline and order are paramount, scholars, isolated from hunger, family, children and women, play the ultra-aesthetic glass bead game. This is Hesse's great novel, which has made a significant contribution to contemporary philosophic literature.

If It Die André Gide

A masterpiece of French prose, *If It Die* is Gide's record of his childhood, his friendships, his travels, his sexual awakening and, above all, the search for truth which characterizes his whole life and all his writing.

Dark as the Grave wherein my Friend is Laid Malcolm Lowry

A Dantean descent into hell, into the infernal landscape of Mexico, the same Mexico as Lowry's *Under the Volcano*, a country of mental terrors and spiritual chasms.

The Collected Short Stories Katherine Mansfield

'She could discern in a trivial event or an insignificant person some moving revelation or motive or destiny . . . There is an abundance of that tender and delicate art which penetrates the appearances of life to discover the elusive causes of happiness and grief' – W. E. Williams in his Introduction to *The Garden Party and Other Stories*

Sanctuary William Faulkner

Faulkner draws America's Deep South exactly as he saw it: seething with life and corruption; and *Sanctuary* asserts itself as a compulsive and unsparing vision of human nature.

The Expelled and Other Novellas Samuel Beckett

Rich in verbal and situational humour, the four stories in this volume offer the reader a fascinating insight into Beckett's preoccupation with the helpless individual consciousness, a preoccupation which has remained constant throughout Beckett's work.